WORLD TREE GIRL

A SHADOW VALLEY MANOR MYSTERY

KERRY SCHAFER

KERRY SCHAFER LLC
Write at the Edge

Published by Write at the Edge publishing, Colville Washington

Book cover design by ebooklaunch.com

To my Grandpa George, who taught me that age is no barrier to new adventures.

ONE

In the uncharted territory along the boundary of life and death, time has no meaning. Souls cross, or don't cross, without consideration for humanity's ticking clocks.

Sophronia has been sitting in this unforgiving chair for hours, waiting. The knobs of her spine feel bruised, and her lower back aches. She shifts her weight, leaning forward and easing from her right hip to her left, careful not to jostle the small, sun-browned hand clasped in hers.

The child's eyelids flutter and he peers up at her, his pupils enormous, his eyes glazed by opiates and sleep.

His chin sets in a scowl. "I don't want to go. You can't make me."

"I'll wait," she says, very gently. He is terribly young. Sometimes she gets impatient with the old ones when they cling and refuse to let go. They've had all the time in the world to do what they were sent here to do, and as far as she can see, there's no reason for them to hang around. But even those who are bedridden and senile sometimes hold on well past the time they should be moving on.

This child is only six and has all the reasons in the world to linger. His parents, who are at home sleeping, love him deeply. Reminders of their attentiveness are everywhere in this otherwise sterile room. Stuffed animals. Picture books. A notebook loaded with games. Music. DVDs.

If they knew that this was his last night, no power on earth would keep them from his bedside. She suspects they will spend the rest of their lives feeling guilty that they left him alone, even though they've gone home firmly believing that he's getting better and will be coming home tomorrow. Even though they are exhausted.

Even the nurses aren't worried about him. They check his vital signs every four hours, and Sophronia hasn't been here that long. If someone comes in and finds her, there will be questions, but she hopes to be gone before then.

To her eyes the boy looks healthy enough. He's had minor surgery, nothing that should kill him, but she knows it's his time, all the same. The call began as it always does, as an uneasiness deep in her belly, something like hunger, growing in intensity and need until it drove her here. She knows, as deeply as she ever knows anything, that she is in the right place at the right time. But this is her first crossing with a child. He is so young, so beautiful, so unfinished. It's not like he's bald from chemo, or wheezing from pneumonia, and she can't help wondering if maybe she was wrong about this one.

His eyelids drift closed and she watches him dream, the eyeballs beneath the thin lids darting side to side. His breath hitches from time to time, and his head moves on the pillow. His hair darkens with sweat. And then his eyes fly open, wide and frightened. His hand tightens on hers. She can feel the pressure of each thin finger digging into her skin.

"Easy," she whispers. "I've got you."

His rib cage expands as he tries to suck in all the oxygen in the room, enough to feed his body through what he senses is coming. There is a short pause. And then all the breath empties out of him in a slow, deep sigh as he trusts his soul into her keeping. It is a gift and a responsibility, one that tracks tears down her cheeks even as she carries him all the way to the crossing, and releases him into what lies beyond.

He will be fine, she tells herself, although she always wonders. She's not allowed to look, to know what comes next. She's always trusted that what she does is right and necessary, but how can she be sure? There are too many mysteries. Souls cross without assistance every day. She's not present for every death in Shadow Valley, and while there are a few unquiet spirits hanging around, there aren't all that many.

Task completed, she opens her eyes to the world of hard-edged realities. A tiny body lies empty on the white bed, the chest no longer rising and falling, the eyes closed. Her own body is cramped and bruised, and the exhaustion is so overwhelming she's tempted to lie down on the bed beside the child and go to sleep.

But things will be bad enough without being found here with the dead. If someone sees her there will be talk again, the familiar whispers behind her back.

Witch.

Ghoul.

Soul stealer.

Time to go, before somebody looks in. She needs to eat something and make her body move, to ground herself in feeling human before this other part of her carries her away.

TWO

Miracle Road is aptly named.

It's a miracle that anybody actually lives out here and a greater miracle that an ordinary vehicle can navigate what passes for a road. There is no shoulder, no ditch, only an unbroken wall of trees marking the boundary between road and not-road. I cling to the door handle, rattling around like a shotgun shell in an ammo can as the state-issued pickup truck bounces and lurches through ruts and potholes.

Sheriff Jake Callahan, both hands tethered to the steering wheel, long legs grounding him to the floorboards, is too intent on driving to be generous with details. So far, all I know is that an individual named Dason Williams, male, age twenty-four, was found unexpectedly dead. No details, other than that the reporting party who called 911 was hysterical and female.

I'm hoping for a murder. If we're really lucky, the killer will be hanging around looking for trouble. It's been over a month since I've seen any action, and I'm itching for a target in need of killing.

Technically, of course, I'm a civilian and not allowed to shoot anybody. I'm only here because Jake said he needed backup and none of his deputies were available. It's a flimsy excuse and I'm suspicious that he's merely taken pity on my boredom. We both know that the FBI badge I still carry is no longer valid. The Paranormal Unit I spent nearly forty years of my life working for has no use for a woman of my age, especially one who knows too many secrets and can no longer be trusted to keep them.

Badge or no badge, I'm good with both guns and investigations. It's not the first time Jake's brought me in, unofficially, to help with a case. So far they've all been dry and ordinary, but I'm always optimistic that we'll catch a weird one.

The ruts and mud holes give way to a steep, one-lane dirt trail, so narrow that branches screech against the sides of the truck as we crawl upward. When we level out and emerge into a clearing, a view of the valley is spoiled by old cars and junk. A battered Ford pickup, so thoroughly rusted I can see daylight from one side of the bed to the other, is parked beside an old but serviceable Jeep Liberty and a black SUV.

The ground is hard packed dirt, but weeds have persevered, healthier and hardier than the half-dead geraniums in a cracked plastic planter. In the middle of the yard stands what might once have been a nice little house, long neglected. The paint is peeling. The roof is patched with different colors of tin. One of the windows has plywood nailed over it. A black and white mutt of a dog lies on the porch, muzzle resting on his paws, not bothering to even prick his ears at us.

"Motive isn't likely to be robbery," I say.

"You'd be surprised what people hide in a place like this."
Jake gets out of the truck and slams his door. I follow, noting the
cement-like quality of the packed earth. We won't be casting
tire tracks to help us find a suspect. It would take a military
tank to leave any kind of impression.

We are the first responders on site, which is the way I like
it. Everything still raw and untouched, nobody else messing up
the scene or pre-loading witnesses with ideas about what
happened.

The dog stirs, barks once in a half-hearted sort of way, then
comes loping over to check us out. His tongue lolls and his tail
is wagging, so I figure he's not going to bite. Jake pats him on the
head and he trails at our heels as we approach the house.

It's Jake's crime scene and I'm not here in any official capacity, so I let him take the lead. He hands me a camera, and I snap
a few quick pictures of the exterior. The vehicles, with their
license plates. The dirt yard. The front door and the closed
windows.

When I'm done, I nod at him and he steps up on the porch.
I draw my gun as he knocks. He'd object if he weren't focused
in the other direction, but you never know who—or what—is
waiting behind a closed door.

Footsteps approach.

The door opens.

A wall of stench hits me from three paces back, hard
enough to stagger me. Jake's hand goes to cover his nose, but I
don't bother. You can't mouth-breathe away a stink like that, it
registers on your tongue, coats your throat. I can taste grease,
garlic, and something putrefied I don't want to name. I breathe
in again, deeper and on purpose this time, analyzing the various
odors.

Definitely a whiff of dead body, but it's competing with dog shit, trash, old food, cigarette smoke, and sour laundry.

All of these make an interesting backdrop for the woman who stands waiting in the doorway.

She looks like she's walked out of a casting call for *stiff, starched church lady of older generation*. A beige turtle-necked sweater and tweed skirt cover her from chin to mid-calf. Her gray hair is cut short and styled in a frizzy perm. Her eyes are clear and bright with curiosity and a little touch of something that looks like excitement. When she speaks, her voice is distinctive, low for a woman, reedlike.

"You were quick. Thank you so much for coming right over."

"Are you the caller?" Jake sounds nasal and a little choked.

"Good gracious, no. That was Geneva who called. The boy's mother." One hand reaches up to pat her perfect hair. "Terrible, isn't it?"

Jake stands there, waiting.

"Oh, I'm sorry. I'm Mrs. Hemsley. The pastor's wife. I couldn't believe it when Geneva called to tell me, and of course I came right over."

"I imagine it's quite a shock for you."

Her hand goes to her heart. "Lord have mercy, yes. Geneva's just—well, losing a child, you know? Especially this way. Shot himself in the head, can you believe it? God have mercy on his soul. It's Dason who's dead, with a D, you know, as in dog. Not Jason. I do wish parents would just name their kids normally, don't you? So confusing for everybody. But listen to me, nattering along. What can I do?"

"Direct us to the body, if you would," Jake says.

"Oh, yes. Of course. I'm just so disturbed I can't think straight at all."

We follow her down a hallway narrowed by boxes of empty beer bottles stacked on top of each other on one side, old newspapers on the other. I feel like a cow in a branding chute. If somebody stood in the door behind us to take a shot, we'd have no room to duck or maneuver. I look back over my shoulder. The door has been left open, presumably for ventilation purposes, and all I see is a rectangle of hard packed dirt crowned by a strip of blue sky.

A few more steps lead us into what passes for a living area. The carpet is buried under bits of paper, candy wrappers, and plates of stale food. A pile of something brown and nasty lurks under a coffee table.

Jake wades in, undeterred, and I follow, straight toward the woman who sits huddled on the couch, holding a cigarette in a shaking hand.

Her hair is greasy and strings around her face in unpleasant wisps. The couch she sits on is black with dirt and matted with pet hair. She glances up as we walk in, then returns her gaze to nothing.

"Did you call this in, ma'am?" Jake asks.

She looks up at him, eyes wide and dry. "He's just sitting there," she says, her voice flat and expressionless. "Like he's working on his computer. I took him a cup of coffee and some cookies. But he didn't turn around. Wouldn't answer me. Something wrong with the boy..."

Mrs. Hemsley, to give her credit, sits down on that filthy couch and puts her arm around the woman's shoulders.

"Now, Geneva dear, you know he can't answer you. He's dead."

"Doesn't get much more wrong than that," the woman says. She tries to take another drag of the smoking cigarette, but her hands are shaking so hard she can't get it to her mouth. Her face contorts, the corners of her lips pulling down, her eyes creasing almost shut, and I brace myself for tears. But the spasm passes and she draws a deep breath and resumes smoking.

"He's tired," she says. "Been working way too hard. That boss of his, she's a slave driver. I've no use for a woman like that. She should stay home with her own kids, not be driving other people's boys to the brink of exhaustion."

Mrs. Hemsley looks up at us and shrugs. "You see how it is," she says.

"I'll be wanting to talk to his boss." Jake pulls out his notepad and pen again, but the woman just stares off into space.

"He works in Spokane," Mrs. Hemsley volunteers. "Just came home for a few days off. He does that. Comes home to help out."

I use my pocket camera to snap a few shots of the room. The clutter on the floor. The women side by side on the couch. I can't imagine what sort of help the young man in question has provided; it looks like the house has been burying itself in debris for years.

"Takes time, after a shock," Jake answers. "Maybe we'll just go—have a word with the boy. Dason, you said?"

"He's a good boy," Geneva murmurs. "Don't ever let nobody tell you different."

"I'm sure. Where is he?"

Geneva doesn't answer, drifting off into space again. I can't tell if she's high, or drunk, or merely in a state of shock.

"Down in the basement," Mrs. Hemsley says. "Stairs go down off the kitchen. I'd show you, but I really don't want to see that sight again."

"That's fine. You stay here with his mother. See if you can get her to drink some water, will you? That will help allay the shock."

The stairs have death trap written all over them. One lone bulb dangles from its wires to light a steep wooden staircase. Boxes are stacked on both sides, thick with dust. A damp smell of mildew and rot is overpowered by the stench of decay. There are no railings, and unstable stacks of boxes prevent me from holding on to the wall for support.

My bad leg doesn't like stairs at the best of times. If I fall, I'm going down like a human bowling ball and taking Jake out with me. My skin prickles as I put my foot on the fifth step. I know this feeling all too well. We've got a ghost. Can't tell if it's Dason's or something older, but it puts me on high alert. Usually, the spooks are harmless, but some have enough rage to do damage. In this case it wouldn't take much—just a box shifting enough to trip me, and down I'll go.

Jake stops at the bottom of the stairs, flashlight on. He's using the blue filter that will show up blood or fluids or flare bright on areas where bleach has been applied. By the smell, I'm pretty sure there's no history of bleach in this basement, but he starts exploring. Cobwebs cling to my face, and I get my own flashlight out and shine it around.

Dust. Mouse turds. Piles of boxes, once stacked neatly, have toppled, spewing their contents out onto the floor.

The door to Dason's room marks the threshold of a whole new world order. Unlike the rest of the house, it's not only clean, it's organized.

Everything has a place, and everything is in its place. Star Wars action figures line shelves constructed from bricks and boards. The narrow bed is neatly made, spread with a comforter that features R2-D2 and C-3P0.

Jake stands motionless. His gaze is fixed not on the body slumped over the desk, but at the posters covering every inch of the walls. Dason's interest didn't run to flowers or fruit baskets.

"Maybe we should check the freezer for body parts," I say, spinning around for the panoramic view.

Jake doesn't answer, just steps forward to see better. I join him, moving from picture to picture, not sure what to make of what I'm seeing: Dead bodies at car crashes. Bodies naked on autopsy tables. Bodies splayed open with their organs exposed. On first glance it looks like crude voyeurism at best, sadistic necrophilia at worst, but on closer inspection I don't find the images alarming or disturbing. The photographer has managed, by some stroke of genius, to capture a certain beauty even in the ugliest of deaths.

In the place of honor, dead center of the display wall, hang two poster-sized prints of a naked girl, front and back. She is young. No longer a child, but still in her teens by my best guess. Her hair is buzzed short, little more than dark stubble over a well-shaped skull. Her face is beautiful, with lovely bones that might have been carved from flawless marble by a master hand. High cheekbones, lips full but not pouty, eyes spaced just wide enough for interest with an upturned slant that hints at an Eurasian heritage. Even in death her skin looks airbrushed and seems to glow from within.

But from the jawline down she is covered in tattoos; part artist's canvas, part mystery.

A world tree sprouts from her navel, the trunk running up

the center of her torso. Branches spread outward, twining up onto her shoulders and down her arms. Flowers and birds are woven into the branches. On her back is the mirror image. Roots trace the length of her thighs and calves, tiny earth dwelling creatures cradled among them.

"Now what is our World Tree Girl doing here?" Jake's thoughts echo my own. He takes the camera from me and snaps pictures of the wall, close-up and from a distance.

Nearly a month ago, these very same pictures were brought to our attention by Sophronia, the undertaker's daughter, after they surfaced on a blog she follows called *Underground Weird*. The blog listed autopsy findings so bizarre they could be easily dismissed as sensational fiction. A bloodless body. Veins filled with a gelatinous substance of unknown composition. No apparent cause of death.

I have reason to know that this isn't fiction. There is one paranormal who kills like this, a creature nicknamed the Medusa, thanks to the clear jelly she injects into the veins of her victims. She is also the one paranormal I've encountered that I don't know how to kill.

Jake and I, along with Sophronia and Matt, the cook at the Manor, have done our best to track down the identity of the dead girl and the host of *Underground Weird*. Between the four of us, we have access to multiple law enforcement and FBI databases and cutting-edge technological know-how, and yet all our efforts so far have yielded nothing.

"Maybe we've finally found our blogger," Jake says, now.

"If so, somebody found him first."

By common consent, we turn to examine the body.

Dason sits in an office chair, slumped forward, left hand resting in his lap, right dangling down to the floor. Beside the chair, directly beneath his limp, blood-blackened fingers, rests a small handgun.

His head is bent forward onto his chest. On the right hand side of his skull, where the bullet entered, there's only a small hole. It's the left side that's ruined, where the hollow point did the most damage on exit. His eye is missing, the socket shattered. His face, what's left of it, is smooth-shaven and soft. He's neither lean nor gone to fat, like his mother. He is neatly dressed, nothing fancy, but the blue jeans and button-up shirt look clean in the spaces unmarked by blood.

On the desk is a laptop, closed, plugged into the charger.

"Hell," Jake says. "Not much of a life. Work sucks, boss is riding him, and he can never quite get away from all this. That Hemsley woman is probably right about suicide."

"Why would he come back here to do that? Revenge against mommy and a disgusting childhood?"

"He could have killed the girl and then himself out of remorse." Jake stalks across the room, careful to avoid stepping on blood spatter or disturbing the scene.

I stay where I am, thinking.

"She's a lot younger than he is," Jake says. "Maybe he seduced her, had sex with her, then killed her out of guilt."

"If he felt guilty about killing her, he wouldn't have put her pictures up on the blog."

"We don't know that he did that," Jake protests. "Evidence, Maureen. Somebody else could have done the blog. Whatever the reason, there's no reason to think this is murder."

"Evidence is for court. He's our blogger and somebody killed him."

"Oh, come on, Maureen. Gun's right there. Look around the room—he never moved on from adolescence. Probably hasn't ever had a girlfriend. And he obviously had a sick fascination with death."

I can't argue with any of this, but at the same time I can't help seeing the photographs as something beautiful, not the product of a sick mind. And something else about this scene is bothering me, though I can't put my finger on what. "I don't see a suicide note, do you?"

"Most people don't bother to write one. Especially this kid. Who's going to read it?"

But even as he says this, he picks his way around the edge of the room to get a look at the desk. "Nothing here."

"Maybe it's in the laptop."

Jake's eyes narrow and I keep my own face innocent and open. "He was a geek. And a millennial. Everything's electronic for them."

Jake starts taking pictures again, making a photographic record. The position of the body. The laptop. The gun. Details of the kid's face and hands. And then he puts on a pair of gloves and gingerly opens the laptop, careful not to disturb its placement on the desk.

The laptop must have been closed when Dason died. The only blood on the screen is from drops that seeped in around the edges, forming a macabre picture frame around a whole lot of nothing.

The only icons are for basic, run-of-the-mill software. Not a single window is open. Jake closes the lid and glances in my direction. "What?"

"I never said anything."

"You don't have to. You're thinking very loudly."

"Well, first off, I think it's weird that not only are all the windows closed, he's exited all the programs."

"He was finished with everything. Done. He liked things neat and tidy, you can see that."

"But wouldn't he want to have a connection to somebody or something? A last Facebook post, a goodbye of some kind?"

He fixes me with a withering glare. "The laptop is evidence. And you are not on the evidence team."

"So, deputize me."

"It was a suicide, Maureen. Evidence is going to bear that out."

"Bets?"

He sighs. "Everything is not some elaborate FBI setup. This is a small town. People kill themselves. Especially young white males afflicted with parental units like Geneva."

"You're not even going to investigate?"

"It's the coroner's call. Speak of the devil," he says, as heavy booted footsteps reverberate on the stairs. A large man in biker leathers and a red bandanna blocks the doorway.

"Tell me you haven't moved that body." His voice positively booms into the room, a deep basso profundo that vibrates down into my toes. In my experience, a voice like that is usually incongruously connected to some skinny sapling that looks like I could snap him in half with my bare hands. Not this time. This guy is at least six foot four and built like a linebacker. Straight black hair in a braid, brown eyes, skin the color of mahogany. A small tattoo marks the angle of his jaw, but I can't make out what it is from here.

"We're just looking," Jake says, evenly. "Not touching. How's it going, Mac?"

The man stays planted in the doorway, eyes probing into every nook, corner, and cranny of the room. "Eh, it's been better, it's been worse. I want to take some pictures. Without you in them."

He's got a professional grade camera slung around his neck, and carries what looks like a toolbox in his right hand. He sets this down in a blood-free space and gets to work. I watch with approval as he pulls out plastic numbers and sets them up around the room, marking the obvious evidence. Looks like he's going to do this right.

"Well, I'll leave you to it," Jake says. "We'll go have another chat with the mother."

"Good luck with that one. If Geneva's got two brain cells left to rub together after all the years of booze, I'll be a ballerina. Not that she had a lot to start with."

"You know her then?" I ask.

The gaze that turns on me is intense and scrutinizing. "Not well, but it's a small county. You, I don't know at all."

"She's with me," Jake says. "Mac, this is Maureen. Maureen, meet our new coroner."

Mac grunts, his face revealing nothing, then turns his back and takes another photo. Definitely a professional upgrade from our last coroner, who was a curvy, giggly blonde. She also murdered my former partner, Phil, and then ran off to Europe.

"This isn't suicide," I say.

Mac lowers the camera with exaggerated slowness and turns to glare at me. "Evidence first. Go theorize elsewhere."

THREE

Elsewhere leads me back upstairs, where Geneva sits, unmoving, a steaming mug in her hands.

"Drink up, dear. It's chamomile. It will help to relax you." Mrs. Hemsley sinks down beside her and puts a comforting arm around her shoulders.

Geneva moves like a wound-up automaton, taking a sip on command. She lowers the cup in the same mechanical fashion, staring into the depths of the beverage as if she has no idea what it is or why she is holding it.

"Maybe something a little stronger?" she asks. "To take the edge off."

The older woman stiffens. "Alcohol is not the solution. This is the time to turn to the good Lord—"

"Listen here, Evelyn Hemsley, when your son is dead in your basement, feel free to preach to me. I want a drink. Don't you think about throwing it away. I know how you are."

"I'm just trying to help. Bending over backward. Don't you think—"

"Ladies, please." Jake lifts a pile of unfolded laundry out of the chair across from Geneva, uprooting something small and black from the tangle of clothes that scuttles across the seat and disappears over the side.

He sits down. I stay on my feet.

"Now. I need a little bit of information from you, okay?" Jake's tone is gentle.

Geneva's eyes are blank, but she nods. His voice brings her back enough that she remembers the cup and takes a small sip of the tea.

"That's the ticket," Jake says, nodding approvingly. "Now, did Dason still live with you?"

"He's got an apartment in Spokane. Just came home for..." Her voice quivers. She takes a deep breath. "He got fired. That bitch let him go."

Her face crumples. When her hands start shaking, Mrs. Hemsley takes the cup from her.

"Need a smoke. Just a sec." Geneva fumbles a cigarette out of the package. Jake lights it for her. The smoke wreathes up around her head.

"Okay. Dason's boss let him go," Jake says, ever patient. "He came home when?"

"I was away. For the weekend. Sister bought tickets to Vegas."

My imagination tries to capture this wreckage of a woman on a plane, then in a casino. Well, that part fits. I can picture her, cigarette in one hand, the other pulling the slots, and all the while sonny boy is lying dead in the basement at home.

"Loved his job, although I can't say why. Called me to say

she'd let him go, and some upset he was by that. I should have been here for him. And maybe he wouldn't have..."

The grief breaks through with the sudden violence of a wrecking ball. Great wrenching sobs suck all the oxygen out of the room. She drops the cigarette, lit, on top of a newspaper and tears at her hair, wailing loudly.

A flicker of bright flame erupts from the edge of the paper. Mrs. Hemsley jerks it onto the floor, where it ignites a fabric softener sheet and a candy wrapper. I stomp the fire out with both feet, feeling a *squish* and a small *pop* of something buried beneath the litter.

Jake grabs the still smoldering cigarette and stabs it out in an overflowing ashtray. I stamp on the paper one more time, just to be sure. Mrs. Hemsley pats the mother's shoulder and makes little clucking noises.

When the wails ease to sobs, Jake leans forward and takes one of Geneva's hands.

"Bear with me a little bit. Just a few more questions, okay?"

She nods, gulping in air and making a little whimpering sound.

"Where did he work? I'd like to talk to his former boss, maybe his coworkers."

Her brow draws down so low it nearly obscures her eyes. Her fists clench. "I'll kill the bitch if I ever get my hands on her."

This is too much for Mrs. Hemsley. "Now, now, Geneva dear. Forgiveness is of the Lord."

"Fuck that," Geneva says. "She killed my baby, sure as she murdered him with her own hands."

"I'll look into that for you," Jake says. "I promise. But you have to tell me who she is."

"She deserves the chair. I want to hear her flesh sizzle." Geneva leans forward, her fleshy face wobbling, tears and snot dripping. "Her name is Kate something or other. She's the ME at the city morgue in Spokane."

Jake's body goes tense, although to his credit the expression on his face doesn't change. "What is it about her that is so evil? Apart from the fact that she fired Dason?"

"She was always on his case. A few little photographs of dead bodies and you'd think he killed somebody. What do dead people need with privacy? He wasn't hurting a soul."

"So the posters in his room," I ask her, "he took those?"

"Walmart wouldn't let him print them posters at their store. Like it's any of their business, you know? He had to send away to get them posters made. He was an artist. Nobody understood him."

"So he'd have been upset about getting fired then."

Geneva shakes her head. "I expected that. He loved that job. But he said he was onto something big and it didn't matter. Somebody wanted to buy his pictures, he said. He was all full of himself with that. 'How'd you like to move into a real house, Mom?' And now he's..." She can't bring herself to say the word and reaches for the cigarette pack instead.

Jake sighs, pushes back his chair, and gets to his feet.

"We are going to do a full investigation," he says, not looking at me. "There's going to be a crime scene team coming in."

"Like CSI?"

"Sort of. It's very important that you stay out of the basement."

Both women shiver, as if on cue. Geneva starts crying again.

"Is that really necessary?" Mrs. Hemsley asks. "I mean, it seems quite clear what happened. Not that I looked very closely, of course, it's all so terribly gruesome and sad." Her voice drifts away, and she sniffs and digs in a capacious purse for a tissue.

"Do you know if anybody came to the house while you were away?" Jake asks. "Mailman, neighbors, anybody at all?"

"No reason for anybody to come up here, is there?" Geneva replies. "I mean, Evelyn stopped by to check on things, but that's all."

"Did you see anything suspicious while Geneva was away?"

"Nothing," Mrs. Helmsley answers. "But I must confess I didn't come in. Let's be honest, it's not the most comfortable environment. And then I saw that Dason's truck was here, so I saw no point in checking again. If only I had come in sooner, maybe everything would have been different."

There's nothing to be said in response to that. I get up and follow Jake out the door, the sound of weeping loud in my ears even after we're in Jake's truck and driving away.

WE DRIVE for a good fifteen minutes before we say a word to each other. Jake calls in details to dispatch and asks for the crime scene unit. I watch the trees go by, and wait, letting him bring up the issue that hangs heavy between us.

"We have to follow protocols," he says, finally. "You know this."

"They'll rule it a suicide."

"Maybe it is." But he sounds less certain than he did a while ago.

"And if the ME is involved? You going to send the body up to her for an autopsy?"

"What do you expect me to do? Spirit away the body and the evidence? Pretend it didn't happen? Dispatch knows I went to the scene. Once she gets over the shock, Geneva is going to blab all over the community. She's the sort of woman who will embrace grief as a status changer. As for the Hemsley person, she's probably already notified the prayer chain. We can't pretend it didn't happen. Can't you do something? What about your people?"

Jake means the super-secret X-files-type FBI unit I used to work for.

Used to.

Before a paranormal damn near killed me during a stake-out. Before I was too old and damaged to be of value. Before the Medusa surfaced and I became a liability because I knew too much about their involvement in her origins.

I stare at him in disbelief. "You're kidding, right? 'My people' took out a hit on me, in case that has slipped your mind. Dason was going to sell pictures of the World Tree Girl. If we're right in guessing the Medusa killed her, then *my* people are at the top of *my* suspect list."

Jake swears a long, elaborate string of fluent curses that raises my spirits. In fact, I'm feeling better than I have in a good long while.

"So, about the ME—" I venture, when he stops to take a breath.

"I can't do anything about that. I can hardly refuse to send the body to the ME in Spokane without making all kinds of wild accusations."

"How well do you know the new coroner?"

"Mac? Seems like a pretty solid guy, as far as his community reputation goes. He grew up in this area, but I don't know him personally."

"And Charlene was a well-respected physician. Look how that ended up."

Jake shrugs. "Every man—or woman—has a price, I suppose."

"Maybe we should hold the body here, at the funeral parlor. Set a deputy to watch it."

"If I do that, am I putting my people at risk?"

He already knows the answer.

"We'll have to update Matt and Sophie."

Jake's jaw tightens. "I've already broken all the rules by bringing you in." He holds up a hand to stop my objection. "I know, I know. When it comes to paranormal investigations, the rules do not apply. Let's call a meeting at the Manor, then, as soon as I get the body squared away."

"I'll set it up."

We drive in silence the rest of the way, each of us busy with our own deductions and considerations. Neither one of us is big on trust, but if we're going to solve this case, we're going to have to work together.

When Jake drops me at the Manor, I stand outside to watch him drive away, shivering in a cold November wind. The air smells like snow, and a few random flakes sift down from a leaden sky. They melt as soon as they touch the ground, but my aching bones and the metal plate in my leg tell me it won't be long before winter comes to stay.

Still, I pull out a cigarette and light it, letting the clean air wash away the stink of that house while I scope out the parking lot. Sophronia's van, with its lurid depiction of a cremation urn, is parked next to Matt's nondescript Ford pickup. My Jag sits where I left it, off to the far edge where it's unlikely to get dinged by a careless driver. There's the usual scattering of cars belonging to Manor residents who still drive, and a few afternoon visitors.

One car looks out of place among the pickups, Subarus, and other vehicles appropriate for navigating Shadow Valley roads. It's a small black sedan, recently washed. No dealer frame around the license plate, which is otherwise standard Washington State. No bumper stickers. Nothing hanging from the rearview mirror.

I walk over for a closer look. A set of high-end luggage—one medium suitcase and a carry-on— in the back seat. A Starbucks cup in the holder. That's it. No clutter of receipts or mail or snack wrappers. No loose change. And then I see the bar code sticker on the driver's side window that marks it as a rental car. Could be somebody flew into Spokane and drove up to visit mom or dad. Could be a sales rep.

Or, it could be trouble.

In my experience, trouble tends to be the most likely option.

Energized by the promise of action, I snuff out my smoke, unfinished, and enter Shadow Valley Manor Retirement Home. Inside, everything appears normal. Voices drift down the hallway from the games room. Somebody's TV blares from behind a closed door. A warm smell of roasting beef winds down the corridor from the kitchen and sets my mouth to watering. I'm suddenly ravenous, even though there are still a couple of hours left before dinner.

Matt, the Manor cook, does exquisite things with roast beef. He's also ex-special forces and the guy my former Unit hired to kill me.

In his defense, they'd fed him a string of propaganda that made him believe he was doing the world a favor by eliminating me. In the end, he helped to save my life when he could have taken it. He's now a double agent, working with me at the Manor, while the FBI still thinks he's their man, planted here to keep an eye on me.

It seems like years ago that I first traversed this hallway with no real idea of what I was getting into. A small undercover assignment, I was told. Nothing complicated. All I had to do was rest and recover from the paranormal encounter that almost killed me while keeping my eyes and ears open and reporting to my long-ago partner, Phil Evers.

Phil's involvement was my first clue that the Manor might prove to be more exciting—and dangerous—than the average retirement home. When I knew him, Phil was a legend in his own time, the 007 of the paranormal world. He'd dropped out of sight years ago but suddenly surfaced, buying Shadow Valley Manor and asking my FBI contact to bring me in on an unsanctioned operation. He got himself killed before he had a chance to brief me, leaving me walking blind into a web of dangerous secrets stretching far back into my past.

Phil foresaw the possibility of his own death and bequeathed Shadow Valley Manor to my care and keeping. Owning and operating a retirement home is about the last thing in the world I want to do, but this one comes with certain compensations, including a secret laboratory, and a propensity for paranormal activity.

As usual, I avoid the elevator and take the stairs. Riding in elevators is stupid, like volunteering to be a fish in a barrel when you know damn well somebody is standing by with a shotgun. Thanks to the paranormal slug that gnawed a hole in my belly and the bullet that blew through my right thigh, climbing two flights of stairs to the third floor is now my personal Mount Everest, but I do it anyway. I'm not one for mollycoddling an injury, and I figure stairs are a form of physical therapy. Today I'm on high alert for trouble, but everything seems to be in order until I reach the hallway leading to my new suite.

The Manor offers a variety of rooms, priced according to size and amenities. When I first moved in, I commandeered one of two large suites situated at the end of the third-floor hallway. It was empty at the time, and I figured it was kept that way on purpose to prevent discovery of a secret passage leading out of the closet and down into the basement. As it turns out, secret passages can lead to boring places. All that's at the end of the seemingly mysterious stairway is storage for the residents and a boiler room for the hot water. A perfectly ordinary stairway accesses the same space.

The real secret passage is hidden in the suite that used to belong to an old vampire named Gerry Vermeer. For obvious reason, I've claimed his suite, too, but the process of moving has been slow and gradual, and I'm still in a state of disarray. Tomorrow a moving company is slated to bring the personal belongings that my soon-to-be ex-husband moved into storage for me.

Right now, the door to my former suite is open and it shouldn't be.

Drawing my .38 from the small of the back holster where I keep it, I move as silently as I can, cursing my slowness and the hitch in my gait. When I peer around the doorframe into the suite, it appears to be empty of everything but the furnishings. Bed, chairs, table. The drapes are drawn, the way I left them.

I come around the corner with the gun out and ready, but nothing moves in the main living space. Bathroom, clear. Closet, clear. To be sure, I make my way down the secret staircase into the basement and clear that, too, cursing my damaged leg all the way. Nobody hiding in the storage area or the boiler room, nothing out of order. By the time I drag myself back up the steep and narrow staircase, I'm tired, sweaty, and buzzing with irritation like a nest full of wasps on a hot afternoon.

I'd pay for a fight just now, and it seems I may be in luck. When I cross the hall to my new suite I hear voices behind the door I left locked with six sets of deadbolts.

FOUR

Adrenaline zings through my body. It feels good, familiar, the return of an old friend. The last month, spent mostly behind a desk, stretches behind me like a long desert of boredom.

The door is unlocked. Nudging it open just a crack, I peer in.

The suite is chaos. Furniture and packing boxes are all mixed up together as if they've been dropped through a coal chute. A wave of perfume assaults my nostrils, expensive and overpowering. I press the back of my hand against my nose to block a sneeze.

Sophronia stands in the middle of the mess, face to face with a stranger. The unknown woman's back is to me. It's an exquisitely tailored back, a fitted suit coat over a skirt that smoothes lean hips and ends at the knee. Her dark hair is twisted up into a chignon. Diamonds dangle from her ears. Stiletto heels make long, elegant legs look even longer.

The two of them are engaged in a tug-of-war over some object, hidden from me by the woman's body.

"Give it to me," Sophronia demands. Her eyes glow like a cat's in the dark, and her hair swirls in a weather system all its own. The stranger would be wise to be frightened, but she hangs on.

"Let go. You've got no right—"

"More right than you have, you—"

"You are going to call me names? You? An insolent little Goth girl—"

Time to put a stop to this before Sophie does.

Gun at the ready, I burst into the room. "Drop it. Both of you."

Both heads swivel in my direction. Two sets of hands go up in the air. The item of contention falls, bounces once on the carpet, cracks against the edge of the kitchenette counter, and spills sand all over my floor.

The strange woman kneels, hands hovering over the mess, but not touching. "Oh *mon Dieu*, how horrible," she wails. "Look what you've done."

"I knew you weren't to be trusted." Sophronia grabs my coffee pot, the only ready container in my kitchen, and begins scooping sand into it.

The broken object is reasonably intact, and the large pieces, if reassembled, would be about the size and shape of a funerary urn. As the instant of shock passes, I realize that the mess strewn all over the floor isn't sand, and although we've met only once and that was many years ago, this woman isn't really a stranger.

She's still kneeling on the floor, one hand covering her mouth, exuding enough drama for a daytime soap. I train the gun on her. "Get up, Jill," I order. "But first, take off those shoes. Nice and slow."

"I believe the usual greeting under the circumstances would be, 'I'm sorry for your loss,'" she says.

"The shoes. Sophronia, step back."

"One sec. I need to get Phil contained and—"

"Now."

Sophie's stubborn, but not stupid. Clutching the coffee pot to her breast, she scoots back and away.

Jill is also stubborn, but the gun is persuasive. She slips off one shoe and slides it across the floor and out of my reach.

"Hand the other one to me. Hold it by the heel."

She complies. I give the shoe a quick inspection. No hidden triggers, no hairline cracks that would indicate it's packed with explosives or contains a switchblade. It is, of course, a lethal weapon all on its own. I throw it across the room to join its mate.

"Now, get up. Nice and slow. Sophronia is going to check you for weapons."

As the daughter of an undertaker, Sophie is well versed in caring for the dead but not so much in frisking for guns. She's slow and awkward and comes up empty. I'm not convinced.

"What's with the welcoming committee?" Jill says. "I came for my father."

"Took you long enough to get around to it." Sophie retrieves the broom and dustpan from the storage cupboard and starts sweeping up the remaining ashes. "Can't believe Craig signed Phil's ashes over to you. You don't deserve to have them."

"I was in France," Jill protests. "I had many affairs to put in order before I could come."

Sophie sniffs and dumps the ashes into my coffee pot.

"That doesn't explain what you're doing, *here*," I say. "In my apartment."

"We need to talk," Jill says.

"I can't imagine what we have to talk about."

"Him," she says, simply. "Look, do you mind if I sit? It's been a hellishly long flight and then that drive here from Spokane through absolutely nowhere... I'm exhausted."

"Make yourself at home."

Not that there are a lot of seating options available—two high-backed wooden chairs, antiques that I fell in love with at a secondhand store but Ed always hated. One armchair, almost as old as I am, and losing stuffing out of one arm. A rocking chair that I've never seen before which has somehow gotten mixed in with my belongings.

"The movers came early?" I ask Sophronia.

"I hope you don't mind that I let them in. I tried to call."

Our eyes meet and hold. She knows, and I know, that if she has keys to my suite it's not because I gave them to her. We'll discuss that later. Solidarity in front of the interloper is more important.

"Another thing." Sophie fidgets and twists a strand of her long black hair around her fingers. "It wasn't a moving company, exactly."

Jill takes advantage of my distraction to settle down into my favorite armchair, which may be old, but is damned comfortable and the one I want for myself. My leg aches. I need coffee and a long, hot shower. But I don't trust Jill as far as I can spit, and Phil is now resting peacefully in my coffee pot, which is a problem on so many levels I can't begin to encompass them all. The sudden advent of my belongings isn't helping.

"Skip the riddles, Soph. Spit it out."

"An old guy brought your stuff in a U-Haul. Your husband, he said. Well, ex, to be precise."

"Ed came here?"

"He had a woman with him. Said they decided to drive the stuff here themselves."

I can't picture Ed and Glenda here at Shadow Valley. And I certainly don't see either of them carting boxes and furniture around.

"They'd hired a couple of boys from the high school to move the stuff up from the truck," Sophie says. "Don't worry, though. I was here the whole time. I supervised everything." Her eyes move expressively to my closet door and back, signaling that secrets have been kept.

Jill looks like a cat who has managed to snag a whole cage full of canaries. "I'm sorry I missed your husband. Does he know about you and Phil?"

"Oh, he's not gone," Sophie volunteers. "Wants to talk to you, Maureen. They're staying at a hotel."

The room temperature drops like a stone into a well. Goose bumps run up and down my spine. At first I think it's just my reaction to the idea of talking to Ed, but then Phil's big orange cat, perched atop a stack of boxes to watch the proceedings, hisses and moans, his ears flattening against his skull. Sophie clutches the coffee pot and its contents in one hand, the broom in the other, and stares at something I can't see.

Perfect. We've got a ghost.

"What's wrong with your cat?" Jill's carefully painted eyebrows arch up in a question.

My eyes gravitate to the coffee pot and the cold settles into my belly. "Sophie, maybe you could take Phil back to the funeral parlor and find him a better container? I'm sure Jill would prefer something more—tasteful—to carry him around in."

Sophie's lips press together in a stubborn line. "Craig signed him out to Jill. She's in possession. They can't go back to the funeral home now."

"Oh, for pity's sake. Sophronia—"

"There are *rules*." She looks fierce enough to make me wonder whether they are rules of this planet or another and I'm not asking in present mixed company.

"It's fine," Jill interjects. "I'll buy an urn or something tomorrow."

I don't like this word "tomorrow."

"Surely you don't want to drive around with your father in a coffee pot. And they won't let you back on the plane without a proper container."

"Oh, I'm not going anywhere. Not for a while. I'm staying here."

"Define here. Hotel? Rental property?"

"No," she says, cool and sleek and dangerous. "Here. At the Manor."

Sophie looks from me to Jill and back again. Her expression has gone remote and priestessy, never a good sign. "I'll ask Matt. Maybe he has a jar or something in the kitchen." She stalks out, still clutching the pot, slamming the door so hard something rattles in the box beside it.

The room warms. The cat stops his unearthly staring and jumps into Jill's designer lap, where he sets to kneading and purring. When she tries to pick him up, he digs in with all his claws, snagging the fabric and scratching her in his ensuing panic to get free. A line of blood wells up on her hand.

"Pleasant creature," she says.

"That is Anubis. He belonged to your father."

"My dad named a cat Anubis?"

"No. Sophie named him."

"Whatever his name is, I really don't care for cats."

This is one thing the two of us have in common, but I stay the course of saying as little as possible. Time drags out like a desert crossing without camels or water.

I light up a smoke and move to the kitchenette, leaning back against the counter to take as much weight as I can off the thrice-damned leg. Just when I think I'm going to have to give in and sit down, Jill sighs and breaks the silence.

"Can I have one?"

"No."

"Look, I know we've not been on the best of terms—"

I snort. "That, my dear, is an understatement."

"But I have questions only you can answer," she continues, as if she hasn't heard me, as if questions make for a good enough reason to traipse across the globe and insert herself into my day.

"Here's what I'm wondering," she says, as if I've told her to go ahead. "What would induce my father to buy a retirement home in a tiny little town? Why on earth would a small-town coroner murder him? And above all, why would he leave the Manor to somebody he hasn't spoken to in years?"

"Since the person in question hasn't spoken to him in years, you'd be much more likely to know the answers to that one."

"We've not exactly been close."

"The picture of you on his nightstand was pretty damn recent."

She blinks at that, her gaze dropping away, and picks cat hair from her skirt. When she looks up again, her face looks younger, almost vulnerable. "I suppose it's a mystery that he left me anything at all. The hostility between you and me complicated our relationship."

"A problem he got past, apparently."

She lifts a slim shoulder in a half shrug. "So, answers?" Her eyes are exactly like Phil's, and I feel a traitorous softening of my heart.

Her father is currently occupying my coffee pot, and her mother died years ago. Maybe I'm being too hard on her.

"It seems your father and the coroner were lovers. She's not the first woman to lose her mind over him and do something stupid." A tactless remark, given that Jill's mother killed herself because of Phil's tendency to wander, but Jill gives no sign that I've struck a nerve.

"And where is this coroner now? I haven't seen any arrest notices."

My turn to shrug. "She took a flight to France, interestingly enough. There is talk of extradition, but they haven't found her yet." I let that hang between us.

Jill still doesn't rise to my bait. She toys with a ring, diamond and ruby. Her face gives away nothing. The pressure to fill the silence grows, and I resist. If I talk now, if I feed her some line about the Manor and make up a reason why Phil bought it or gave it to me, she'll know I'm lying. She's playing the silence the same way I am, watching me for reactions.

I know my tells and focus on keeping my right hand quiet at my side, the left busy with the cigarette, eyes always on her. In the background, though, I'm aware of time passing, and I know I need to get her out of my suite. Soon. When I get down to ash, I crush the butt into an ashtray, and say, casually, "Perhaps he didn't think you'd be the safest around a bunch of help-less old people."

"Right," she retorts. "You're clearly the perfect choice for that."

"Clearly."

"You're really not going to share those smokes?"

"No."

"I have hired an attorney," she says. "To go over the will."

And there it is, finally. The real reason why she's here. When I first discovered Phil had left the Manor to me, I would gladly have turned it over. Not now, though. It holds too many secrets.

"It's a free country," I tell her. "Have at it. But trust me— running the Manor isn't fun and games. Nor is it particularly lucrative."

"What do you want with it then?"

I shrug. "Nothing better to do. Divorce. Nowhere else to be."

"Such a shame," she says, sarcasm piled so thick I can almost see it materialize into a black cloud above her head.

A tap comes at the door.

Whatever is out there, it's not opportunity or salvation.

Another knock, louder this time.

Jill's features sharpen, the patient cat who has finally spotted a mouse. "You look tired, Maureen. Shall I get it for you?"

Without waiting for my response, she dislodges the cat and crosses the room to open the door. When she sees Jake standing there, she spins around back to me.

"How did you do that?"

"How did I do what?"

"Call the cops. You didn't even pick up your phone. Wait. It was that obnoxious teenager, right? She called."

Her behavior, strongly indicative of guilt, is a matter of interest. What has she done, or what is she planning to do, that she thinks the police would be interested in her?

"Come on in, Sheriff," I say, keeping my voice formal and willing Jake to pick up the cues. "This is Jillian. What's your last name, now, Jill? Have you married?"

Jake's sharp eyes take in the chaos of boxes and furniture in one quick sweep, then focus in on Jill. Although he's old enough to be her father, she flashes him a killing smile and drops her voice to a low purr. "I have no idea what they told you, but I can assure you I'm not making trouble. At least not that kind of trouble."

Her accent is suddenly more French. She even looks more French.

"You would be Phil Evers's daughter," Jake says.

She bats her eyelashes at him. "Oh, trés bien. How did you guess?"

"He had a picture of you on his nightstand."

For just a fraction of an instant her face darkens with what might be grief, the expression gone before I can pin it down.

"I would love to have this photograph. Is it with his personal effects? And must I come to the station to pick these up?"

"No need," Jake says. "All of his belongings remain in his home. I'll get you the key and you can go over there any time you wish."

"Now would be good," I say, burning a hole into Jake with my eyes. "She needs a place to stay."

"Oh, I don't think so. I am so very tired," Jill says. "I don't think I'm safe to drive."

"I'm pretty sure Jake would give you a lift."

Her eyes, the same damn shade of ice blue as Phil's, well up with tears and she sniffs, pitifully.

"I'm sorry," she says, her voice breaking. "But I just—I can't face that now. Not yet, so soon after my trip. And to be there alone all night in the place where he died..." She shivers, dramatically.

Jake's face softens. I roll my eyes. "Fine. Let's get you a hotel at once."

"I tried to make a reservation before I left France," she says, very nearly swooning with sudden onset weakness. "All the hotels are booked. Some sort of a convention, I understand. I'm on a waiting list, but nobody has called."

"What kind of convention could possibly be happening in Shadow Valley?"

"Wildlife management," Jake says. "Every year."

"Apparently Ed managed to get a hotel."

Jake blinks. "Who is Ed?"

I draw a deep breath. "My husband."

"Ah," he says, noncommittally. An awkward silence threatens.

"I'd love to stay here, at the Manor. Maureen and I have so many things to talk about." Jillian smiles bravely, tears glistening beautifully on her cheeks. She presents the perfect expression of a weary, bereaved damsel in distress. "And I'm here already, n'est-ce pas? Surely that's the easiest thing. I noticed an empty suite across the hall? It's old-fashioned, but clean. I'm sure it will do for a few days."

Hellfire and damnation, she's good. Jake looks torn between

her misery and me. And I've got no valid objection to make. At least if she's across the hall, I can keep an eye on her. If she finds the secret passage in that room, it won't lead her to anything more exciting than the junk Shadow Valley residents have hoarded away in the basement.

She reads acquiescence in my silence. "*Bien*. Good. Are there sheets for the bed? Towels?"

"This is not a hotel."

"She's a stranded traveler. Surely we can scare up some bedding and a towel," Jake says.

"Fine, I'll have sheets and towels brought up, but you'll have to make the bed yourself. Dinner is at five, downstairs in the dining room. Please be prompt."

"You can count on it. Do you think someone could bring up my bags? I truly am just so exhausted."

"Leave me your keys. I'll ask Matt."

Jill shrugs and hands over the car keys. When she leaves the room, the cat makes to follow her, but I scoop him up and keep him with me. He knows too much, and I don't trust the two of them alone in a room together.

FIVE

"What was that all about?" Jake asks, as soon as the door closes behind her. "Good God, Maureen, the woman is grieving her father. You're acting like she's a terrorist about to blow up the whole damn place."

"Wouldn't put it past her."

"What did you do to her?"

"Me? How on earth is this my fault?"

"Only reason I can think of that she'd be out to get you is if you did something to her."

I sigh. "She's Phil's daughter. Who knows what he might have taught her? If she's half as smart as he was, she's more of a nuclear warhead than a suicide bomber."

His eyes soften. "Her showing up must open a whole can of worms for you."

He means grief. There is that, too, if I'm honest, but he has no idea the can of worms that Jill represents. Mutant worms. Teeth. Fangs.

Fortunately, there's no need to explain things further, as he's distracted by the state of my suite. "Lovely place you've got here. What sort of discount moving company did you hire?"

Ed and Glenda is not a topic I care to address with the sheriff, or with anybody, for that matter. I can't begin to imagine what possessed the man to drive a moving truck to Shadow Valley. Fortunately, Jake's question was only rhetorical and he's already moved on to practical matters.

"I'm feeling a draft. Is that slider sealing properly?"

He makes his way through the mess to check the door, but I know that's not the source of the lingering chill. "Looks okay. Are we on for the meeting?"

"As far as I know. Sophie went to find a container for Phil."

"You might need to explain that," Jake says.

"What?"

I'm wading through the boxes, each one identified with a list of contents written in Ed's strong, precise hand. Maybe something will be useful for this investigation.

"Why does Phil need a suitable container?" Jake says. "He's still dead, I presume?"

There's just a hint of a question mark behind the sarcasm. Poor Jake has had a steep learning curve about the paranormal world.

"Oh, that. Yes. As far as I know. Sophie and Jill just spilled him all over the floor in a tug-of-war over possession of the ashes. Which reminds me, I should probably vacuum up what's left."

Jake, who is standing pretty much where the spill happened, looks down at his feet and then back at me. Before he can say anything else or I can look for the vacuum cleaner, there's a sharp knock at the door, repeated at precisely five seconds once, and then again.

Matt and Sophie come in together, Sophie clutching a large plastic container labeled POTATO SALAD.

"It's only temporary," she says. "Where is she?"

"If by she you mean Jill, she was last seen entering the suite across the hall."

"You're going to let her stay here?" Sophie asks, incredulous. "Don't say I didn't warn you."

She stalks through the room, into my walk-in closet, and I hear a creak as the secret door opens.

"That needs some WD-40," Matt says. "What's up with Soph?"

"Who ever knows? Come on, let's go."

Matt and Jake follow Sophie. I take the time to lock all of my deadbolts and set my security system. If anybody tries to break in, there will be no warning lights or alarms, just a discreet buzzing in my pocket. If Jill decides to come back into my suite for some snooping, I'll know all about it, but still, I take care to close the closet door behind me, and then the secret passage doorway in turn. The last thing in the world that we need is for her to find her way down to the laboratory.

According to my best guess, the underground passages in Shadow Valley Manor originated as fallout shelters. The building itself was built as a Cold War military installation. When it was decommissioned, it became the Home for Unwed Mothers (known to the locals as HUM) before it was repurposed into a retirement home for seniors. In reality it's more of a high-end boarding home complete with meals, laundry service, cleaning, and a 24-7 staff member to respond to any other needs.

The secret stairway built into the closet in this suite leads to a warren of small rooms and then a long passageway that culminates in a clandestine laboratory. The operators of HUM used it to conduct human-paranormal research on the fetuses of the young pregnant girls who came here seeking shelter.

This laboratory is where my new Paranormal Investigative Team—composed of me, Jake, Matt, and Sophronia—holds its regular meetings. Sophie says we need an interior decorator, and I'll admit that this room looks harsh and a little creepy. A clandestine lab is a clandestine lab, and there's not a lot you can do to change that.

I have visions of getting some decent forensic equipment in as soon as we can scrounge up the money. My wish list includes a powerful computer, fingerprint equipment, chemical analysis, maybe even a DNA sequencer.

For now, we get by with bulletin boards, a laptop, and a projector. We've brought in a card table and four folding chairs.

By the time I arrive, a coffee maker gurgles cheerfully on the counter beside an antiquated centrifuge, and the others are all seated and waiting for me.

"So the blogger's been murdered?" Sophie asks, before I even get settled into my chair.

"We don't know that," Jake protests. "It looks like a suicide. And we don't know if he's our blogger."

"He's our blogger. And it wasn't suicide." I load crime scene photos onto my laptop from the camera's SD card and project the images onto the wall one at a time.

"First lead we've had since that blog popped up a month ago," Matt says. "If these pictures are identical to the ones on *Underground Weird*, then I think we can assume there's at least a connection between our new vic and the World Tree Girl."

"Suicide," Jakes says. "Until we have a reason to believe otherwise." He holds up his hand to stop my protest. "A real reason. Something other than one of Maureen's hunches."

I cue up the *Underground Weird* post on my laptop, scrolling through the photos and then making a split screen for comparison.

"They look like the same pics to me."

Jake makes a noncommittal sound in his throat. "Let's look at that article again."

I scroll back to the top.

The blog header features a tasteful drawing of a crow with a bloody eyeball dangling from its beak. A human heart sits on one side of a balancing scale, a black feather on the other. I have no objection to the imagery, but the article was written by an idiot:

In the darkness where the creepy crawlies lurk something is afoot. Gather round, children, and let me tell you a tale. Don't be misled here by the pretty face; this is clearly the body of an alien who has chosen to de-animate. The Medical Examiner is looking for a killer, but we know better.

Look for the ligature mark around the neck. See it? No, because there is none. Deformities caused by broken bones? A caved in skull? So much as a bruise beneath all of those tattoos? No. Not a mark. Healthy brain. Healthy heart, lungs, stomach, kidneys.

So what happened, then? The official verdict? Exsanguination.

A reasonable conclusion, given that there is no blood

in the body. But it's a conclusion based on a faulty premise, and therefore it's erroneous.

Let me ask you this—where did all that blood go? How did it leave the body?

Again, there is not a mark to be seen on her skin. No laceration, either internal or external, that would result in bleeding. Even if her throat had been slit, there would still be blood in the arteries and veins, a little pooling in the heart. But there is NONE. Only a strange, clear jelly that has yet to be identified by the geek squad at the forensic lab...

The blog post is unsigned. When I conducted a WHO IS search it yielded the name Duncan Donut, with an address that doesn't exist. Every trick I've tried to identify the blogger has led me to a dead end.

"Good thing we have screen shots," Sophie says. "Because as of this morning, the blog is gone."

"Nothing's ever gone on the Internet," Jake says.

"Well, this is. Poof. DNS address does not exist."

"That sounds like the Unit," I say. "Take out Dason, obliterate the blog, erase all traces of evidence."

Jake rolls his eyes but refrains from comment.

Anubis picks his way across the table and pours himself down into Sophie's lap. She tickles his chin and he starts to purr.

"What do we know about this dead guy?" Matt asks. "Where would he have seen the World Tree Girl?"

"That's the interesting thing," I tell him. "Up until a few days ago, he worked at the city morgue in Spokane. According to his mother, the ME worked him to the bone and then fired him for no reason."

"Taking personal pictures of crime scenes and dead people not being sufficient, of course," Jake adds.

The coffee pot glugs and gasps and goes silent. Matt gets up to fill our mugs. "If he had access to autopsies and we have evidence that photographing dead people was his thing, I'm with Maureen. He's a good bet for the blogger."

"Bets are not enough," Jake says. "We need evidence. Maybe he took the pictures and somebody else did the blogging. Mama said he was trying to sell the photos of our World Tree Girl."

"At least this narrows the geographical area," Matt says. "Probably Spokane County. If it had happened here in Shadow Valley, Jake would have been involved."

"Could have happened in Stevens, Ferry, or Pend Oreille," Jake says. "All of those counties use Spokane for forensics. Plus, sometimes autopsies are done privately, which widens the field again."

"Well, at least we can rule out foreign countries, and the rest of the US. Evidence points to somewhere in Northeast Washington. I need a look at Dason's laptop."

Jake glares at me. I hold his gaze, waiting, not sure just yet where he'll draw the lines between our collaboration and his legal duties. I feel hamstrung. I'm used to working cases with the full power of the Unit behind me. The feds have all the cool toys and access to any database they take a fancy to. Now I'm limited not only to what Jake can access, legally, from a rural sheriff's office, but to what he chooses to share with me. Of course I can hack into the Internet, even into FBI files if I'm so inclined, but that's like playing ding dong ditch on their front porch. I'd rather they believe I'm just wasting away here at Shadow Valley Manor, for now at least.

"If the Unit killed Dason," I say, after Jake fails to offer access to Dason's laptop, "then they'll be covering up the World Tree Girl's death as much as possible. Keeping it quiet."

The Unit hushes up anything related to a paranormal attack. This is justified by the level of panic that would explode if the normal population ever discovers what is lurking in the world around them. Best to keep the sheep in the dark and let them think of paranormals as sheer fantasy they can be frightened by on TV shows or read about in books.

"Sophie, do you have an inside track with the ME in Spokane?" Jake asks.

"Kate? Are you kidding? Kate probably follows a manual on how to properly brush your teeth. If she knows anything, she'll take it to her grave rather than break protocol."

Jake leans back in his chair. Anubis pads across the table and steps into my lap, where he begins purring like a steam engine.

"Shoo." I shove him with my hands, but the inevitable claws come out and I know better than to fight. "Maybe we could drive up to Spokane tomorrow and give it a try," I say. "She might be persuaded to talk to you, a sheriff. Outside of that, I don't know what to do."

"Please tell me you haven't forgotten about dinner with the middle schoolers tomorrow," Matt says.

I stare at him in dismay. "Oh, hell. Is that tomorrow?"

"I've been trying to talk to you about it all week."

"Can't we cancel?"

"It's a little late now."

"But we have a lead!" I look from Matt, to Sophie, to Jake,

and can see they are all arrayed against me. Apparently the descent of the middle school kids upon the Manor at Thanksgiving is a community tradition I'm not supposed to breach.

"If you want to cancel, Maureen, you need to make the call," Jake says. "It's your Manor. I'm not going to be the one to tell Joanna Schrader that we're killing her holiday tradition."

"Not killing it. Just giving it a moratorium. Maybe we could do Christmas." I can't quite repress a shudder. Kids that age are unruly savages. The thought of them mixing in with the old people and running wild through the Manor is a terrifying thing. I'd much rather single handedly pursue the Medusa.

Matt doodles a skull and crossbones around and through the words "Middle School Menu" at the top of his notepad, which makes it look like he's planning to cook and serve children. "Yes or no?" he asks.

"We can't just sit around eating pie and waiting for somebody else to get murdered."

"We don't know that Dason was murdered," Jake objects.

"He didn't kill himself. And the Medusa killed the World Tree Girl."

"The girl died over a month ago." Matt adds flames to the design he's been drawing. "I really hate to say this, but are we sure the Medusa killed her?"

"Do we know of anything else that sucks all the blood out of somebody and leaves slime behind?" Sophie sounds more curious than disgusted by the idea.

"Or maybe the Medusa has siblings," Matt replies. "How do we know there wasn't a batch of the creatures?"

"How about we stick with the evidence?" Jake suggests. "We have photos of a dead girl. We don't know who posted them on *Underground Weird*. Neither do we know if her physical condition was accurately described by the blogger. We don't know if Dason killed himself, or if somebody killed him. And if it was the Medusa who killed the girl, it's been over a month since it happened and there have been no other such deaths."

"That we know of," I mutter.

Jake's going to rupture an optic nerve if he keeps rolling his eyes like that. I smile at him. "Look, what would it hurt for you and me to drive up to Spokane in the morning? We could be back in time for dinner. I want to have a look at Dason's apartment, talk to his friends."

"It's outside our jurisdiction," Jake protests.

"He was killed in your jurisdiction."

"Probably a suicide. We're still waiting for the coroner to rule."

Matt slams his pencil down onto the table. "Look. I'm as keen on catching the Medusa as anybody. But since I work here at the Manor, and part of my job seems to be this infernal dinner, I need to know if we're having it or not. There are groceries to be bought. I need help in the kitchen. Help serving. We've done nothing to prepare."

"I don't understand why you all are so wound up about this dinner thing. So we cancel at the last minute. How is this a national crisis?"

"Have you met Mrs. Schrader?" Sophie asks.

"Community relations," Matt says.

"Since when do we care what anybody thinks?"

"Old people die, Maureen. Who do you think is going to replace this crew when they drop off?"

"We haven't had a problem so far. We've filled all vacancies within a day or two."

"And you've never called off the Thanksgiving dinner. You don't want to read the Yelp reviews if you cancel this event."

"Plus, we don't want to call any attention to either the Manor or its new ownership," Jake says. "We managed to skate after that fiasco with the Medusa, despite a few dead bodies. But we're on the radar now. Next time it won't be so easy."

"Fine. All right. We'll have the dinner. But I can't imagine why the residents want all those kids up here. You'd think they'd be extra thankful if we called the whole thing off."

"Not fond of kids?" Matt grins.

"There is no paranormal more frightening than a twelve-year-old. Except maybe the Medusa. Speaking of which, can we get on with trying to find her, or do we have to spend the rest of our time talking about turkey and pumpkin pie?"

"Give me a budget, get me some help, and I'll take care of it."

"Done. Now, can we get back to the Medusa? Until we have evidence to support another theory, let's assume she's responsible for the World Tree Girl and that she will kill again. As for Dason, if he's not our *Underground Weird* blogger, he has a connection to whomever is. And this whole situation stinks of activity from the Unit. There should be a description of the World Tree Girl on the missing child database. There ought to be a coroner's report, an autopsy report, a police report. Jake has searched the official channels from the sheriff's office. I've hacked into everything short of the FBI database, done extensive searches. Nothing. It's been hushed up, and maybe Dason has also been hushed up."

Jake rubs his forehead. "If—and this is pure speculation, but I'll go along for the ride—if the Unit silenced Dason, what about everybody else at the morgue? The ME? Other staff? Are they at risk?"

"None of them are selling photos or blabbing about autopsy findings. My guess is Dason signed his death warrant when he tried to sell that picture."

Jake is looking at me in a way I don't entirely like, as though I'm some sort of bug under a magnifying lens. "Did you do that sort of thing when you were with the Unit? Wipe out targets to keep them quiet?"

"No. I engaged in a little gentle persuasion, usually more bribery than fear based. Set up witness protection programs, that sort of thing. Killing seems to be something that happened around the time Matt signed on."

"I have a new person to report to," Matt volunteers. "Goes by Charlie. He apologized, more or less, for what happened to Phil and Abel. Said there was objection in the ranks to the actions that led to the regrettable deaths of valuable agents. Leadership has changed and I'm to stay where I am and keep my eyes open."

By keeping his eyes open, he means keeping me in his sight. The Unit planted him here at the Manor, with a license to kill and a head full of lies. He's on our team now, walking the fine line of a double agent, and the stress is beginning to show.

There are dark shadows under his eyes, new lines in his face. My heart softens, treacherously, but I harden it. I can't afford to get too attached; one of these days I might need to kill him.

"Does this Charlie person drop any hints about this girl, or thoughts that Medusa killed her?" I ask him.

"Not a word. But then they don't exactly trust me."

"I really thought we'd killed that thing," Jake says.

"I really hoped we had," I answer.

The four of us watched the Medusa melt, poisoned by silver dust and burned by lasers. She'd certainly seemed dead. But when you're dealing with a paranormal that can go invisible, you can't trust the evidence of your eyes.

We threw every weapon we had at her, and if she's still alive, as I firmly believe, I have no idea what we're going to do when we *do* find her. The best we might hope for is to make ourselves decoys.

This is a reality I'm not willing to accept. There has got to be a way to find the creature and to kill her. I fully intend to do both.

SIX

By the time dinner rolls around, I'm knee deep in unpacking. I'm hungry, and I should go down to keep an eye on Jill if nothing else, but I have just discovered a box with a label marked CHINA & SUNDRIES. Ed, my ex-in-progress, knows full well I have no use for either china or sundries. It's not his handwriting on the label.

I open the box with caution. Inside, a handwritten note rests on top of an expensive bone china tea set. It's written in a flowing script with lavender ink.

Maureen, it must be so difficult to leave your home and resettle at this time of life. Please allow me to send a little house-warming gift. I do hope someday we might be friends.

Glenda

Clearly, Ed's new woman is either brain damaged or evil in the cold-blooded way of snakes. I'm contemplating the satisfying way the teapot would explode if I use it for target practice when Jake knocks on my door.

He doesn't flinch at the gun in my hand, just looks from it, to me, to the box, and says, "Let me take you away from all this."

"Twice in one day?"

"What can I say? I'm a romantic."

"My husband's new love has sent me a tea set. She'd like to be friends."

He makes a face. "Forget all that. I need you."

"I can't leave Jill here on her own."

"You don't want a look at the body?"

"Dason's? Oh, hell, you're a cruel man, Jake Callahan."

"Think of me as your knight in shining armor. Come on. Mac is there waiting for us. Jill is a grown woman. I'm sure she can survive without you, even surrounded by a bunch of old people."

"That's not what I meant."

"I know what you meant. She's just here to settle her father's estate. Not everybody has ulterior motives. Lock up tight. I have coffee waiting for you in the car. And a donut."

I can't argue with the logic of coffee and donuts. And he's probably even right about Jill.

When we pull up to Frank's Funeral Parlor and Cremato-rium, there's a sheriff's cruiser parked in the lot. There's also a hard-ridden Harley, the black gas tank painted with a horde of ghosts and skeletons, apparently all trying to strangle or beat each other into a second and more permanent death.

The front doors are locked and Jake taps at them.

I hear footsteps. The door opens theatrically on a skeletal face calculated to send mourners fleeing. Half of the head is bald, with blotchy, discolored skin pulled tight over the skull. The other half sports thick, wavy brown hair. The face has no eyebrows, which emphasizes a bony ridge of high forehead. One eye is milky white and clearly blind, but the other is a brilliant blue that checks me over with keen intelligence. Two open nostrils mark the spot where a nose should be. The mouth has no lips, and the skin of the entire face is a collage of textures and colors, from blanched white to beefy red.

"Hey, Craig," Jake says.

No pipe organ music and scuttling rats. This is just an unfortunate man who has had a close encounter with fire.

"Come on in. They're waiting for you." He has a lovely voice and his tone is polite, as if my rude staring hasn't bothered him. The little bell at the door rings as we enter. Craig locks up behind us.

"We're closed," he says, in explanation. "Lysander is throwing fits. Come on, they're in the prep room."

Jake motions for me to follow, and he brings up the rear. In the viewing room where I once found Sophie holding a ceremony to help a dead woman cross, everything is brightly lit and clinical. No candlesticks, no piles of jewelry and food and wine. We follow our guide through a maze of hallways, stopping when we reach a deputy standing outside a metal door. Female, medium height, solid muscle, dark hair cut short.

"Everything okay, Grace?" Jake asks.

She nods. "Yes, sir. Nobody in or out. Except him." She casts a glance at Craig, but stops short of eye contact.

"Craig works here," Jake says, and there's an edge to his voice that Grace would be smart to pay attention to.

Craig's face reveals nothing. "Take care, Jake. Ma'am." He nods at me.

I nod back, then follow Jake into a cool room brightly lit by fluorescents. A concrete floor slopes down to a drain at the center. The ripe smell of a well-fermented body permeates the air. Sinks, hoses, suction pumps, and all of the embalmers' tools and equipment are on display.

Dason lies on a preparation table at the center of the room, naked. A camera and computer are set up on a table beside him. Lysander, Sophronia's father and the owner of this establishment, stands guard, jaw jutting like a bulldog. His legs are spread wide apart, his hands curled almost into fists. Mac towers over him, his face and body language expressing boredom and complete indifference to the other man's rage.

Lysander redirects his temper to me. "You. I should have known you were involved. Tell them this building is not a storage facility for disputed bodies."

"I don't give orders to cops and coroners, Lysander. What's coaxed you out of hiding?"

"Don't lie to me. You brought them here. I know what you are. This—thing"—he gestures at the body on the table—"does not belong here. Too late for embalming. Either it gets buried at once, or it goes to the ME where it belongs."

He might as well be a puff of hot air for all the attention the other two men pay his words.

"Sending the body to Spokane seemed—unwise—given the circumstances. Mac thought it best to keep it here, until we talk to Kate," Jake says.

I cross over to the camera setup. The computer is open to a telemed link, ready to dial. "What's the plan?"

Mac's face looks as innocent as a biker's face can look, which makes him look guilty as hell. "We want Kate's opinion on the body, while keeping it safe here from any—tampering."

"I object," Lysander shouts. "This is all against protocol. It's probably illegal."

"You can complain to the ME," Mac says. He walks over to stand behind me. "Jake tells me you're good with technology. Can you run this? I can do it, but technology goes wonky around me. This needs to go off smooth as silk."

"I can."

Mac grunts, approvingly. Up close, I can see the tattoo on his jaw is a raven. His eyes are so dark they seem to absorb the light.

"Shall we do this?" he asks.

"Whenever you're ready."

"Get the camera on me, first, and screen the body out. Right. Can you get a close-up when we need it?"

I look at the controls. "Affirmative." To demonstrate, I zoom the camera in until only Mac's nose shows on the screen. Under magnification it looks cratered, more like the moon's surface than human skin. I dial the zoom back just until he fills the screen, all solid muscle and black leather.

He gives me a thumbs-up and I initiate the connection.

A woman comes on screen. If she tops five feet, I'll be surprised, and she carries not an extra ounce of weight on her bones. Her long, dark hair is perfectly braided and coiled around her head. She wears a pristine lab coat, pencil skirt, and high heels. Her name tag is not only visible, but pinned to her coat so that it lies perfectly square.

"Make it quick, Mac. I'm very busy. Your e-mail was vague and incoherent. I'm attending this appointment only because I understand it must be difficult for an inexperienced coroner to manage a questionable death. Tell me now, again, what is the problem with this body?" Her voice is tinged faintly with an accent.

"It looks like suicide, but I have my doubts."

"Send the body to me. This is customary. I do not understand what the problem is. If we follow protocol, then we do not have these interruptions and disturbances. I can give you two more minutes, and that is all."

Timing is everything. I'm already working the zoom before Mac gestures to me. He steps aside and I focus the camera in on the side of Dason's face that still looks like Dason. Kate responds with silence. No intake of breath. No sudden exclamation. She leans forward, peering into the screen for a better look at the victim.

"You see my problem," Mac says, after a long moment.

"Quite right," she answers, her voice still clinical and cool. "You've done precisely the correct thing. I'd ask what happened, but that would be inappropriate. Please be sure not to give any information away that I should not know."

"I take it you knew the deceased?" Jake asks the question.

Kate's gaze sharpens as she dissects him with her eyes, top to bottom.

"Sheriff," she says, coolly. "You already know that I knew him, or we wouldn't be having this conversation. Yes. His name is Dason Williams, and I fired him last week."

"Care to tell me why?"

"Do I need an attorney?"

"It looks like suicide. But if you think you need to lawyer up, we can certainly make this official."

She says nothing, and Jake goes on. "Did the two of you have conflict?"

"Absolutely not."

"He was difficult? A bad employee?"

"He was a quiet, unassuming sort. Tended to be lost in his own thoughts."

"Is that why you fired him?"

"No. I fired him because he broke protocol."

"What were his duties, precisely?"

"He washed the bodies after autopsy. He was also good with a camera, and I had him take photos for me to illustrate certain points during a post mortem."

"Sounds like a valuable employee."

"He was."

"But you fired him."

She sighs, glances off camera to what I'm guessing is a clock, and adjusts her already perfectly aligned badge. "His job was to take photographs I requested using the designated equipment. All photos were to remain within the morgue, or be disseminated as I saw fit, according to legal requirements and privacy laws. I caught him taking pictures with his own camera."

"It seems he had been taking pictures for some time," Mac says. "Maureen?"

I've used the time to connect my own notebook to the system and pull up images of the photos we found in Dason's room. "Do any of these look familiar?"

Kate's face darkens with anger. "I had no idea he'd been doing it so long."

"You recognize some of these, then?"

"Yes. Go back. One more. That one. That boy died last year. I should have had Dason arrested. My reputation, the reputation of my morgue has been compromised!"

"Are you sure you didn't know?" Jake says, conversationally. "Maybe you found out. You fired him, and he refused to promise to keep the pictures to himself, so you killed him."

"Now you're being ridiculous. I quite understand what

you're insinuating, and why. If you care to tell me when he was murdered, then I will see if I have an alibi. Push this further and I will find an attorney."

"You see why it's not appropriate that we send him to you."

"Of course. I'll ask Trevor in Coeur d'Alaine to take a look at the body. Do you have reason to think it's murder and not suicide? No, wait. Don't answer that. Don't answer anything. We're through here."

Her hand reaches for the Disconnect button on her unit.

Jake's voice stops her. "Please. One more question."

"One, Sheriff, but no guarantee that I will answer."

"I was wondering if you had seen this girl at all in your morgue." He nods at me, and I bring up a photo of the World Tree Girl.

Kate's face changes, hardens. Her pupils dilate. Color washes out of her cheeks.

She's good, though; it's only a second before she waves away the picture as though it is nothing more than an annoying fly.

"Really, showing me pictures of cases outside your purview crosses the boundary. I am not at liberty to discuss any of the deceased who are outside of your jurisdiction and unrelated to this case. And you have made me very late with my schedule. I must go now. I will have Trevor call you for arrangements about the post mortem."

A click of a button, and her half of the split screen goes dark.

"What the hell was that?" Mac glares at me, then Jake.

"She didn't like it much," Jake says.

"But she's definitely seen it." We all stare at the photo still up on the screen.

"The tattoo work is amazing," Mac says. "Beautiful." Mac rubs a hand over his jaw. "Think Kate knew what Dason was up to all along? Huge problem for her if that gets out."

"I've known her for years," Jake says. "I doubt it. She's totally by the book." He shifts his gaze from me to Mac and back again, brows raised in a question. I shake my head. Mac seems like a good guy and a solid and intelligent man. But where this story is going to lead, he doesn't need to go. There are already enough people involved, and the less he knows, the more likely he is to be alive in the end. We've already said too much.

I yawn, deliberately, and stretch, or try to. There's a stitch in my belly that is perpetually tight these days and refuses to give. Maybe I should do the physical therapy the doctor prescribed, after all, only I have no faith it will help.

"Well, this has been interesting, but it's been a long day at the Manor. I have work to do before I go to bed. And I'm starving."

"I'll take you home," Jake says.

I half expect Lysander to be waiting right outside the door, ready to barge back in shouting and throwing a fit, but he's nowhere to be seen. Craig doesn't make an appearance, either. There is only Grace, standing guard.

Jake says nothing until we've exited the building and are all the way to his car. "What do you think?"

"If Kate hadn't seen the body, she would have said so. Lies are not in her vocabulary. She's scared."

"Should she be?"

"Damn straight. She's been warned to keep it quiet. We should all be watching our backs right now."

"You realize our whole theory is built on speculation." He

opens the car door for me and refrains from offering a hand as I bend my complaining body and climb in.

"Speculation is where it all starts. At least it's something."

"You have a point." Jake slams the door and walks around the back of the car to climb in on his side. "I'll do a search of murders in Spokane within the last few months and see what comes up."

"My bet is you'll get nothing. The autopsy report and the investigation report will all have vanished just like the blog post."

"Do you think her body is still at the morgue in Spokane?"

I shake my head. "Too risky. Either they've cremated it, or taken it to their own laboratory for further analysis."

"I hope you're wrong."

"Me, too."

"You said you were hungry. I could buy you dinner." His eyes are on the road, his voice carefully bland.

"I really need to check in on Jill. And I've got boxes to move before I can sleep tonight. Matt will find me some leftovers."

Before I can get out of the car at the Manor, Jake stops me with a hand on my arm. "Look, I know you're indestructible, but be careful, will you?"

I grin at him. "Life's so much more interesting when there's risk. You know what would be awesome about now?"

"A smoke?"

"That, too. I was thinking about access to Phil's weapons."

"Maureen—"

"Yeah, yeah. They're evidence and his murder isn't truly solved until we catch Charlene. Rules. Protocols. All wonderful things until they kill you." I pull out my pack of cigarettes and offer him one.

He shakes his head. "I'm quitting."

"Me, too." I grin at him. "Not tonight, though. Life's short. Might be the last one I get. Would be a sad, sad, thing if one of Phil's contraptions could have saved me."

Jake is a good man, but he's a cop, first and last. His face falls into the lines of his reserved, professional persona. "Good night, Maureen."

"Good night, Jake. Let me know what you don't find."

I watch him drive away, unlit cigarette in hand, still feeling, for no good reason, the warmth of his hand on my arm.

SEVEN

I'm not at all surprised when Ed calls. I've been expecting it. I'm only surprised that I answer.

"We need to talk."

Four simple words, but they erase the cushion of time between us as if we'd spoken yesterday. The sharp twist of his betrayal stabs my heart as if the wound is new and fresh. Apparently a couple of months of time apart can't uproot the emotions engendered by twenty-five years of marriage.

"Maureen?"

"We're talking," I say.

"In person. Can we meet somewhere?"

I look at the wilderness of stuff clamoring to be unpacked and organized, and a wave of exhaustion rolls over me. There are things I wouldn't mind saying to Ed, but not now. Not tonight. I evade with a question.

"How did you manage to get a hotel, anyway? I hear they're all booked up."

"About that," he says, and I drop down onto a packing box, knowing what's coming.

"We reserved a room a month ago. Tried to check in and a rather rude young man at the service desk informed us our room had been given to somebody else."

A mushroom cloud of silence hovers over my head. Ed keeps talking.

"We've tried every hotel in town. There are no rooms to be had for love nor money."

"Pity. Well, Spokane's not that far. Better get headed back. Watch out for deer."

He clears his throat. "Glenda's dead set on staying here tonight. She's asking for a tour of the Manor."

In the background a female voice chimes in: "Just ask her, Ed. I'm sure it will be fine."

In the silence that follows, I know he's put his hand over the receiver and is mouthing something at her. Amusement at his predicament of being trapped between her and me revives me better than a tonic.

"Ask me what, Ed?"

"We were wondering if we might stay there. At the Manor. Just for tonight." His voice is heavy with reluctance, and I can picture the hand signals and whispered instructions he's receiving. I almost feel sorry for him.

Almost.

"A sleepover?" I ask. "Or a threesome? Hey, maybe I could scare up a partner and we could have a swinger party. That's a swell idea."

"Maureen—"

His voice is overridden by a woman's in the background.

"Let me talk to her." A sound of scuffling follows, and then Glenda comes on the line.

"Men are so bad at explaining things, don't you find? We were going to drive up to Canada tomorrow. Can you believe that I've never been there? Crazy, right? So it would be terribly disappointing to drive back now, when we're so close. Besides, just between you and me, Ed's eyes are not so good for night driving anymore, but you know how he is."

I ignore this invitation for us to bond over the peccadilloes of my husband, letting the silence do my work for me.

Glenda emits a small, ladylike cough. "Anyway. I'd also just love to spend some time with you. We haven't had a chance to get to know each other *at all*. I think—"

Her voice breaks off on a sharply drawn breath and Ed comes back on. "Maureen—"

"It's a wonderful idea. I can't imagine why I didn't think of it myself. As it happens, we do have a vacant room right now. You two kids make yourselves right at home. I'll let the night staff know."

He starts to protest, but I hang up on him, and when the phone rings again, I don't answer.

Sleep is now out of the question. I buzz Darcy, the night shift aide, to let her know about Ed and Glenda, and then set to work on unpacking. It's midnight when I finally fall into bed, exhausted, and it seems my head has barely hit the pillow when a knock at my door jolts me awake. The room is pitch dark and I'm disoriented and confused. New suite, the floor plan a reverse from the old one. Furniture scattered in random positions. Packing boxes all over the floor. I map it all out in my head, waiting for the knock to come again and fumbling for my gun.

This all takes longer than it should. I'm slipping. Twenty years ago, even ten, it would have been effortless and instantaneous. I'm going to have to start doing memory games or something to keep my brain sharp. Living in the Manor with a bunch of zebras is softening me.

Anubis hisses when I shift him so I can move my legs. Without turning on any lights, I limp along the path I've made through the boxes and peer out through my security peephole.

Jill.

She knocks again. Her hands are empty. No purse, no obvious bulges indicating a weapon. Of course, a weapon can be disguised as anything.

I open the door, but don't invite her in.

"Did you need something?"

"Is that necessary?" She stares pointedly at the gun in my hand.

I just raise my eyebrows.

"Maureen. I'm not a child anymore. I'm not going to stab you."

"Adults are generally considered more dangerous than children, not less. What time is it, anyway?"

She brushes past me. "Two? Three? I lost track. Can't sleep." Light floods the room as she locates a switch and flicks it on. I blink, temporarily blinded, bringing up the gun in reflex and aiming it where I last heard her voice. She's moved on, though, and doesn't even notice, her back to me as if it's never even occurred to her that I might really pull the trigger.

The clock confirms her time estimate. Ten past three.

"*I* was sleeping just fine," I tell her. "Can you go and not sleep in your own space?"

She starts opening cupboards in the kitchenette. "You've got to have something to drink. Ah, here we are."

She plunks a bottle of scotch down on the counter. I sigh. "Glasses are in the cupboard above the sink. Pour me one while you're at it."

I watch her pour, but there are no sleight-of-hand maneuvers or sly attempts to slip something into my drink. She sets them both down on the counter, side by side, with no attempt to steer me toward one or the other.

She's still wearing the suit and jacket, considerably worse for wear, and she hasn't removed her makeup. Her eyes are bloodshot and puffy, as if she's been weeping, mascara smeared into raccoon eyes.

Exhaustion, I tell myself. Jetlag. Not tears.

I select a glass and she picks up the other, crossing over to the French doors that lead out to the balcony.

"Mind if I open the blinds? I need to see the sky." Without waiting for my consent, she pulls the cord, and then stands there, staring out into the night. A full moon pours light across the floor, bright enough to turn the world outside into light and shadow.

"Tell me about my father," she says.

"What do you want to know?"

Her shoulders lift in a shrug. "Anything. Everything. I hardly knew him."

If she'd opened fire with a handgun or come at me with a knife, I'd have been prepared and would have an answer. I don't know what to say to this.

"Nobody knew him well."

She turns then, and there are tears on her cheeks. Oh, hell.

"He sent me cards. He took me on vacations to resorts in

out-of-the way places. When I was young, he called to ask me about school, or if I was dating boys. As I got older, he asked fewer questions. He never talked about himself. And I never asked him. And then, after..." She swallows what's in her glass and goes to the counter for a refill.

"I haven't seen your father in years. People change. You probably knew him better than I did."

"You're just as evasive as he was," she says. "What would it hurt you to talk about him?"

It's a loaded question. Anything I tell her about Phil is also giving her a piece of me. My heart aches with memories, all of which culminate with me standing in the funeral home holding a cardboard box of still warm ashes.

"I could have come home," she says, after a long silence. "Right after he died. I wasn't really tied up with anything, just loitering in Paris. I was angry at him, I think, for dying before I had a chance to know him. And then I found out he'd been murdered, and that he'd left you the Manor..." She drains half the glass in one long swallow. "Maybe you can tell me that. Explain to me why he would leave you an entire business property?"

I can't tell her, much as she maybe deserves to know. So I just shrug. "Maybe he thought I'd be a better manager."

Jill snorts. "If you're not going to answer that one, try this. What kind of man gets a woman pregnant and then abandons her and the baby? My mother thought he loved her."

"Every woman thought he loved her."

"And that's supposed to make it okay? He loved her and left her, and she killed herself over him."

"And you blame me for that?"

"You're the one he left her for."

"If you really believe that, you're right. You didn't know him at all."

"I know that after you were done with him, he never settled down."

"Good Lord, are you still sixteen? He was always like that. Before your mother, after your mother, and certainly before and after me. There were always women. He loved and left them. You don't see me cutting my wrists in the bathtub, do you?"

"You're a bitch." She crosses to the kitchenette to pour herself more booze, her steps wandering a little.

"Never pretended to be otherwise. Nobody invited you here. Feel free to leave."

"I never said being a bitch was a bad thing." Her face breaks into an unexpected smile—Phil's smile. She raises her glass to me. "I'm one myself. Now, tell me something else about him. I've already been enlightened."

"Jill. I don't owe you answers or anything else. Go back to bed."

And then a thought occurs to me, something I can't believe I've overlooked already. "I have a question for *you*."

"What?"

I take a sip of my drink. It goes down warm and smooth. "You were sixteen last time I saw you. Faces change over time. What if you're not really Jill?"

"Oh, come on. You said you saw my picture on his nightstand."

"I saw *a* picture on his nightstand. I assumed it was you. It matches you. Which is really meaningless."

"Want to see my passport?"

I dismiss this with a wave of my hand. Passports can be faked. "No. Tell me about the last—and only—time we met."

"Surely that's not the only time in your life somebody has tried to kill you."

She's right. I tend to bring out that quality in people somehow. "That's beside the point. Talk to me. Tell me about that stabbing, something nobody else would know, or I say not another word about your father."

Jill sits down in the chair and thumps her glass down on my only end table, hard enough that a wave of amber liquid washes over the edge. It will leave a ring, but I let it be.

"I tracked down your apartment. You opened your door when I rang, and I stabbed you without saying a word. Went for the heart and missed. You did some ninja thing and flipped me onto my back on the floor before I could try again. And then you zip-tied me to a chair. There was blood on your hands, blood all over me by the time you were done. And then you called Dad. He left me there in the chair, tied up, while he stitched you up without an anesthetic and made me watch."

"Tell me about the knife."

"That's not enough? Nobody could know what I've just told you. You both said you'd never tell anybody—"

"Doesn't mean you—or Jill if you're not her—didn't talk."

"Fine. The knife was a gift from Phil. Other girls got jewelry and clothes. He sent me knives and weird-ass gizmos I couldn't understand the use of. Obviously I wasn't very good with the knife. The handle was carved out of some sort of bone, I think."

Bending down, I draw the knife in question out of my ankle sheath. "This look familiar?"

Her eyes widen. "You still have my knife?"

"It's a great little knife. Saved my life a time or two and more than earned its keep." I toss it in the air and catch it, loving the weight and balance of it in my hand.

"Can I have it back?"

"Maybe when you're several continents away from me, I'll consider sending it to you. What are you really doing here, Jillian?"

"Exactly what I said. I came home to get my father's ashes, and to ask you questions about him. Apparently I'm next of kin. Do I have brothers and sisters somewhere?"

"Nope. He got himself snipped after your mother got pregnant. Said he had no intention of settling down and it wasn't fair to bring kids into the world."

What he also said, and what I'm not telling Jill, is that kids could be used as pawns, as leverage, as hostages. In his business, and especially after he and I incurred the scrutiny of the Unit by refusing to participate in a Paranormal/Human research project, this was one of the reasons he managed to live as long as he did.

Me, I'm still playing the life game, but my continued survival is against the odds. Meanwhile, I've got two dead bodies on my radar and the Medusa on the loose. No more time for sparring with Jill. "Look. Maybe you don't require sleep, but I do. Go to bed. We'll talk in the morning."

"No way. I've learned more about Dad in the last hour than I have in my entire lifetime. Tell me more." She gets up and goes to pour another glass, then shrugs and swigs right out of the bottle.

My patience is done. "He liked the color green. Whiskey was his favorite drink, but he'd only drink when he had a partner with him who was sober and could watch his back.

Women were his undoing. There's nothing else I can tell you."

"How about this. What was he, exactly? Some sort of spy, right. FBI? CIA? He always said he couldn't tell me."

"If he wouldn't tell you, I'm certainly not going to."

She shuffles back to the chair, very carefully now, bottle in hand. "He's dead. No need to protect him anymore. Tell me the so-big secret that kept my father from being my father. *Tell me why he chose you over me.*"

Her voice wobbles on these last words, and comprehension floods through me. I can see how it would look that way to a teenager. Phil was a fantastic agent and an amazing lover. Not so great in the commitment department.

Just like I'm not great in the capacity of counselor and advisor.

"Don't be ridiculous," I tell her. "He loved you. Let that be enough."

"It's not enough. It will never be enough. I have a right to know—"

"You don't have a right to anything he didn't give you. It's not enough for you that he left you a couple of million? Go look through his house. Maybe there are answers there."

Somebody taps on my door. It's quiet, something you wouldn't hear if you were sound asleep. Or even wide awake in the room across the hall. I want to ignore the door, but Jill is already staggering onto her feet. "Shall I get that?"

"It's my door. I'll get it. Give me your gun first."

"I have no idea what—"

"Left leg. Ankle holster. Sit down. Let me get it."

The tap at the door comes again. Jill sinks back down on the couch, laughing like a maniac. "Of course I have a gun. Phil taught me how to shoot. He had me sent to Juvie for stabbing you. Did you know that? And when I got out, he said I clearly needed discipline and training. We went to the shooting range. He bought me martial arts lessons, too. What sort of man teaches a sixteen-year-old to shoot a gun and use a knife after she's just tried to kill somebody?"

"You lied to me. You said you hardly knew him." I kneel down, biting back a groan and a curse as every muscle in my body sends up a full-scale rebellion. Once we solve this Medusa thing, I need to go on some sort of healing retreat and teach my body to mind its manners.

"A few hours on the shooting range don't exactly constitute a close relationship."

The gun is a sweet little .22, lightweight and nicely balanced. Spoils of war, I figure. I'll take it out and see how it shoots. If I still like it, it's mine. I slide the cartridge out before I cross to the door. Even so, I feel exposed when I turn my back to Jill. There's no rule that says she can't be carrying another. Or that she doesn't have a knife in her pajama pocket and finely honed throwing skills.

Sophie stands outside my door, the old dog we rescued at her side, the potato salad container clasped in her arms.

Hell. I am not the shelter for strays.

Behind me, Jill is slumped down on the couch, the bottle loosely cradled in both hands and resting on her lap, her head tipped back, eyes closed. I crack the door, intending to tell Sophie to go away and come back later, but she shoves it open, barging into the room without even looking first. The dog scrabbles on the hardwood for traction, sliding slow motion into a box. As soon as he's back on his feet, he goes after the cat, barking like it's the end of all things. Anubis stands his ground, hissing.

A cold draft brushes over my skin, and I know we have company.

"We've got a problem," Sophronia says, then stops, catching sight of my visitor. Her eyebrows draw together, her eyes flare green. "What is she doing here?"

"Asking questions. What are you doing here? It's four in the morning."

"Couldn't sleep. What are you drinking? Can I have some?"

"Absolutely not. Look, whatever the problem, you should come back when..."

But she's already bounced across the room and is standing over Jill.

"Sophie, don't—"

She spins around and fixes me with a glare. Her night-black hair drifts around her as if blowing in a breeze. There is no breeze in my room, and I know what it means when Sophie begins having an atmosphere of her own. "What exactly do you think I'm going to do?"

Jillian takes one good look at Sophie and shields her face with both arms. The bottle crashes onto the floor. Scotch puddles around her feet. "I'm not ready," she wails.

"Neither was Phil," Sophie says, her voice eerie and very nearly echoing. If this were a movie, there would be an effects unit applied. The electricity flickers. Sophie's green eyes glow with a light of their own. "You cremated him. No time for him to be ready, for his soul to adapt. And that is a problem."

"I'm sorry," Jill says. "I couldn't be there. That coroner, Charlene—"

"His murderer," Sophie says. "His murderer suggested you rush into burning his body. And you went right along with that."

I can't imagine being drunk and having an angry Sophie show up. I'd be enjoying the show if I didn't know exactly what this girl is capable of, should she ever cross the line.

Jill leans forward and pukes. All over my floor. All over Sophie's feet. Before I can stop it, the dog skitters across the floor and starts lapping up the mess.

That action snaps Sophie out of her avenging spirit mode. She takes a breath. Her eyes go back to human. "Ewwww," she says, stepping back. "My shoes."

"You shouldn't go scaring drunk people like that." I take a deep breath and wish I hadn't. "You want to tell me what this is all about?"

"Phil," Sophie says, her voice bereft now, and very young. "He's—Phil doesn't want to cross."

EIGHT

"What do you mean he won't cross?"

I've only had a sip of scotch, so I know it's not that, but all at once I need to sit down. The dog comes over and tries to lick my hands.

"Get away from me. I know where that mouth has been. Sit, or whatever."

He ignores me.

"Morpheus, sit," Sophie says, and the dog obeys, plopping down on his haunches right in front of me, tongue lolling. He smells strongly of whiskey and lists a little to one side.

"I've been coaxing him for weeks," Sophie says, sinking down into the armchair. "Phil, not the dog. I've tried every ceremony I could think of. Offered him wine, gold coins, sang him songs, told him stories. He won't go."

Jill pushes herself upright and blinks at Sophie. "Wait. Just a minute. I'm a little drunk, so say that again. My dad is—"

"Refusing to cross."

"Cross what? Cross where? I'm not familiar with undertaker language so 'splain it to me."

Sophie telegraphs a question to me and I shrug. "Might as well tell her."

"Sometimes," Sophie explains, still looking at me and not at Jill, who is focusing so hard her forehead is about to implode, "when someone dies—especially if they die suddenly, or they're murdered, or feel they have left something undone..." She lets that hang, staring off into space.

Anubis, up on the counter to get away from the dog, makes one of those eerie noises only a cat can make. The room temperature plummets.

"Huh. That's interesting," Sophie says.

"What?" I cross the room and grab the sweater I left hanging on the bedpost.

"They usually stay downstairs. I've never seen them up here before."

Jill glances from Sophie to me, mouth hanging slightly open. "Why is it so cold in here?"

"Old building," I lie. The only thing I know of that drops the temperature like that belongs in a grave. "Go on, Soph."

She startles, as if I'd poked her. "Right. Anyway—when those things happen, and especially if the deceased is buried precipitately, or their body is cremated while they're still around to watch—they refuse to go into the spirit world."

Jill processes this, cogs turning, but slowly. "Wait. Just a minute." She holds up one hand in an overdramatic stop signal. "Are you trying to tell me that my father—the infamous Phil Evers—is now a ghost?"

"I wouldn't say ghost, exactly," Sophie says. "Spirit, maybe—"

She doesn't get any further, because Jillian bursts into laughter. Tears pour down her cheeks, and her face flushes crimson.

Sophie glares at her. "It's so far from funny I can't even—"

"I'm sorry." Jill sucks in a deep breath, gets her face in order, but then breaks up again. Her foot stomps on the floor. Another whoosh of laughter escapes her. "A ghost. Really. You can't make this shit up."

Sophie looks exhausted. There are dark shadows under her eyes. Her cheekbones jut out under her skin, which is even paler than usual. A tiny piece of me comprehends what Jill is finding amusing, but the rest of me is wrapped in a dark, anticipatory dread. Phil, with all his extensive knowledge of all things in the spirit world, would make a formidable ghost if he took a turn toward the dark side.

Jill's laughter ebbs, and she wipes her eyes with her hands. "Hoo boy," she says. "Haven't laughed like that in months."

Ignoring her, Sophie turns back to me. "Tonight, I tried to force him. I figured she's here for his ashes. So far he's at least stayed tethered to them. But if she's taking them, then he needs to be safely through the crossing. I thought I was strong enough. I should have been."

"Women," Jill says. "You forgot to bribe him with women. Maybe if you'd promised him the seventy-two virgins, he'd be willing to go." Drunk as she is, her laughter fades as she peers at Sophie's serious expression, then mine. "You're not honestly scared of a ghost, Maureen?"

"He could get out of hand," I say, carefully. "Spirits are unpredictable."

"Something happens when they hang around too long," Sophie adds. "They forget. Without the body to help them remember emotions, they lose them all, one by one, except for whatever it is that's keeping them here. Have you seen *Poltergeist*? Or *The Shining*?"

Jill's face works as if she's caught between laughter and tears. And then she leans forward and pukes on the floor again. The dog is no longer in cleanup mode; he's lying stretched out flat and snoring like a wino.

By the time I clean up the mess and get Jillian across the hall and tucked into her bed, Sophie has fallen asleep in mine. Not that there's any point in going to bed now anyway. Not much time before dawn, and the day isn't going to wait while I try to get some sleep.

So I go back to work unpacking boxes and making some sense of my living space. When my cell rings, I check it automatically, thinking it's Jake. Maybe he's working late. Or early, whichever way you look at it.

When I see the number displayed on the screen, I drop the phone. It clunks onto the floor and skitters under the chair. This wakes the dog, who staggers to his feet, looking positively hung over. Anubis hisses at him. Cursing vigorously, I crouch down, and then work my way over onto my knees, bending down to peer under the chair. I can't quite reach, unless I get flat and stretch.

"What are you doing?"

I crane my neck to see Sophie peering down at me.

"Dropped something. Did you have a nice sleep?"

"Your pillows suck."

My fingers catch the edge of the phone, just enough to send it out of reach. "You could always sleep in your own bed."

She sinks down onto the chair, the mutt climbing up into her lap. He's way too big to be a lapdog. Too hairy, too.

"No dogs on the furniture." Either she doesn't hear me or chooses to ignore me, and I go back to my fishing expedition.

"I can't sleep," she says. "They won't let me."

"Is that normal?"

"No."

"So, is Dason here, too? Hanging out with Phil? Or is he with his body?"

"He's here."

I retrieve the phone, but stay on the floor, not entirely sure I can get to my feet without help.

"I wish it was like the movies, and he could talk to me," Sophie says.

"Wishing is for people with time and money and nothing better to do."

"Maureen? I'm not sure letting Phil out of the funeral parlor was a good idea."

Her face is averted, her hands playing with the dog's ears. I get an image of an angry and invisible Phil, with no remaining remorse or compassion as ballast, loose in the Manor. There are already a few ghosts hanging around here, thanks to the experiments performed when it was the Home for Unwed Mothers. One spirit on its own is limited in strength. But if they get together and form a coalition, God help us all.

"It will be okay," I tell her. "Go home. Get some rest. Let me think about this."

"Think fast," she says.

"A word of advice—don't try to force Phil into anything. Alive or dead, he's got a will that isn't going to bend. Don't bother trying to coax him, either. He'll go when he's ready."

"That's what scares me."

I'd like to comfort her, but the truth is, she's probably not scared enough. I need to talk to Matt and get Thanksgiving dinner canceled. The Manor is going to be no place for kids.

Sophie yawns, stretches, and trails toward the door. "Come on, Morpheus."

The dog scratches at what had better not be a flea, and then follows her.

As soon as they are out, I sit down and stare at the message on my phone. Two little words that make my skin crawl and my blood run cold.

Hi Jinx.

It's been thirty years since I've seen those two words together in a message directed to me. Even Ed, for all the years we spent together, doesn't know about Jinx. The only person who ever called me that is dead and currently occupying a potato salad container.

NINE

I hold the phone like a ticking time bomb about to explode. And then it occurs to me that maybe it *is* a ticking time bomb about to explode. Scarcely breathing, holding my hands as steady as I can, I remove the battery cover. The battery looks innocent and normal, but I know damn well this is the tricky part.

Using just the tip of my fingernail I catch the edge and flip it up and out, holding the phone in one hand, the battery in the other. Waiting.

Nothing happens, and I dare to take a full breath.

My hands shake as I set the gutted phone down on the table. Somewhere, in this mess, there ought to be a locked toolbox. It takes a minute of sorting through boxes before I find it. I enter the combination code and pull out my full-size electronic scanner. My pocket-sized bug sweeper isn't going to cut it. Setting the unit up on the table, I proceed to go over every inch of the suite, looking for tiny microphones or cameras.

I pay special attention to all the places Jill has been, especially the couch. That whole drunk thing could have been an act, the perfect opportunity for her to plant something.

On the off chance there's some new technology my sweeper doesn't recognize, I tear the couch apart, even though I'm fond of it. If everything blows up, it will be ruined anyway. I do make the cuts on the backs of the sofa cushions so I can disguise the damage, throwing each one on the floor when I'm done with it. My search reveals nothing.

Anubis emerges from under the bed, where he took refuge from Morpheus, and sticks his inquisitive nose inside one of the slashed cushions.

Somebody knocks at the door.

Goddamn it, this place is like Grand Central Station. What does a woman have to do to get a few minutes of privacy? I stalk across the floor, check who is out there, and fling the door open.

"What?"

"Hello to you, too," Jake says, taking in the chaos. "Are you re-upholstering?" He hands me a grande coffee cup. For me, this is the equivalent of roses and chocolate, and I smile despite myself.

"You look like miles of hard road," he says.

"Thank you so much. And you're Prince Charming." All sarcasm aside, he does look amazing. The man has got to be sixty, given his hair and the lines life has carved into his face, but he clearly works out. The uniform emphasizes lean muscle and brings out the gray in his eyes.

I turn away before my face can reveal what I'm thinking. "No sleep. Since you're here, help me out a minute, would you?"

He follows me into the room, setting down the briefcase

he's carrying on the table, where he pauses to take note of my gutted phone and the snooper device.

His eyebrows go up like an elevator, but he takes the hint and doesn't say anything, just goes to the other end of the sofa and helps me turn it upside down. My leg has had about enough of all the exercise, and the muscles spasm when I kneel. An involuntary hiss of pain escapes me.

"Let me do that." Jake takes the knife from me without making any fuss or offering assistance. Which is wise. Even when you've brought coffee, never offer sympathy to an angry woman with a naked blade in her hand.

He slices the fabric along the bottom of the sofa in one neat incision. I hand him a small flashlight and he peers into all the corners before rocking back onto his heels and shaking his head. "Nothing. What triggered all this?"

"Spring house cleaning. What are you doing here?"

"Brought you something."

"Besides coffee?"

Crossing to the table, he opens the briefcase and pulls out a laptop.

Not just any laptop. The blood spatter on the cover looks like an asymmetrical Rorschach test. I see a Cthulu if I squint up my eyes. The whole thing is sealed into an extra-large plastic bag and is labeled and tagged. Last time I saw this computer, it was in the middle of a crime scene.

"For me?" I beam up at him and clasp my hands like one of the soppy girls in a diamond commercial.

"It will be weeks before any CSI person will really look at it. And even then, they'll give it a cursory once-over and that will be it. They're pretty convinced this was a suicide and there's no reason to think otherwise."

This bending-the-rules business is hard on Jake, poor man. The strain is evident in his voice.

I pull on a pair of cotton gloves before lifting the cover and turning on the power. Jake pulls up a chair and sits down across the table, resting his chin in both hands.

I sit and stare at the screen, not touching any keys.

"What?" Jake asks.

"For starters—no password."

"Most people don't bother. Trust me. I deal in stolen computers more than you'd think. People are stupid."

"This kid was stupid enough to take photos in the city morgue. Of evidence. But he got away with it for at least a year before he got caught, so he's not a complete idiot. Plus, look at the background."

Jake pushes himself up from the table and comes around to stand behind me, so close I can feel the warmth of him on my skin. He smells like soap, with a hint of aftershave and leather. "I don't see what's wrong with that—he was an artistic sort."

"It's generic, comes with the OS for Macs. You think a kid who decorates his room with personal posters of dead bodies is going to put a generic Monet as his background?"

Carefully, I tap a few buttons and bring up the screen saver. "Same thing, see? Generic."

"That's all I've got on my computer."

"You're not a millennial, thank God. Let's see what he's got for files."

What I find is a whole bunch of nothing. No photograph files, no documents, no music. Not so much as Photoshop or an equivalent program. It's not that he's stored them in the Cloud, or Dropbox, either, unless he's done it from another computer. This one's so clean it squeaks.

"Could it be brand-new and recently set up?" Jakes echoes my thoughts.

"Possible. If so, that's a strike against the suicide theory. Think about it. Millennial kid springs for a brand-new laptop, sets it up, then shoots himself in the head before doing anything with it? There's not even anything left in the cache."

"He could have wiped it himself," Jake says.

"Could have. But why? If he was going to be dead anyway, why bother? Protecting his mother from his infamy?"

Wiping computers was my job when I worked for the Unit. I was good at it. Still am. In fact, if I didn't know better, I'd say this was my work, all the way down to the choice of background and screen saver. Not the first one on the list. Not the last. Somewhere in the middle.

"I don't suppose there were any fingerprints."

Jake shakes his head. "Not a thing."

"So, rather than leaving a goodbye message, or recording his death on the camera, he erases and reinstalls all the software files. Empties the cache. Ditches all of the documents. And then wipes the whole thing carefully for fingerprints— not easy with a laptop. All those key edges, the spaces in between. And when he's done, he closes it up, pulls out a gun, and shoots himself in the head."

Jake sighs. He's bent over my shoulder, hands resting on the back of my chair, his warm breath brushing my cheek.

My heart is beating faster than it ought to, and I keep my eyes on the blank screen instead of turning around to look at him.

"Why are you so all fired fixated on making this out to be a suicide?" I ask.

"Because of what it means if it's not."

The words lie heavy between us. He knows, and I know, that if the Unit is still trying to hush this up, in an effort to clean up their own mess and keep the public in a state of ignorance, then we are playing a game with lethal stakes.

Jake's been open with me. He's brought me the laptop despite the fact that this is breaking the evidence chain. I should tell him about the message on my phone. Instead, I ask, "How's the crime scene processing coming along?"

"Slow. Mac's calling for an inquest. Spokane has three high-level homicides to investigate right now, and they'll be hogging the resources. It will be months before we get anything back beyond the basics."

"Gun powder residue on his fingers?"

"Yes. But that's easy enough for a murderer to plant. Mac says the lividity is consistent with the position Dason was found in. Most likely the body wasn't moved after death. Mac also grabbed a blood sample and got someone at the hospital lab to run a tox screen. No drugs or common poisons on board."

His radio crackles and dispatch comes on.

"Domestic disturbance, 1211 Nightingale."

Jake looks at the laptop, then at me. "Well, hell."

"Go, save the world," I tell him. "This will keep. I promise to take very good care of it."

His brow creases into deep furrows as he turns to survey the demolished couch. "You still didn't tell me what happened."

"Bugs," I say. "Or bombs. Searching for. Didn't find any."

He shakes his head. "You are a fascinating woman, Maureen Keslyn. Paranoid, but fascinating."

I lock the door behind him with every single one of the deadbolts before I sit down and search through the laptop's programming, seeking traces of anything left behind. Again, I come up empty.

My stomach is also empty. It growls, and I look at the clock. Damn. If I want to catch the official breakfast, I have just enough time to run a comb through my hair and slip into clean clothes. Of course, there are perks to running the Manor. Well, one perk anyway. Matt will feed me breakfast even if I'm late. But I do like to keep an eye on things, and the best way to do that is to eat with the rest of the herd.

If I take Jill with me, it won't matter if I leave the laptop unattended. But just as I start to strip off my gloves, a chat window pops up with an invitation. Maybe it's one of Dason's friends, somebody who hasn't heard the news that he's dead.

A lot can be learned from a person's friends.

A glance at the clock. One sad thought for breakfast, and I sit back down and click Accept.

The chat balloon pops up:

Hi Jinx.

I freeze, then type, *Who the hell is this?*

Incorrect response. Try again.

I've never known a ghost to type electronic messages. Which means somebody knows I have Dason's laptop. Somebody knows not only Phil's old signal to me, but that there was a counter code. I'm not falling for it.

Nobody here named Jinx.

Incorrect response. Try again.

I take a slow deep breath, my brain racing. Anything is possible. I flex my fingers, then type in the familiar code reply:

The rational response to an irrational situation.

The world is not rational, my dear.

And there it is, the entire code sequence Phil and I used to use. Nobody else knew. I certainly never told anybody, and Phil wasn't one for blabbing secrets.

Anubis hisses, tail puffed up, ears back.

I'm not afraid of ghosts, at least I never have been. I'm not afraid of Phil. And if it isn't him, it won't hurt for whoever is playing games to believe I think it's him. I'll play.

Damn it, Phil, what did you go and get yourself killed for?

I missed you too.

What's with the fun and games?

Easier than wall tapping. Quieter.

I think about this one for a minute.

I want to hear some tapping.

That sort of thing is exhausting.

Indulge me.

Not an impostor.

Tap.

I can almost hear the theatrical sigh. All is quiet. The cursor blinks on the screen.

A cold chill chases itself up and down my spine.

And then the closet door slams. Three times loudly. Then three times softly.

Anubis streaks across the room and hides under the sofa.

Three more loud slams.

Silence again.

The windows are closed. There's no draft. And I know that closet door was closed; I keep it that way. Anubis pokes his head out with his ears back, hisses once, and retreats again.

I look at the laptop. Waiting. It's a full sixty seconds by my count before the next message.

Too tired now. Later. Watch…

I'm so focused I jump when an entirely different kind of knock comes at my door.

"Maureen? Everything okay in there?"

Damn it, it's Jill. I close the screen, slide the laptop into its plastic bag, and tuck it under my mattress.

I crack the door, ready to drop and roll if a gun materializes from her handbag. She's still wearing the same skirt and fitted jacket, both rumpled, as if she slept in them. Which she probably did. I certainly didn't undress her before I shoved her onto the bed and left her there to sleep off my good booze.

She squints past me into the room. "I heard banging."

"All quiet in here. You're imagining things."

"No. I heard it. Sounded like an SOS. Very loud." She presses a shaking hand against her head and slumps against the wall for support. "I feel terrible."

"You drank an entire bottle of scotch. What do you expect?"

"Can I come in?"

"Now? Oh, no. I was just on my way to breakfast. You might as well come with me." I edge out the door, forcing her back, and lock all five deadbolts behind me. I didn't have a chance to set my alarm, which is aggravating, but at least Jill will be with me.

TEN

Breakfast at the Manor is an event. Matt serves it up in style— white tablecloths, real china, fabulous coffee. Sunday mornings everybody gets mimosas. Most of the residents dress up for the occasion, fully coiffed and with diamonds on display. By the time I arrive with Jill in tow, the plates are already half empty, and the gossip is in full swing.

All eyes focus on us when we reach the door. Hands stop on the way to mouths. Stories stop short of spilling the good stuff. Jill looks like a half-drunk Kardashian, and I can see the questions spinning in the residents' heads. Is she a movie star on a bender or just an ordinary crazy person? Either way, what is she doing at the Manor and how long will she be staying?

Since they are all staring anyway, and the room has gone quiet, I raise my voice to a decibel calculated to reach the hard of hearing. "Hey everybody, this is Jillian, Phil Evers's daughter. She wanted to see the Manor."

A low murmur wells up in the wake of my words.

Jill winces at the volume of my voice, and I can see the "new kid in the cafeteria" awkwardness take hold of her, weakened as she is by a hangover and lack of sleep. Probably, she expected a room full of the drooling demented, rather than this group of intelligent and wealthy oldsters.

I walk over to my table and the only two empty seats in the room.

"Jill, meet Chuck, Ginny, Julia, and Val."

Jill stands like a statue, eyes invisible behind the dark glasses. Chuck lumbers up onto his feet and pulls out her chair. "Have a seat, beautiful lady. Welcome to the Manor."

She sits, a little hard, probably because he shoves the chair into the back of her knees before she's quite ready. One hand flies to her head, and she inhales sharply.

"Are you all right, dear?" Ginny pats her crimson lips with a napkin, her sharp eyes not missing one detail of Jill's appearance. "I'm so sorry for your loss."

"Bit of a headache," Jill manages to say. "Thank you."

Ginny shifts her attention to me and shakes her head. "Maureen, have you even combed your hair? You look pale. It would take only a few seconds to at least put on a little blush."

As usual, her own elegant face is perfectly painted. She's wearing something soft and drapey and obviously expensive.

"It was not a good night. Where's Matt? I need coffee."

"He's around here, somewhere. Jill, that handbag is gorgeous. Gucci, no?" Julia goes easy on the makeup because of her hand tremors, compensating heavily with designer clothes and extravagant diamonds.

Jill attempts a smile that just makes her look more like she's about to puke. "Yes, actually. I bought it in Paris."

Julia clasps her hands. "Oh, you've come from Paris? I haven't been in years. I do adore that city. Can I see?"

Jill passes the handbag over and both Julia and Ginny ooh and aah over it. To me, it looks awkward and about as useful as carrying around a Kleenex box, but the ways of these women escape me.

Val just watches everything. She's a thin, wiry woman with skin that is nearly ebony and shrewd brown eyes that miss nothing. Seventy-four, with a face that could pass for fifty. Hair like white cotton. She was a high-powered criminal attorney until a stroke attacked her language centers. What speech she retains is limited to fragments of song and poetry quoted from memory, making communication with her complex and time consuming. Her children, as soon as they had guardianship, packed her up and sent her here. Now, her eyes travel to the purse and the women gaping over it. Then her gaze meets mine, and in one electric moment of connection I see laughter and disdain as her lips quirk up on one side and she shakes her head slightly. God help her, she's fully alive in there.

Jill, misguided but more perceptive than I would have given her credit for, says, "Val, did you want to see?"

The mean girl mentality doesn't end with high school. Ginny hands the purse back to Jill. "I hardly think she'd be interested, dear."

Julia snickers, cruelly. "She's probably more the Walmart type, don't you think?"

Matt arrives just in time to prevent me from bloodshed. He's got two mugs of coffee, setting them down carefully in front of us.

"I see you have a guest," he says. "What can I get you?"

Despite the dark glasses and the hangover, I can tell Jill is not immune to either his looks or his charm. Before she can say a word, I answer for both of us: "Lots of coffee. And yes, breakfast."

A long swallow of coffee sends caffeine rushing into all the little cells of my body, and I feel better immediately.

"So sad about your father," Chuck says. "Murdered. I can't imagine how you feel about that."

"Because you're not capable of feeling," Julia retorts.

"I can't believe that trampy little coroner got away with it," Ginny chimes in. "Who would expect the coroner to go around murdering people? They say she grew up here and everything."

"Were you close?" Chuck loads up a fork and shovels it in, oblivious to the bits of egg that fall on his shirt front.

"What sort of question is that?" Ginny objects. "He was her *father*."

"That doesn't necessarily mean anything," Julia says. "I wouldn't exactly be devastated if something happened to mine."

Val says nothing. She eats neatly, one precise bite at a time, her dark eyes not missing a thing.

Matt comes back with two plates of food and a tall glass of what looks like tomato juice. Jill looks at it dubiously, but he leans down and whispers, "Good for what ails you. Drink up."

She sniffs, then sips. "Bless you. *Tu es un ange.*"

"Hair of the dog, eh?" Chuck says. "Poor child. I understand about finding comfort in the bottle."

Jill tries to smile and nearly succeeds, aided by the drink. "I'm afraid I did drink too much last night. It's been difficult."

"I'm well acquainted with morning afters." Chuck pats her shoulder. His hand lingers and slides down onto her back.

I kick him in the shins, accidentally of course, in the act of stretching a kink out of my leg. He drops his cane with a loud clatter. Jill winces visibly, both hands going to her head. I have no sympathy. That was my good scotch she drank, my sleep she disturbed. A little pain won't kill her.

"You've barely tasted your eggs, Jillian," I tell her. "Eat up."

"Have you taken any aspirin, honey?" Ginny says. "That always helps."

"I'm sure I've got something." Chuck roots around in his pocket and comes out with a bottle. "Here, dear. Take a couple of these."

He pauses in the act of shaking pills into his hand, staring toward the door. "More company?"

"Looky-loos," Ginny answers. "And clearly not the sort we're looking for at the Manor."

I'd forgotten all about Ed and Glenda. They stand in the doorway, holding hands, looking like Disneyland tourists who've accidentally wandered into a Park Avenue gala. They're wearing matching sweatshirts, cherry red, with a picture of a cartoon sheep and the words "I survived the Valley of the Shadow" emblazoned across the chest. Glenda even has a camera dangling from a strap around her neck.

Once again, all talk in the dining room dies away. The residents are enjoying the interruptions in their routine, and the weight of their collective curiosity is palpable. As owner of the Manor, it's my job to find the newcomers somewhere to sit, but I'm too busy wallowing in mean spirited enjoyment of their dilemma. Glenda, however, is not about to let a little social awkwardness get in her way.

She sweeps toward me with her arms outstretched. "Maureen! There you are!"

Hemmed in by chairs, limited by my damaged mobility,

there's no way short of shooting the woman to avoid being enveloped in a perfume-scented hug. Fortunately, she's one of those people who need both hands to talk and she releases me before I'm forced to elbow my way free.

"Such a lovely facility. Thank you for letting us stay. What do we do about breakfast? Is there a charge? Aren't you hungry, Eddy?"

Ed, who was never called Eddy even as a child, remains in the doorway. His face is set in the grim lines of a man watching his beloved play roulette with a fully loaded six-shooter. He tries to signal her with hands and eyes, but she's oblivious.

All around us, hands adjust hearing aids. Infrequently used glasses appear out of pockets and purses. Nobody wants to miss a single moment of the show.

Matt appears with two extra chairs, his timing so perfect he could have been waiting in the wings for his cue. "I'll have your food right out. Coffee?"

Glenda sits, waving semaphore code at Ed with such vehemence he has no choice but to come and join us.

Jill bats her eyelashes and thickens her French accent. "Oh, enchantée! You are Maureen's husband? I am Jillian. Phil Evers' daughter."

She reaches her hand up to him as if she expects him to kiss it. Ed, visibly confused, is a polite man, but he's not given to romantic gestures. He accepts the hand, shakes it once, and then carefully lowers it to the table, as if it's a fragile object she's offered up for his inspection. He cuts a glance at me, his eyes a question I don't even try to answer.

Instead, I push back my chair and abandon a perfectly good breakfast. I take my coffee with me.

"Leaving?" Jill asks, all innocent concern. "You've barely eaten a thing."

"I have work to do. And a hotel room to find for you. Enjoy your breakfast."

My attempt at a smooth exit is marred by Ed, who follows me to the door. Despite the fact that I ignore him, he stays with me all the way down the hall. Unconsciously my steps synchronize with his, a familiar cadence that my body remembers despite all my efforts to forget.

"Aren't you forgetting something, Eddy?" I shorten my steps, deliberately breaking the rhythm.

Matching sweatshirt and diminutive nickname aside, Ed is not a zebra. He spent too many years with me, absorbed too much of what I do, to ever be complacent about the lions. He's also direct when he wants to know something, one of the qualities I've always appreciated.

"How much danger are we in?" he asks, now.

I plant my feet and stop, waiting until he turns to face me. "Is that why you brought her here? Afraid to leave her home alone?"

"You called last month and told me to take her out of the country."

"Well wishes for the new couple. Did you enjoy it?"

"It was lovely," he says. "Glenda is easy to travel with. Who is this Phil Evers? Am I supposed to know him?"

"It's a long story."

"I have time."

Time is not the issue here. Trust is an issue. Betrayal, abandonment. Those are issues.

"Phil's dead, for starters."

"I'm sorry." He means it, and that throws me off balance.

"And I haven't seen him in thirty years." We both let that sink in. I didn't have an affair that will let Ed off the hook for his. I can tell he was hoping and was also prepared to be outraged.

Now he deflates. "Can we get breakfast somewhere else? Just the two of us. We should talk, at least once."

"Are you sure we shouldn't bring Glenda?"

"Maureen. Please."

I TAKE him to *House of Joe*, where the coffee is excellent and the food is well salted and full of bacon. We find seats in a back corner, where our conversation will be covered by the country music blaring overhead and the voices of other patrons.

Ed doesn't waste time. The minute our food is on the table and the waitress off to other customers, he asks, "Well?"

"I find it difficult to talk about the Unit while I'm looking at that shirt."

"Don't." His voice is a warning.

I bat my eyelashes and clasp my hands like a lovestruck schoolgirl. "I didn't know Shadow Valley had tourist paraphernalia. It's adorable. The two of you make the cutest couple."

"Maureen—"

"What did you expect, Ed? You moved her into our house— my house—while I was in the hospital. And then the two of you waltz in here looking like the Bobbsey Twins on vacation and you expect me to be civil. You're slipping."

His fork hovers over a plate of eggs and bacon, never landing. "Five minutes. You get five minutes to tell me what a bastard I am. Then you can tell me what sort of mess you've

gotten yourself involved in and how it's likely to affect me—us
—and then I'll load up and get Glenda out of your hair."

I anchor both hands around my coffee mug and keep them
there, where they can't betray me.

"This whole thing would be easier if I were a man."

Ed blinks, twice. "Seems like this whole thing wouldn't be
happening, were that the case."

"I don't suppose I could interest you in a fistfight or a duel?"

"Fight it out like gentlemen, you mean? You'd win,
Maureen. You'd kick my ass to kingdom come. We both
know it."

"It would be damn satisfying." I take a sip of my already
cooling coffee. Even thinking about kicking Ed's ass eases my
anger enough to answer the question that brought us here.

"I am no longer working for the Unit."

"Excuse me if I'm skeptical. Running a retirement home is
not exactly in your skill set."

"Phil left the Manor to me in his will."

"And Phil is who again? Besides dead?"

I hide my face in my coffee mug for a good long swallow,
thinking about how much to share. "Phil Evers *was* my partner,
and yes, my lover, when I first joined the Unit. I hadn't heard
anything of him for years, but he brought me to the Manor on a
rogue assignment, something the Unit wasn't exactly in favor
of. They eliminated him."

"Jesus, Maureen."

"That's when I called and told you to get out of the country. Phil willed the Manor to me and it makes sense for me to
live here, home not being an option."

I expect this rough summary to elicit more questions, but
not the one Ed asks.

"Do you realize you were never home? In all the years of our marriage, you spent more time hunting monsters than you spent with me. Even when you were home, your mind was somewhere else."

"Hunting monsters, Ed. Not men. Never Phil."

"Thank you for that." He smiles, but his eyes are sad. "I always wondered."

"You never asked." I take a bite of country fried steak. It's perfect. Greasy, crunchy, salty, and as unhealthy as it comes. "I thought they might come after you to get to me. You're safe for now, I think."

"That's comforting. What on earth did you do?"

"It's what I didn't do. The less you know the better."

"I'd like to be the judge of that. And I don't believe for a minute you're not still working."

It's hard to lie to Ed, but not impossible. I level my gaze, focus all my will and attention, and look directly into his eyes. "Why on earth would I work for a Unit that wanted to kill me?"

"You wouldn't. You'd try to get back at them for what they did to this Phil guy. And you don't think that puts me and Glenda in danger? Jesus, Maureen, tell me the truth for once. Our entire marriage had been built around secrets."

"And its dissolution should yield sudden truth?"

"Why not? Fresh start. Clean slate."

He's right about the secrets. I never let myself wonder about his, as I wasn't about to tell him mine. His choice of a new woman is certainly not something I had predicted. Looking at him now, sitting across from me in that tourist shirt, a bowl of oatmeal in front of him instead of bacon and eggs, he looks like a stranger. How can you be married to somebody for twenty-five years and not know them at all?

"Maureen?"

I realize that I've been staring, trying to reconstruct the foreign lines of his face into familiar territory. I'd like to tell him the truth now, one last gift, the closest thing to an apology he'll ever get from me.

I can't. It might get him killed.

The truth has been an invisible guillotine hovering over my head since the day Phil and I walked away from a paranormal research program we judged to be unethical and evil. The price of our freedom—and our lives—was our silence.

I kept mine.

Phil didn't. He went underground and staged a resistance that finally got him killed. His death drives me now, along with the deaths of innocent civilians killed by monsters the Unit created in a project they are still trying to hush up. I'm motivated by guilt. Revenge. Reparation.

In light of all this, Ed's questions, the fate of our marriage, are small considerations. He's going to have to make friends with his questions.

"That's it, Ed. There's nothing else to tell. Rather sad and boring, really. I'm not working for the Unit. I'm running the Manor to stay busy."

"So that's it, then?"

"That's it."

I watch acceptance settle over him. Not belief—he knows full well I'm not telling him the truth—but acknowledgment that nothing is about to change between us. He pushes back his plate, wipes his lip with his napkin, carefully folds it, and lines it up beside his bowl.

"I should be getting back to Glenda."

We drive back to the Manor in silence.

"Goodbye, Maureen. Try not to get yourself killed." Ed leans over and kisses my cheek, and then he's gone, walking away from me toward the Manor, toward his new woman and his new life.

I open my window and call him back.

"Ed!"

He turns his head back over his shoulder, slows his steps, but keeps walking.

"If I die suddenly, you might want to consider an ex-pat community. Belize, maybe. Or France."

"Jesus, Maureen," he says. He doesn't stop. Doesn't come back. Doesn't even tell me to make an effort to stay safe.

When the front door of the Manor closes behind him, loss hits me hard enough to steal my breath away, but it only lasts a minute. I would suffocate in the domesticated air of the life he deserves, has deserved all these years. I have work to do. First on the list is the task of thwarting the Middle School Invasion.

ELEVEN

Joanna Schrader, sixth grade teacher at Shadow Valley Middle School, is teaching a class and unavailable to come to the phone. The young woman who takes my call is either challenged in the department of brains, or hoping I'll change my message. Or both.

"Are you sure?" she asks me, after I've repeated myself for the third time.

"I'm sure. Maybe next year."

"Mrs. Schrader was planning on today."

"Yes. Which is why I am calling. The dinner at the Manor is off. There has been a complication."

Silence on the other end, marked by panicked breathing.

"Hello? Can you give her the message?"

"I can't tell her that."

"It's pretty straightforward."

"You don't understand," the girl says.

"Tell Mrs. Schrader not to shoot the messenger and—"

"Oh, God. Do you think she would? Shoot me, I mean? I know she'll be mad, but. Oh, God. I can't—"

"Look. She's not going to shoot you. Write it down on a piece of paper. Leave it on her desk. Don't sign your name. Just make sure she gets it, okay?"

"But—"

I hang up. Putting Joanna Schrader and the Middle School Invasion out of my mind, I get to work on letting the rest of my team know the plan.

Their enthusiasm is lacking.

"You told Ms. Schrader *what*?" Jake sounds incredulous over the phone. "I don't think anybody has ever told her no before. To anything."

"Who is this woman that she has everybody cowering in terror? An ogress? Does she boil kids and eat them for dinner?"

"You haven't met her," is Jake's response. "It's your funeral, Maureen. I can meet you in the lab at three."

"What am I going to do with all the food?" Matt asks, when I tell him. He doesn't know Mrs. Schrader, so at least it's not another fear reaction.

"Freeze it. Make it into multiple meals. I don't know, Matt, you're the cook."

I'm rewarded with a glare at first, but then his eyes light up and he grins. "A good ghost hunt should be fun. Do you have equipment? What's the plan?"

"Jake will be here at three. Meet us in the lab."

Matt's face clouds over. "I still have to make dinner for the residents."

"Pizza," I tell him. "Order it now. Talk them into delivery."

"What's this about pizza?"

Jill stands in the kitchen doorway. She's made a dramatic

recovery. Her hair's been washed and twisted into a sleek knob at the back of her head. She's wearing black spandex, an outfit that might be meant as exercise gear, but to my eyes all she needs is a mask to fit the role of a B-movie cat burglar. She smiles at Matt—Phil's smile, the one designed to charm and disarm— and insinuates herself between us, directly in his line of vision.

"I haven't had pizza in so many years. They don't make it right in France. Can I help?"

"We're ordering it in, Jillian. Matt's busy."

"I could still help," she says, ignoring me. "With ordering pizza. Or food preparation. I'm good with a knife."

"I was thinking we'd get you up to your dad's place today," I tell her.

"I'm not ready." Two perfectly matched crystal tears well up and spill onto her cheeks. She turns her head so the light catches them and sniffs pathetically. "I need distraction. Let me do some work in the kitchen."

I haven't had a chance to warn Matt about Jill, and I hesitate. I have things to do and if she's with him, at least she's not under my feet. He has skills; he should be able to handle her.

My gut doesn't sit right with this, but she who hesitates is lost.

"What I'm going to do," Matt says, with a caustic glance in my direction, "is chop up all this turkey breast I was going to cook for the middle school dinner and put it in the freezer."

"Let me help you," Jill pleads.

"Awesome." Matt pulls a knife out of his stash and hands it to her. My eyes gravitate to the sight of a sharp blade in those hands, and I can't suppress a quick flashback. Pain, blood, a whole lot of drama. Another memory, another body, this time

Matt's handiwork, comes into my mind. I shrug. Matt's a big boy. He can take care of himself. Maybe the two of them even deserve each other.

"Play nice, kids," is all I say.

I've got a lot to do before we go ghost hunting, but, as usual, the universe has plans of its own that get in the way. When I get back to my suite, the door is unlocked.

Damn it. I knew I shouldn't have walked away without setting my alarm. Jill and Ed have seriously disrupted my focus. I spin the chamber in my revolver so the silver bullet will be up first. I loosen the knife in my ankle sheath and the one I carry at my hip. Then I turn the doorknob and kick the door open with my foot, staying sheltered in the hallway with my back flat against the wall.

No sound. No movement.

All I can see is a whole lot of chaos, just like I left it: packing boxes and random furniture strewn about without rhyme or reason. My own breath held, I can hear panting. Not human, then, whatever it is. I launch myself around the corner, finger on the trigger. Something four-legged and hairy hits me in the kneecaps and nearly knocks me off my feet.

"Don't shoot!" Sophie's voice calls out from the chair at the obscured corner of the room.

The furry creature, which is nothing more than Morpheus, dances around my feet, whining and wagging his tail. Sophie sits in the chair, Anubis curled in her lap. Both sets of green eyes fix me with a glare.

"Put that thing away before somebody gets hurt." She sounds like my mother, which does nothing to settle all the fight-fueled adrenaline coursing around in my body.

"If you're going to make a habit of barging in like this, I'll get you a set of keys."

"Obviously I've already made one."

Obviously. I open my mouth to unleash a torrent of sarcasm, but then she sniffles, and I look at her more closely. Her eyelids are swollen and red, all the usual kohl liner washed away. A sodden wad of used tissues sits on the end table beside her.

Hellfire and damnation. Preserve me from teenage girls and their emotions.

I holster the gun. Slam the door. Slide the deadbolts into place.

"What's happened?"

Her only answer is more sniffling. Morpheus trots over to lie down at her feet, licking her hand. Anubis swears and swats at him.

I'm going to need fortification for whatever this is. I pull out my bag of coffee beans and then remember I have no coffee pot.

"What have you done with Phil?"

"Nothing. Yet." Her tone makes this sound ominous.

"At your earliest convenience, I'd like my coffee pot back." Even as I say it, I realize that even for me, reusing that pot might be a stretch. I'm going to need a new one. With a sigh, I plunk down onto one of the wooden chairs. "Talk to me. What happened?"

"Jamie Bergstrom," she says, as if this should have meaning to me.

At my blank look, she takes a quavering breath and tries again. "He's six. Was six. I helped him cross on Sunday morning. And now they..." She presses the back of her hand over her mouth, her face crumpling.

"One of the nurses saw me leaving his room. They've banned me from the hospital. I needed to go up there this morning—I tried. Marie said she'd call security if I didn't leave."

I'm the wrong person for this conversation. Anybody else would handle it better. Jake. Matt. Jill, probably. Even Mrs. Schrader.

"What are people saying?"

She lifts one shoulder in a half shrug, burying her face in the cat.

"Sophie? What are they saying?" If there's going to be mob action, we need to be prepared.

"The nurses? I don't know. They're just whispering. But gossip runs fast in Shadow Valley, you know? I ran into some of the kids from my class. Kayley called me Death Girl. Gage laughed. And—" Her voice breaks again.

"Did anybody threaten you?"

She hasn't thought of that. Her head jerks up, tear-filled eyes wide with surprise. "No. Nothing like that."

"They sound like stupid kids. Why do you care what they think? Didn't you drop out, anyway?"

"They've always hated me. I've never had any friends. Everybody already thinks I'm some weirdo because of the undertaker thing. A bunch of them at school used to hold their noses when I walked by, saying I stink like dead people. Because of my dad. But nobody has ever called me *that*. And now—" Her voice breaks and she buries her face in the cat again, sobbing. Anubis objects, wriggling out from beneath her and taking refuge under the bed. The dog, a much better creature than either me or the cat, presses up against her, licking away tears.

She sighs tragically, wrapping her arms around his neck.

"I'm sorry, Soph. Life's tough sometimes."

She sniffles, face buried in dog fur. "Maureen? I'm scared."

"Of some idiot kids?"

Her arms tighten around the dog's neck. He whimpers and tries to wriggle out from her grip. She makes a choking noise and lets him go. I walk over and push back the screening fall of hair, taking her chin in one hand and turning her face up to mine so she has to stop hiding.

"What really happened?"

She swallows, twice. "I—when Kaylee called me Death Girl, I was mad. It would have been so easy. I could feel her soul. All I had to do was slurp it out of her and send it across. *Poof.* No more Kaley. And nobody laughing at me anymore."

I wait. Not saying anything, not yet. Comfort isn't what Sophie needs, although she hasn't realized it yet.

"They're right about me. I'm weird. They could make a superhero movie about me, only I'd be the villain. Death Girl."

I say nothing, still holding her face and making her look at me. Letting the silence grow, waiting for her to come to the true root of her problem.

Finally, she draws a deep, quavering breath and whispers the words I've been waiting for.

"I'm scared of myself."

"Good. You should be."

"I can't believe you just said that."

"What am I supposed to do? Pat you on the back, say 'there, there, you're harmless?' You are goddamn fucking dangerous and you'd better know it."

"You are the weirdest adult ever."

"And you're a weird kid. So there we are. Look. Why

would I lie to you? That serves no purpose. Tell me, why didn't you just slurp out Kayley's soul, as you put it? Teach all those kids a little lesson?"

"I didn't think I could live with myself, after, if I did that."

"So what did you do?"

"I stared at her for a minute and walked away. Totally lame. They think I'm a weird idiot freak."

"You are."

"Oh my God! You are so bad at this!"

"It's good to know what you are. Spiderman was a freak. So was Superman and all those heroes the kids think are awesome on TV. Even Buffy the Vampire Slayer was weird. People laugh at what they don't understand, because it's different and scares them. You are what you are. Best accept that."

The kid probably needs a hug, but the best I can manage is an awkward pat on the shoulder. "Look—your wonderful, brave, weird Death Girl self saved my life. And Matt's, and Jake's. If that had been Kaylee or one of the others in the lab that day, none of us would be here. Understand?"

Instead of looking encouraged, her shoulders slump a little more and she turns her face away from me.

I curse my own self for an idiot. Sophie took a life to save ours that day, slurped the soul right out of a paranormal-human hybrid.

"Look. I'm not going to say that I know how you feel—I don't. But I do remember the first time I felt guilty about killing a paranormal. It was a werewolf. It had been on a killing streak for a couple of nights in wolf form. Phil showed me what was left of the dead bodies—a couple of mangled teenagers. A little kid. And then he took me out hunting. We caught up with the monster just at sunrise, and it shifted back to human when I put a silver bullet in its belly.

"I knew it was a monster. I saw what it had done. But in human form it was this teenage girl, with acne and big brown eyes. She was scared and screaming with the pain, hands pressed against her belly, trying to stop the blood, begging me to help her. I stood there frozen, unable to do anything. And then I fell down on my knees and put my hands over the wound.

"Phil put his pistol against the side of her head and pulled the trigger."

Sophie gasps. "How could he?"

"That's what I said. He ignored me for a minute—got down on his knees beside me, closed her eyes, ever so gently, and then picked her up like a sleeping child. 'What would you have us do, Maureen?' he said to me. 'She's got a taste for human blood. She'll shift again. She'll kill. We can see her locked up for the rest of her life. Or we can kill her. Sometimes, killing is a mercy.'

"And that was it. We never talked about it again."

Sophie plays with the dog's ears, her face averted. "You don't think you could have—I don't know—changed her? Saved her?"

"I don't have an answer. We need research. Science is *still* debating the nature versus nurture question with humans. We haven't even begun to delve into paranormal behavior."

She exhales, as if she's been holding her breath, and nods once. "Maureen? There's another thing."

"What's that?"

"We have a ghost problem."

"I'd noticed."

"I mean, really. I'm seeing spirits I've never seen before.

Some of them aren't even connected to the Manor. I don't know why they're here, and they're agitated. None of them are interested in crossing."

"Which is why we are all meeting in the lab at three."

"We are?"

"I tried to call you. You didn't answer your phone. "

"It's not working." She pulls it out of her pocket and taps the screen. "Too much energetic interference. Not the first time. What about the dinner thing?"

"Canceled."

She blinks. "You canceled? On Mrs. Schrader?" She couldn't sound more shocked if I'd invited a tribe of vampires over for dinner.

"You think we should have a bunch of kids up here with spirit activity manifesting all over the place?"

"Well, no, but..."

"What is it with this Mrs. Schrader? I'm sure she'd appreciate the fact that we're looking out for her kids. There was palpable paranormal activity at breakfast. Something needs to be done. You're sure you can't talk to them?"

"If I could, you don't think maybe I'd have done that already? I keep telling you I'm not a medium."

"There must be some way to communicate."

"They are not so good with language. I think it's one of the first things to go when they die. Maybe that's why some are so angry. They need to communicate something and have no way to do it."

I think about my conversation with Phil, and decide it's not something Sophie needs to know. "What about Ouija board and all that?" I ask.

She shrugs. "All I know is that spirits never even try to talk to me."

There are other ways to communicate.

Just like that, the overhead lights blink on and off. The dog points his muzzle up to the ceiling and lets out a mournful, melancholy howl, worthy of his wild forebears. Every hair on my head stands up as if there's an electromagnet hovering there, or I'm about to be struck by lightning.

A burner on the stove turns itself on and glows cherry red with heat. They're going to burn down the Manor if they keep this up.

"Listen, whoever you are," I warn. "Turn that burner off, now, or I get the salt sprayer out. I mean it."

A moment, and then the red hot glow fades.

"Thank you. Now behave yourselves." I turn to Sophie. "Meeting at three. Don't be late."

She gets up to go, the dog at her heels, his hackles raised and a low growl pulsing in his throat. "Phil has to cross, Maureen. I'm telling you again. He's like a beacon for the others."

I think about the unfinished chat conversation again. I'm not ready to let him go. I want to talk to him one more time. "He'll go when he's ready," I tell her. "You can't make him do anything."

"Are you ready to do what needs to be done if he doesn't?" Her skin is always pale, but her face looks bloodless, green eyes enormous.

"You mean, erase him completely?"

"If there's no other way," she says. "There are spirits here from across the country, Maureen. They are drawn to him. They keep coming. None of them will cross."

I've been involved with eliminating a spirit who refused to be tamed. It was unpleasant, but in that case, it wasn't somebody I'd known and loved. It was easy enough to tell myself the soul had always been evil, that elimination was an act of good will. But this is Phil we're talking about. A man I've slept with, worked with, trusted my life to.

"There's always another way," I say, after a minute.

She nods, as if I've just said something meaningful, and leaves me there, closing the door firmly behind her.

Before I start digging in boxes for all the ghost hunting paraphernalia I own, I check in with Dason's laptop, wanting desperately to connect with Phil. Surely I can still reason with him. Ask him to help with this situation, even. But the chat window is empty. Worse, there's no transcript of our previous conversation. The laptop is inert, sterile, wiped clean of any trace of either me or Dason.

TWELVE

The temperature in the lab is so frigid, despite two space heaters turned on high, that I can see my own breath. Both Matt and Jake are hunched up, hands tucked under their arms for warmth. Sophie is late.

"She'll show up. Let's get started," Jake says. "It's not like she needs any of this equipment."

I hand him a pair of infrared goggles, an energy sensor, and a recording device.

"What am I supposed to do with these?"

"Ghosts leave an energy signature. You can see it with the glasses."

"And detect it with the energy scanner, I suppose." Jake switches on the handheld, and it goes crazy. He switches it off. "This is an old government installation. How do you know I'm not just registering radiation or some such?"

His natural-born skepticism is held in check by the inexplicable things he's been part of recently. When you've been almost killed by an invisible jelly-thing, scoffing at the idea of ghosts is a luxury you can't really afford. But he's still having a problem with the concept of a ghost hunt.

"Put the goggles on," I tell him. "Have a look. And then please tell me there's a way to get the weapons you confiscated from Phil's house, because we are going to need them."

He adjusts the googles into place and looks around the room. "Oh, Shit. Not good, I take it?"

I put on my own pair of goggles and survey the impending disaster. In all my years, I've never seen anything like it.

Ghosts throng the room. Most of them are lined up around the walls, like high school kids at the beginning of a formal dance. A few roam freely, one of them touching Jake's cheek and evoking a shiver. Even as I watch, two new ones drift down from the ceiling.

"I don't think we'll need to do much hunting," Matt says. "What do they want?"

"That's what I'd like to know. Sophie thinks it's Phil."

"Can't she talk to them?"

"Apparently not."

"It is Phil," Sophie says from the doorway. She stands there, unmoving, the potato salad container clutched to her chest.

As if to emphasize her point, all of the spirits swirl toward her in a paranormal cloud, as if she's a cosmic vacuum cleaner sucking them in.

"Back off!" she commands, as if she's talking to a pack of dogs. "I'm walking here." The cloud parts to let her move, closing in behind her as she proceeds to the back of the room. She sets down the container on the table beside the old lab equipment. It is instantly surrounded by a cloud of activity, and the spirits stay there when Sophie walks over to join us.

"I wanted all of you to see. It's not me they're thronging to. It's Phil."

"Why is he in a potato salad container?" Jake sounds thoroughly shaken. I can't blame him.

Sophie returns to the container, carries it across the lab, and sets it carefully in the hallway. Then she closes the door between it and us and pours a mound of salt across the threshold. Most of the spirits remain out in the hallway, although a few still drift around the room.

"Phil needs to cross, or he needs to be eliminated," Sophie says, in a clear, emotionless voice. "Maureen isn't able to see this, but I'm sure the two of you can. He is no longer the man she knew and worked with. And he needs to be stopped before somebody gets hurt."

"Like *Ghostbusters*?" Jake asks, reaching for humor and falling flat.

"This is not some stupid movie. What they could do in these numbers is terrifying. Besides, they're not meant to be here. They need to move on. And as long as Phil is here, they won't go."

As if to emphasize her words, the lights go out.

We're equipped with flashlights, but they only serve to make the dark look darker. A blue glow illuminates the cracks where the door doesn't quite seal.

"It's a drastic measure," Matt says quietly. "Wiping somebody out forever like that. Do you know what's in the Beyond, Sophie? I'm not sure I'm comfortable with that."

"Comfortable?" she asks, her voice breaking. "You think I'm comfortable? Souls are my *job*. Destroying one is like the worst sin I could commit. I just don't know what else to do."

Relieved to hear humanity and emotion back in her voice, I

draw a deep breath and a little of the tension I'm holding eases out, enough that my toes uncurl. "That's what this meeting is for," I tell her. "So we can figure it out, together."

"Has he done anything awful?" Jake asks. "Visibly campaigning for a ghost uprising, doing something to draw them in?"

"Not that I can tell," Sophie says. "They just keep coming."

To illustrate her point, a ghostly flicker emanates from one of the walls and trails across the room, hovering in front of the door that bars it from Phil.

"We need a medium," I say. "But since we don't have one, I've brought some possible communication devices. We'll run recorders constantly; sometimes they pick something up. Everybody carry a small one with you as you move through the Manor. While you're at it, keep scanning for energy." I dole out the small recorders and EDI scanners. "Be sure to make notes of time and place of any manifestation. And take pictures. I have one full-spectrum camera, but cell phones work surprisingly well."

I hand the camera to Matt, who gets busy photographing the lab.

"Now, for communication purposes." I open the laptop and pull up a blank Word document.

"What if they can't type?" Jake asks. Before I can answer, he waves me away. "I know, I know. Electronic signals, or whatever. And I assume the flour is not for a baking project."

"Every possible opportunity." I spread a cup full out on the table. "Are we set?"

"What happens if they get out of hand?" Jake asks. "I mean, can they hurt people? Are they dangerous?"

"Yes," Sophie says. "They could."

"Let's not get melodramatic," I object. "They might manifest, which scares people. They can tear up a room and throw things around. But we've got the salt sprayer. They don't like salt. And we've got Sophie. Let's stay in pairs. Sophie goes with Matt. Jake is with me. Okay? First, let's see what we can pick up. Sophie, bring Phil back in here."

"This is a bad idea," she says, but does it anyway.

When the door is open and the spirits move freely again throughout the lab, I switch on my recorder. "You want to talk to them, Sophie?"

"Not particularly."

"Fine." I clear my throat. Talking to ghosts seems like talking to myself. I feel unusually self-conscious and theatrical, as if I should be speaking in Latin. Still, I get to my feet. "Hey, Phil. If you and your friends have something to say, we'd really like to hear it. We're listening."

The room goes weirdly quiet. All motion stops. With the goggles on I can see ghostly faces turning toward me, too many to count. I can't make out individual features, don't know which one belongs to Phil. The cold sets into my bones.

And then my walkie-talkie hums a warning, and Cathy's voice comes through. "Maureen?"

"I'm busy."

"Yes, well, what do you want me to do about the middle schoolers?"

"That's been canceled."

Silence.

"Cathy?"

"Um, they're here."

"Tell them to go away."

"I sort of let them in."

"You did what?"

"Mrs. Schrader insisted. She wants to talk to you. And there are kids—" Her voice cuts off sharply and another voice comes on. "Maureen Keslyn? What were you thinking? You can't cancel same day. There are plans."

"We have a ghost infestation. It's not safe."

"Right," she says. "Nice try. Dinner at five."

The walkie-talkie bursts into static, which grows louder and louder until the volume is painful. Jake covers his ears. I fiddle with the knob, trying to turn the accursed thing off, but the radio does not respond. It feels hot. A whisp of blue smoke drifts up out of it, visible in my flashlight beam, and then it makes a sizzling noise and goes completely silent.

"Well, that complicates things," Jake says into the horrified silence.

"Permission to order in pizza?" Matt asks.

"You'd better. I don't suppose they can make you pizza with turkey and dressing?"

"It's four now. It will be a miracle if we can get plain cheese delivered by five. I'll do what I can."

"I don't like this," Sophie says. "I don't like this at all."

THIRTEEN

I don't like it, either.

We need to stick together, or at least work in teams, but Matt has to do something about dinner, and Sophie insists on staying in the lab. She performs her best eye roll, followed by a hair toss. "With all due respect, Maureen, I'm Buffy and you guys are the Scoobies. Who is going to protect whom?"

"What?" Jake says. "Translation?"

"CliffsNotes version—she's the paranormal ass kicker and we're the sidekicks," I tell him. "Look. Soph, even Buffy needed help."

"They're not going to hurt me," she insists. "Leave me a bag of salt, if you're worried. If things get out of control, I'll put myself inside a circle until you come to rescue me. Go on. You just stir them up."

"Me? I stir them up?"

My radio isn't dead after all. It squawks and squeals. Then

Cathy's voice comes again, tinny and far away. "It's getting a little weird up here, Maureen."

None of this bodes well, especially with a Manor full of kids.

"Sophie. Please come with us," I say.

She shakes her head. "This is my life, Maureen. It's what I do."

"All right then. I'll come check on you as soon as I can." Matt is already out the door, running down the corridor. Jake stays with me, and I let him help me up the stairs. It goes against the grain, but there could be lives on the line.

An eerie howling sound echoes down the stairwell, mournful and disturbing enough to make me put on a burst of speed. It's only the dog, Morpheus, sitting in the closet at the top of stairs, his muzzle pointed toward the ceiling.

He whimpers when he sees me, pressing his head against my knees.

"It's okay," I tell him. "She's fine."

He's clearly unconvinced, refusing to budge from his position.

Anubis, unsurprisingly, is nowhere to be seen.

We take time to load up with a few extra supplies. Holy water. My spare crucifix. A couple of stakes. Stakes are useless against ghosts, of course, but paranormal activity attracts other paranormal activity. Right now, the Manor is a blazing signal to any creatures within range.

"Ready?" I ask Jake.

He nods, and I unbolt the door.

I take one step and am almost mowed over by a wheelchair careening around the corner on two wheels. It's occupied by a freckle-faced boy, screaming for his life, pushed by a hellion of a girl who is racing as fast as her skinny legs will move them.

Jake snatches me back from the path of destruction in the nick of time, and forgets to let me go when the danger has passed. His arms are around me, his strong hands holding me by the waist. His body feels warm and solid, dispelling the lingering spirit chill, and it's oh-so-tempting to slip my arms around him and lean my head against his shoulder. I look up into a pair of gray eyes as intent as a cat's.

The expression on his face does something to my heart rate that the entire room full of ghosts failed to do. Before I can make the decision to pull away, Jill's door slams open.

"What is going on out here?"

Jake releases me and I swing around to confront Jill, who blinks at the two of us in confusion.

"I heard shouts. Wheels. Running."

"Normal noises of a retirement home," I tell her, but her eyes take in the pair of goggles perched on my head, the camera slung around my neck, the EDI device Jake is carrying. Just to be helpful, the lights in the hallway flicker on and off, and a ceiling tile loosens and almost hits her on the head.

She ducks and it crumbles at her feet.

"You're on a ghost hunt!" she exclaims. "Like on TV. Let me help."

"You'd be best to stay in your room with the door locked."

Her eyes travel up to the ceiling and down to the broken tile. "I think I'm safer with you."

"It's not your safety I'm concerned about."

"Oh, come on, Maureen. What am I going to do? You've confiscated all my weapons."

She has a point. There's also something to be said for keeping her in my line of sight.

"All right. But you stay with me, and do whatever I tell you. Clear?"

"Yes, ma'am!" She salutes, mocking me. Which is fine. She hasn't seen anything yet.

"Can I wear the goggle things?"

I hand her my pair and lead the way toward the stairs; there is no way I am setting foot inside an elevator during a spirit storm of this magnitude. The three of us trail down the hallway, Jill lollygagging behind as she takes in the sights through her ghost vision goggles.

Downstairs, things are not going smoothly.

Matt is on the phone in the kitchen, his voice raised. "Yes, I know it's outside your normal delivery area. I promise a hefty tip."

The fluorescents are misbehaving. They flicker. Once, twice, three times. Then they go into a slow fade, dimming to almost dark before gradually growing brighter.

And brighter.

A loud buzzing fills the kitchen. An incandescent flare of white light blinds me. There's a sizzle and a pop and then darkness.

"Hello?" Matt's voice says from somewhere out of the dark. "Hello? Damn it. Phone's dead."

Once the light stops dancing in my eyes, I can see the small red glow of the instrument panel on the back of the stove. The green light of the coffee pot is on. Lights are still on out in the hall. Only the kitchen fluorescents have blown.

"What do you want me to do?" Matt asks.

"Try your cell."

"No dice. That was dead before the landline."

"Somebody needs to go down there in person. And one of you needs to corral the Schrader woman. Because if I go talk to her right now, it's not going to end well."

"I'll get the pizza," Matt and Jake say simultaneously.

"Seriously?" I play my light over the two of them while I make a decision. "Jake, you've less experience with the ghosties, so how about if you go after the pizza? Take my credit card. Pay them whatever it takes. Matt, go charm the teacher. How bad can she really be?"

"Right. Throw me to the wolves," Matt complains.

Jake claps him on the shoulder in sympathy as he beats a quick retreat.

Matt sighs. "Where do you think she's at?"

"Beats me. If I see her, I'll tackle her myself. Mission one is just keep all the kids safe."

"I'll go with Matt," Jill says, her voice as sultry as any B-movie actress about to be ravished by a ghost.

"No, you'll stay with me. Go on, Matt. Try the talkie. If it doesn't work, come find me. I'll be running patrols."

He salutes and heads toward the lobby. When I step out into the hallway, nothing seems out of order. The temperature is reasonable. The lights are on. One of the women from Table One is shuffling along with her walker. Her name is Nora, and she's a kind, grandmotherly type, despite the legion of diamonds that always adorn her.

"Maureen dear, thank you so much for bringing in these children." She gets hold of me with both of her cool, blue-veined hands. She smells of powder, and up close I can see it settled into the crinkles on her face like fine, white dust.

"I hardly know my own grandchildren. They would be,

what, ten and twelve years old now? My son moved to Europe two years ago. He comes home for a visit once a year, but he never brings the children."

She's going to go on forever, and an alarmed shout from the vicinity of the games room tells me we don't have that kind of time. Neither can I leave her wandering around the Manor untended.

"Let's go see what the darlings are up to, shall we?"

"But I was going to my room to freshen up before dinner," she protests.

More shouts. A shriek.

"Can I tell you a secret?" I lean in close to her ear. "Jill and I are both terrible with children. From the sounds of things, they need a little managing. Will you come and help us?"

Nora smiles at that. "Well, surely, dear. If I can be of assistance."

Fortunately, she uses the walker mostly for balance and can move a little faster than a full shuffle. When we reach the door of the games room, I realize my mistake. I should have locked both women into a room and left them there.

"Merciful heavens," Nora whispers, putting one hand to her heart.

I see nothing of either mercy or heaven in the scene that meets my eyes. A gaggle of kids and seniors huddle together under the shuffleboard table. The kids look excited and scared; the residents seem dazed. There's a wheelchair in the middle of the room, lying on its side with one of the rear wheels spinning crazily. A dart, thrown by an unseen hand, whizzes through the air and strikes the target. Bull's-eye.

One of the kids, seeing me, scrambles out from under the table. A resident grabs her and pulls her back, just as a shuffleboard disc levitates and then drops onto the spot where her head would have been.

That's it. I'm pissed. I don't need special glasses to see what's going on here, but I pause to snap a few photos before going into avenger mode.

"I'm warning you," I say, holding up my salt sprayer. "I'll give you until the count of three."

A dart zooms past my head, so close the feather brushes my cheek, and thunks into the wall.

I start turning the handle, spraying the room indiscriminately with salt.

The floating discs crash down onto table and floor. The darts follow. I wait. When everything stays quiet, I draw Nora into the room. She's shaking, and I hope she's not going to have a heart attack.

At my direction, Jill rights the wheelchair and we ease Nora into it.

"Kids, residents, stay put," I order. "Anybody else, get out now. I've had enough."

"Wow!" Jill says, her eyes alight with excitement. "Is it always like this?"

"No. It's generally very boring."

Eyes stare at me, like I've performed a magic trick.

Using the nozzle on the sprayer I paint a line of salt across the threshold of the doorway as I back out of the room, giving another directive to the humans to stay put.

Grabbing Jill's arm, I tow her away to check the dining room, which is empty with the sole exception of Stanley.

He's a grumpy old cuss at the best of times. Right now he looks ready to stab somebody. "Hate kids," he grumbles. "Was going to stay in my room, but my TV won't work. Keeps turning on and off and changing channels. What the hell is all that about, I'd like to know. Probably the government. We need a new president. Goddamn politicians ruining this country."

"Stay put," I tell him. "Pizza is on the way."

"Where to?" Jill asks.

"2nd floor."

With the elevator out of commission, the only option is the stairs. My leg is already dragging and on the edge of a full Charlie-horse spasm, but I can't baby it now.

Jill gets five steps ahead of me before she turns around to watch me haul myself up, one slow stair at a time.

"Oh, I'm so sorry. Let me help you," she says, in the tone of a girl scout to an old lady crossing the street.

"Just stay out of my way."

"I'm trying to help," she says in saccharine tones.

"Well, don't."

She stomps ahead of me and waits at the landing, arms crossed over her breasts and foot tapping. Raised voices are coming from the library.

Somebody screams, then laughs to cover it up. "What kind of Scrabble game *is* this? I don't even know that word."

"It's quixotic."

"Quicks what?"

"Comes from Don Quixote, meaning—"

"Who is Don Quixote?"

"A character in a book. One you should read."

"There's a word made up after some old dude in a book. I don't—"

"Holy shit. What about that one?"

"Watch your language, young lady."

Six chairs around the coffee table. Four kids, two residents.

Val sits at the far end, peaceful, palms turned up, eyes closed. Dan, the man at the other end of the table, crosses himself. A slip of a girl, her long hair in tangles down her back, a ball cap pressed firmly on her head, leans forward, entranced.

"It's like a Ouija board. Only we didn't ask any questions."

The Scrabble tiles are arranging themselves without the help of human hands. One at a time they slide off the trays, reforming into words that have no connection to triple point squares or intersection with other words.

"My mom will have kittens," one of the boys says. "I'm not even allowed to watch horror movies."

The other two look too scared to say anything.

I lift my camera to take a picture of the Scrabble board. Just as I click the shutter, the lights flicker and go out. I take another picture of the board, using the flash, then several around the room for good measure.

Jill starts beating at apparently invisible air with her hands, shrieking loudly. "Get it off me. Get it off me!"

"What is it? Jill, what is it?"

"Cold and—gooey. I hate slimy things." She collapses to her knees, wailing. All three of the boys are away from the table, stampeding off down the hall. My heart thuds at the thought of the Medusa loose in a Manor full of kids and old people.

Whatever it is, I can't see it. Jill's got the ghost-watching glasses. But I do have Phil's special flashlight hanging from a belt loop. It looks like an everyday thing you could buy at Walmart, but it burned holes in the Medusa during our last encounter. I turn it on and start playing the beam over Jill, just in case. She's stopped fighting and has her arms wrapped around her head, weeping hysterically.

"Jill! Are you all right?"

"It's gone," she sniffles. "I think." Her voice sounds thick and uncertain, but she's still alive. Probably just ordinary ectoplasm, and not the Medusa.

I leave her to recover and turn back to the room. Val's eyes are still closed, but her slim brown hands are moving, arranging Scrabble tiles in a row in front of her.

"Whoa," the girl breathes, watching intently.

Whoa, indeed. The words on the table read:

Deja Vu Jinx

Revelation

Jill gets to her feet, bumping heavily against the table and falling half across it. Tiles cascade onto the floor. Val startles and jerks, her brown eyes open, staring at us in confusion.

"Ow," Jill complains, sitting on top of the Scrabble board and nursing her foot. "I think I broke something."

I ignore her, my focus on Val. "You're a medium," I say, watching her face. She nods. Worry creases her forehead, and she looks down at the table where the words she had spelled are scrambled now.

"You spelled out words," I tell her. "What did it mean?"

Her eyebrows lift in a question. She puts her hand to her throat and makes a humming sound. "Vorpal sword. Snicker-snack." Her hands go to the tiles and she turns them over, looking at them one at a time, then slams both hands on the table in frustration.

"What's wrong with her?" the girl whispers.

"She had a stroke. She has trouble finding the right words."

"My grandma had a stroke. She talks funny now, and she can't walk."

"Well, Val walks fine, and she can understand everything you're saying. She just talks around the edges of things."

"But she was—"

"Right. What's your name, kid?"

"Call me G."

"Is that your name?"

"Does it matter?"

I shrug. "I guess not. Okay, G. I need you to do something for me."

"What?" She's a natural-born skeptic. I can see she's been tricked into agreeing with things before.

"I want you to go back to the—"

"I'm assigned to Val. I'm staying with her."

"You're assigned?"

"Mrs. Schrader. She'll skin me alive if I leave."

"Were the boys assigned, too?" I ask.

G makes a dismissive noise. "They're more scared of ghosts than of Mrs. S. Boys are stupid."

Val gets to her feet and tugs at my hand.

"You want me to go somewhere? Yes? Okay. I'm coming."

"Stay here," I instruct the girl, again. "Jill, stay with her."

"No way." G sweeps the Scrabble tiles back into the bag. "I go with Val. And I'm bringing these with us, just in case."

Jill shudders. "I am not staying here alone. What if that thing comes back?"

Short of tying both of them up, there's nothing I can do to make them stay here. "Fine, then, let's go."

G takes possession of Val's free hand. Jill trails along behind us, so close I can feel her breathing down my neck.

Val leads us down the hallway and up a flight of stairs to the third floor. It's pitch dark, and my flashlight only serves to make the shadows darker and more menacing. We stop outside my suite.

"Are you sure?" I ask.

Val pounds on the door with the flats of both hands, making strangled animal noises low in her throat.

"All right, all right. Hang on." I start unlocking deadbolts.

"You sure have a lot of keys," the kid says, as I fumble with the flashlight, my key ring, and the salt sprayer.

"Here. Hold this. Don't turn the handle." I hand her the sprayer.

"What's the salt for?"

"Ghosts don't like it. What's your name, really?" I ask her, as I finally get the door open. I figure if I lose her, I should at least know how to notify her parents.

She wrinkles her nose. "Guinevere. Don't call me that."

"Oh dear."

"Right? What were they even thinking?"

"Mine named me after a movie star," I tell her. "Parents do these things."

The instant the door is open, Val picks up her pace, towing me along the path between my packing boxes toward the hidden staircase. I plant my feet and brace to resist her. Jill is with us. And G, although cool for a kid, can't be expected to hold her tongue. If I let this happen, then there is a huge risk that word will get out about the secret passage and the lab.

"What is it?" I ask, feigning confusion. "Something in my apartment? I know it's a mess."

Val swings around and slaps me, right across the cheek, like I'm a bratty kid. It's not anger I read in her eyes, though, it's fear. She picks her away across the room and opens the closet door.

Tendrils of mist stream out into the room, snaking through the beam of the flashlight.

Sophie is alone down there. The security breach will have to be dealt with later.

Darting past Val, I open the door at the back of the closet, letting the others follow or not as I move as fast as I dare down the steep stairs. The walls, the steps, are slick with condensation. A cold wind whistles.

"Cool," G says, a note of awe in her voice. "This is the best night ever."

Hoping she lives long enough to rethink that, I proceed, one slow step at a time. If I fall, I'll be no good to Sophronia or anybody.

At the bottom of the stairs I stop to take a breath and poke into the shadows with my flashlight. "You still have that salt sprayer, G?"

"Got it. It's freezing down here," G says, her voice uncertain for the first time. "Look, I can see my breath." She shines her flashlight in front of her face and illuminates a cloud of steam.

Ghosts are known to lower the temperature, but not like this. The walls sparkle where I shine my light. Frost is forming. My skin has goose bumps all over and not just from the cold.

G is quiet and I turn around to check on her. Her eyes are wide, but she looks more excited than scared. Jill, on the other hand, is deathly pale. She's shaking so hard her teeth rattle. Val glides past me, not stopping to wait for me to light her way, straight toward the lab.

When I turn the flashlight beam on her, she looks like she's walking through a tunnel of swirling blue light.

"Here, make yourself useful." I toss the camera to Jill, who fumbles and nearly drops it. "Seriously. Pull yourself together, or go back upstairs. Take the child with you."

"I'm going with Val." G scampers ahead of me down the hallway, the salt sprayer swinging from one hand.

I follow as fast as I'm able, wishing with all my heart that we were dealing with something stake-able. Like vampires.

When we reach the lab, it's lit up with a cold blue light that renders flashlights irrelevant.

Sophronia stands in the center of a circle of salt, clutching the potato salad container and Phil's ashes. Her eyes glow green. The air swirls around here in a visible tornado, the wind of which whips out into the room and intensifies my cold to the point where I can barely remember warmth. Her face looks like Joan of Arc at the stake—a blaze of passionate determination overriding fear.

I stop dead in the doorway, repelled by the cold and the wind and the palpable touch of swirling ectoplasm on my skin. No need for ghost hunting goggles here. I can make out body shapes and the vague outlines of faces with my unaided vision.

"Maureen!" Sophie cries. "I don't know how long I can hold them."

Phantom hands touch my skin. Individual outlines shimmer in and out of focus. Some are children and babies, the most dangerous kind of ghost. For years they've drifted, without any anchor to time or space, forgetting what little they ever knew of warmth and love and human morality.

Now Phil's presence has wakened them with a vengeance.

Or possibly *to* a vengeance. Tiny fingers pinch my cheeks, poke at my eyes. G collapses onto the floor, burying her face in her knees and shouting, "Get your grubby hands off me, or I'll salt you!"

"Wait, G. Hold on."

"Val is a medium," I say, to Sophie, to the ghosts, to anyone or any other thing listening. "Let's talk about this."

I shove my way through the cold and clammy ghosts, twitching off their clutching hands, and dump the Scrabble tiles on the table. Val pulls out a chair and sits. Instantly, crackling electricity traces her entire form with blue flames. Her body shudders and goes rigid, her back arches, her eyes roll back in her head so only the whites are visible.

Small tornadoes of light break off from the big one and spin around the room, knocking over chairs. A wordless wailing echoes off the walls.

I've seen a spirit storm once before, though not so big as this. It's like a forest fire—by this time they've created their own weather system. It can go on gathering power until they are capable of bringing down the entire building and inflicting physical harm on the inhabitants, if that's what they're after. I have to shout to make myself heard above the racket.

"We're listening!" I shout at them. "Let us help you!"

The wind dies down to a few small flurries. Val's muscles loosen and she sags in the chair, head bowed on her chest, unconscious. Scrabble tiles skitter away across the table and back again.

I hold my own breath, watching to see if her chest starts moving. Could they have killed her? It would take a strong heart to withstand that sort of an onslaught, and she's not exactly young. A long moment, far too long, and then she draws a deep breath. Her back straightens. Her hands come up to lie open on the table, palms turned up.

Everything in the room goes still with waiting. And then Val's hands begin to move, selecting one tile after another and putting them in a row, turning them over without looking at them and spelling one word.

GENESIS

God, I hate ghosts. Just once, I wish they'd stop talking in riddles. "Could you be a little more specific?" I say. "What in blazes is that supposed to mean?"

But Val's hands lie still.

The room sounds like it's breathing. All the blue light fades and we are left in the dark, illuminated only by the beam of my flashlight.

Jill kneels down at Val's side. In the small circle of light she looks ghastly, her face smeared with mascara and tears.

"Dad," she says. "Please. Talk to me."

The tiles swirl and rattle around on the table. Ghostly fingers run up and down my spine.

Val's hands begin to move again, sorting through tiles and turning them over, one at a time.

FIX IT

More riddles. Is that a message for Jill or for me? If it weren't for Phil, I'd be tempted to start spraying the lot of them indiscriminately with salt out of sheer frustration.

"Come on, Phil," I say. "You can do better than that. Try. Use your words."

One more message forms.

FREE ME

Sophie still stands inside the salt circle, holding on to Phil's ashes.

She shakes her head. "No, Maureen. They're already out of control. Let this out of the circle and I don't know what will happen."

Before I have the sense to intervene, Jill is up and across the room. She grabs the container. Her feet are on one side of the circle, Sophie's on the other.

"Give him to me."

"Never." Sophie's voice echoes with supernatural power. Jill doesn't take the hint. She leans all her body weight backward, uses all her strength.

Déjà vu, I have time to think. Maybe this is the disaster I'm supposed to prevent. I try to run in their direction, but I'm too slow. My leg seizes up and almost drops me.

Jill is heavier than Sophie and isn't limited by the need to stay within the circle. Her feet, searching purchase, smear through the line of salt. A cry escapes Sophie's lips.

My flashlight sizzles and goes out, plunging the room into total darkness, with one exception. Any lingering doubts as to whether Sophie is fully human are extinguished in that moment. Human eyes can't glow. Not like that. Not with no light to reflect. In the dark there is the sound of feet scuffling on concrete, harsh breathing.

A cold wind blows me backward.

Jill screams.

There is a wet thud, as of something heavy hitting concrete.

And then there is silence.

FOURTEEN

I become aware of warmth. My fingers tingle with returning blood flow. The lights come on.

Val is still at the table. She blinks and runs a hand across her face. G kneels on the floor beside her, smudgy but unharmed. Jill lies unconscious on her back on the concrete, blood pooling around her head, making mud out of her father's ashes strewn on the floor all around her.

I drop to my knees beside her and touch her cheek. "Jill, are you okay?"

She's not, obviously, but this is the universal question they teach you in first aid and CPR courses. I shake her shoulder, which has the effect of making blood gush a little faster out of her head. I look around for Sophie, but she's nowhere to be seen.

G comes over and kneels on the other side of Jill's inert form.

"Is she dead?"

She's breathing, but just barely. I can't see her chest rise and fall, but if I lean down close to her face, I can feel a faint, rhythmic warmth on my cheek. Her heart is beating.

I slide my hand under her head and apply pressure to the bleeding wound.

"Sophie? Sophronia, I need you!"

She is nowhere to be seen and my voice echoes off the walls and concrete. My walkie-talkie is fried and won't turn on. I can't call for help.

Val comes over and stands looking down, as calm as if the events of the evening are an everyday occurrence.

"Did either of you see where Sophie went?"

I don't like the look on Val's face in response to this question. I don't like what's going through my own head.

"G, I need you to help me. Run upstairs and find either Sheriff Callahan or Matt, the cook. Tell them to call an ambulance and then get down here. Don't tell anybody else. Understood?"

The kid nods, her face settling into the serious responsibility of her task. "Yes, ma'am." No wasted words or explanations. She's off, pelting down the hallway. I listen to her echoing footsteps and cross mental fingers that she won't run into trouble on the way.

It seems a lifetime before Jake shows up, but it's probably only about five minutes. In all that time, Jill doesn't move. If it weren't for the beating of her heart and her barely perceptible breath, I'd believe her dead.

"I'm sorry," I whisper, in case Phil is listening. Jill is his daughter, after all. It wouldn't have hurt me to look out for her.

Jake skids into the room, G right behind him. His keen eyes take in the overturned chairs, the Scrabble tiles, Val, and then the problem of Jill.

"Can she be moved?"

"I think so. It was dark. She fell backward, I'm guessing. But if her neck is broken..."

"Does it look broken?"

"No bumps or lumps or obvious bruising."

"We're going to risk it." He bends down, gets his arms under her, and scoops her up. "Let's go."

Jake's in great shape, but he's no spring chicken and Jill is not a small woman. By the time we're halfway down the hall, his breath is already coming short and hard. I have no idea how we're going to get up the stairs. But then footsteps thud overhead, and Matt is descending the steps two at a time.

He takes half of Jill's weight, and between the two of them they get her safely up into my suite and lay her down on the couch. I grab my first aid kit and press a compress to the back of her head, trying to stop the bleeding. Jake elevates her feet. Matt throws a blanket over her. The dog comes over and starts licking her face, but despite all our efforts, she's still unconscious when the ambulance crew shows up.

"You moved her?" one of them asks, leveling a disapproving stare at Jake. "You know better."

"I moved her," Matt lies. "I found her on the floor in the bathroom, must have hit her head on the counter when she fell. It just seemed— indecent—to leave her lying there."

"Never move the victim," the woman EMT says, but her voice softens a little at the sight of Matt's impressively woeful expression. "Rule one."

"God, I hope I didn't hurt her."

His acting skills are impressive. The EMT smiles at him. "Hopefully no harm done." She manages to tear herself away from Matt and joins her partner in getting Jill assessed and stabilized. They check out her vital signs and her pupils, bandage her head, then get her into a cervical collar and backboard and from there onto the stretcher. Anubis, who has been hiding under the bed this whole time, emerges to get under the EMTs' feet and damn near trip them up.

G gives Matt a long, considering look, before turning her attention to Jake and me.

"I won't tell," she says, before she's ever asked. "You can trust me on that."

I see the conflict on Jake's face. I know he's thinking this is a terrible and twisted thing to do to a child. I've seen enough of G in action to be a little less conflicted.

"In exchange for what?" I ask her.

"Maureen!" Jake says. "She's a child."

"I am not a child," G snaps back. "In answer to Maureen's question, I won't tell if you let me help you."

"With what, exactly?" I ask her, since by the way Jake's jaw is working he's not going to arrive at comprehensible speech for a minute or two.

She waves her hands expressively. "Oh, you know. Whatever you're doing in the lab down there. Whatever is going on here in the Manor that you're trying to hide."

"That's out of the question." Jake has recovered his voice.

If Matt is a good actor, G is a brilliant one.

Her shoulders curve and her neck sinks between them, making her look small, vulnerable, and years younger. Tears well up and flood her cheeks, and her lips tremble. In between sobs, in a broken voice, she says, "This night has been horrible. There's a secret tunnel into the basement and an evil scientist lab down there. That's where Jill really fell, but they lied about it—the sheriff and the owner and the cook. They probably tried to kill her themselves, and they told me not to tell anybody, but I'm so scared."

"Are you done?" I ask her.

"That depends," she says, in a normal voice. "I can go on for hours if needed."

"I'm sure you can. What is it, exactly, that you want again?"

"To help."

"It's too dangerous," Matt says. "You can't possibly be seriously considering this, Maureen."

He's right about the danger, and that's where I'm hooked. If anybody finds out what this child knows, then her life is in danger from the Unit. It looks like the best way to keep her quiet, and safe, is directly underfoot.

Val seals the deal by walking over and resting a hand on G's shoulder. Even if I say no, the kid will hang out with Val anyway, snooping around and uncovering secrets on her own.

"All right," I tell her. "Not a word to anybody, you understand? You spent the evening cowering in terror in a corner of the library."

"Behind the curtains," G adds, eagerly, "in case anybody else who was there wonders where I disappeared to."

"Lord have mercy," Jake intones, his eyes rolled heavenward. "Listen, Guinevere—"

"Don't call me that! And don't try Gwen or Vera either." She bristles with fierceness. Val pats her shoulder.

"I don't care what your name is as long as you can follow

directions and keep your mouth shut," I tell her. "You'll come every day after school and help Val. If you have homework, you can do it in her room."

I raise my hand to head her off when I see her mouth open. "There will be long stretches where that is the most exciting thing you will do. That's how it is here. Everybody has a regular job."

"All right," she says finally, digging an object out of her pocket and holding it out to me. "I found this."

We all stare blankly at what she's offering. Just a phone.

"It belongs to that weird girl. The one with the green eyes."

The premonition that hits me then is colder than any spirit storm the ghosts have been able to stir up.

Nobody moves.

"Where is Sophie anyway?" Jake asks.

Matt crosses to the window and looks out at the parking lot. "Her van is gone."

"Last I saw her, she was at the center of the spirit storm. The lights went out. When they came back on, she was nowhere to be seen."

"And?" Jake asks.

Matt, who has been making the blood on my cushions spread into a hopeless pink wash by scrubbing with a wet washcloth, pauses and looks up at both of us.

"Last seen, she was engaged in a tug-of-war with Jillian over Phil's ashes." I want to stop there, but take a breath and add, "Her eyes were glowing. In the dark."

"Damn," Matt says, sinking down onto the bloodstained couch. "This can't be good."

"There's a text message," G says, helpfully. She flushes

under our collective stare. "Okay, I was snooping, but it might be helpful."

A teenage girl Sophie's age, you'd think her phone would be full of text messages, but there are only a few. From me. From Matt. And one from this afternoon.

COME TO ME. *I HAVE ANSWERS.* RAVENNA

FIFTEEN

"Who the hell is Ravenna? Anybody?"

Nobody responds.

Jake takes the phone and dials the number connected to Ravenna's text message, but there's no answer. A helpful robot voice tells us no voicemail has been set up.

"Whoever Ravenna is, she expects Sophie to know where to find her," Matt says, after a long silence.

"Maybe she went home. She was already upset, earlier. And the spirits were very—intense. She has a right to come and go as she pleases."

"Do you believe that?" Jake asks me.

"I want to believe it." Which isn't the same thing, at all. Sophie vanishing at this point is completely out of character.

"You're both forgetting one thing." Matt's voice is dismal.

"What's that?"

"Mrs. Schrader."

He's right. I have forgotten Mrs. Schrader. And despite the presence of G, I've also forgotten the kids.

My own cell phone rings, and I answer it with great misgiving.

Cathy is not amused. "You wouldn't answer your walkie."

"It was malfunctioning."

"Well, you could have checked in! I have a bunch of pizzas, the kids are freaked out, and Mrs. Schrader—"

A voice cuts her off. "Let me talk to that woman at once."

I hang up. When the phone rings again, I don't answer.

"PR Strategy?" Matt asks.

"It was a Haunted House. Everything on purpose, nothing to worry about. Spread out, keep it light. Let's go. The kids will be fine if we feed them."

Everything in the Manor seems pretty much under control. In the library, both kids and seniors are still sitting underneath the table. G scoffs at the boys and they come out under their own steam, full of bravado and far-fetched stories about what really happened. I enlist them to help the seniors, who are less flexible and a little worse for wear from sitting on the hard floor. Same story in the games room.

The lights are still out in the kitchen, but Matt has lit the area with flashlights standing on end. Pizza boxes are stacked on the counter, and the warm, savory smell of tomato, cheese, and pepperoni makes my mouth water.

"Can I have a piece?" I ask.

"After the kids. Help me load up. Let's get them fed and out of here." Matt rolls a food cart over to the counter, and I lift a pizza.

A cutting voice in the hall stops me, cold.

"What I want to know is how this Keslyn woman can feel suffi-
ciently entitled to arrange something like this without any notice to
me or the school at all. First, she leaves me a message—a message,
can you believe it? Canceling. And now this? Irate parents will be
coming out of the woodwork. There could be lawsuits!"

"I understand your concern," Jake's calm voice answers,
"but I'm not clear what you think I should do about it. I don't
think a surprise Haunted House event is illegal."

"It was terrifying! Lights flickering on and off, objects
floating around. I can't imagine how it was done, and I'm
certain these poor children will be scarred for life. If there is no
law against that, then there certainly should be."

"Wonderful things can be done with mirrors and lights,"
Jake says. "Nobody was hurt and surely they are old
enough to—"

"They are children. Trust me on that. I want them rounded
up and out of here, now, and I can tell you that this is the last
time they will be coming up to the Manor. I hope that Keslyn
woman feels good about ending a long tradition."

The Keslyn woman feels great about that, but a warning
glance from Matt reminds me to guard my tongue.

"I've already called the mothers who are transporting,"
Mrs. Schrader says, "and they will be here in fifteen minutes.
This is outrageous, and I will press charges."

"It would be a shame to deprive the kids of their dinner,
especially since the residents do so enjoy having some time
with the young people. I don't know about you, but I'm starving," Jake soothes.

By now she's in the doorway and I get my first glimpse of
her. Boring sweater, drab skirt, flat shoes, wire-rimmed glasses.

Her nose wrinkles. "It smells like pizza. What kind of Thanks-giving dinner smells like pizza?"

Matt turns his most charming smile on her. "Ms. Keslyn figured kids always love pizza, and it's a treat for the residents. Besides, it's difficult to prepare a full Thanksgiving dinner when the electricity is flickering in and out inside a haunted house."

"You must be Mrs. Schrader." I shake her hand without waiting for any participation on her end. "Lovely to meet you. Let's just go straight to the dining room, shall we? It's right this way. Matt will bring the pizza along behind us, and we'll get everybody fed."

I get on the other side of her so she's sandwiched between me and Jake, and take her arm as if I'm in need of assistance.

"Ms. Keslyn. Really. I've called the parents who are trans-porting. We are leaving—"

"Of course you are. Right after dinner. My goodness, it's been a long day. Kids do wear one out so, don't you think? My poor feet are aching like the dickens. I don't know how you manage to deal with them all day, every day, but then you're young yet."

Between Jake on one side and me on the other, we get her moving in the right direction.

A questioning tap comes over the loudspeakers, a new installation I'd thought wise and am suddenly rethinking, but it's followed by Matt's voice, sounding calm and appropriately professional. "Dinner is being served in the dining room. Pizza and pumpkin pie!"

"What is that thing?" Mrs. Schrader gestures at the salt sprayer I'm lugging along in my free hand.

"It's just a prop. For the Haunted House, you know. Kids love things that are weird and improbable, I find. Don't you?"

"Kids love strict boundaries and guidelines," she begins, but fortunately we've reached the dining room. Kids and seniors are settling into chairs. The kids are all chattering animatedly, faces glowing, looking none the worse for a little excitement, with the exception of one boy, the biggest and toughest looking of the lot, who keeps wiping away tears with the back of his hand and sniffling—nothing that a little pie won't cure.

As for my residents, some of them are a little dusty and disheveled, but they look younger and remarkably energized. Even Julia is laughing about something, her face surprisingly attractive, and Ginny uses a napkin to wipe a smudge of dirt off the face of a little blonde waif sitting next to her. G sits at the table beside Val, keeping her promise at least for the moment. There's a glitter of salt in her hair and her face is smudged with dirt, but she's grinning from ear to ear.

While I'm counting heads to make sure everybody else is present and accounted for, I make a little speech thanking Sophronia and Matt for helping to put on such a fabulous surprise Haunted House.

"Special thanks to Mrs. Schrader for bringing the kids, and for the parents who were willing to drive," I say, as I see two flustered looking ladies trot up to the door, panting, wild eyes seeking out their young. "I'm sure Matt has a couple of extra plates, and we'd love to share with you."

A couple of kids wave from across the room. One of the mothers, well trained to know her place in public, stays right at the door. The other swoops across the room and catches her son in an embrace. "Are you all right? Are you hurt? We are leaving right this minute."

The other boys at the table snicker. Dan, one of the intelligent residents in the Manor, reaches out and puts his hand on hers.

"Ma'am, I think you'll see the boy is unscathed. Let him eat. Get some food. Life is short."

The boy seizes the proffered salvation, wriggling out of her grasp and smoothing his hair.

"Mom, I'm fine."

At this opportune moment, I hear the rumble of wheels in the hallway. Matt appears, pushing a food card loaded high with pizza boxes, Cathy right behind him. Jake and I step in to help set up a buffet line.

A handful of other parents arrive. Jake hunts down chairs for them, and they crowd into the overfull tables with good humor, once their fears are at rest. I see a lot of glances aimed at Mrs. Schrader, though, and suspect that she might catch some undeserved flak.

Matt brings me a plate and finds me a chair and a space at one of the tables. Jake doesn't sit, moving around from table to table, chatting with parents, looking safe and reliable and removing doubts.

I love pizza, but my appetite is compromised by worry. Jill is fully grown up and not my responsibility. At all. And yet I can't shake a niggling sense that I owe it to Phil to look out for her. Maybe she is only suffering from a concussion, but my gut tells me it's something much worse.

Sophronia, once we find her, has some explaining to do.

It seems to take forever, but finally everybody runs out of room for pizza and nothing is left of Matt's delectable pumpkin pie but a few crumbs. The oldsters are tired and headed for their rooms. The parents are anxious to collect the kids and get home.

Mrs. Schrader seeks me out before she sails away like a bulky ship on an unsteady sea. "Don't think for a minute I'm going to let this go. I'll be consulting my attorney first thing tomorrow morning."

"Now, Joanna," Jake says, putting a hand on her shoulder. "Of course you can do whatever you want, but I hope you'll change your mind. Come now, let's get you headed home and you can think about this all some more after a little sleep."

Her mouth opens in protest, but Jake is already propelling her out the door and down the hall.

THE THREE OF us reconvene up in my suite.

Morpheus is overjoyed to see us, but I'm not so happy to see him. The fact that Sophie left him here when she vanished worries me; it's completely out of character. Before I can deal with this oddity, I call to check on Jill. The ER nurse isn't eager to talk to me, HIPAA and all that, so I make my voice as creaky as possible and toss in a few sobs for good measure.

"Listen, she's my niece and I'm her only living relative. Her poor sainted father passed a few weeks ago—you may have heard of him. Phil Evers? Murdered in his own bed. Who would have thought such things would happen in Shadow Valley? So you can see that—"

"Ma'am—"

"Poor Jill has nobody, unless it's me, and here I am stuck up at this godforsaken Manor miles away from civilization. Maybe

I can find someone to give me a ride, bless their hearts, but with the wheelchair and the catheter bag and—"

"Ma'am—"

"I just don't know. How late is it okay to visit? Can I bring friends? Maybe we could get the medical transport bus to bring us down in a group, I know she'd love to see—"

"How about I just give you a report over the phone, ma'am. I'd hate to put you out."

"Well, dearie, if you could do that, then that would just be a lovely thing, bless you so much."

"I'm afraid she hasn't recovered consciousness," the nurse says, "but the good news is that we did a CT scan and there's no evidence of brain damage or bleeding. The doctor is hopeful that she'll regain consciousness soon, and we're sending her upstairs to ICU within the hour. So when you're able to make it in, you can visit her *there*."

"Thank you so much, dearie. God bless you. It makes me feel so much better knowing you are taking care of her."

Jake's face is a mixture of laughter at my performance and worry about everything else. "You think Sophie—" Jake shakes his head. "I can't imagine her crossing that line."

"You've never seen her as she was tonight."

"Who would have ever thought she'd go off like that?" he asks.

Matt looks pale and strained. I'd blamed his expression on the episode of Kids Meet the Supernatural we've been engaged in, but now I see it's more.

"Why wouldn't she?" he says. "All that power, and no training. No mentor. No guidance at home, no close friends."

"She's got us..." I start, and then trail away. More guilt. I could have done more to help her. She came to me, and what did I tell her? Oh, the truth, for sure, but the truth doesn't always set you free. Sometimes the truth is what kills you. Or incites you to kill others.

"We let her down," Matt says.

Jake sinks into a chair. He looks stricken: shoulders slumped, the lines in his face deeper than I remember them. "We need to find her. And fast."

"I agree. Any idea who this Ravenna is?"

He shakes his head. "There's something—seems like I've heard her name before, but can't put a finger on it. Maybe Lysander knows."

"I still think maybe Sophie just went home," Matt says, but I can tell he doesn't believe it.

Jake looks up at me, his gray eyes weary. I want to smooth away the lines of tension in his face, and I'm startled by a strong desire to kiss him.

"Either way, we'll need to go pay a visit," he says.

"If she's running away, she'll need food, clothing. Let's go see."

I push back the chair, appalled at how stiff I am and how much pain and effort it takes to get upright and mobile.

"Shouldn't somebody wait for her here? In case she comes back?" Matt asks, beginning to pace.

I think about this and then shake my head. "She won't hurt the old people. Jill, on the other hand..."

Jake's head snaps up, his face goes still. "I hadn't thought of that," he says. "Maybe where I need to be is up at the hospital."

"Are we so very sure," Matt asks, drawing out his words, "that this isn't a case of somebody trying to hurt Sophie?"

No, we don't know that. We don't know if Jill is a victim or has ulterior motives beyond taking over the Manor. We haven't gotten any closer to solving the mystery around Dason's murder and his connection to the World Tree Girl.

All of this fuss and furor of a ghost uprising at the Manor would feel like smoke and mirrors if it wasn't for the glaring reality of Phil and his refusal to cross.

All in all, I'm more than ready to find some answers.

SIXTEEN

I'm relieved to see Sophronia's van parked outside the funeral parlor, but not for long. Nobody answers the chiming of the bell when Matt and I walk through the front door. We find Lysander in the showroom, dusting caskets with one of those Swiffer things. His face is set in a scowl even before he sees us and he downright growls when we walk into the room.

"What now? Another dead body to store in my basement? Maybe I should buy a freezer."

"Mr—Lysander. We're here about your daughter." Matt's tone is polite, deferential. His smile charming.

The effect on the undertaker is alarming. His already florid face turns a mottled, congested color, almost worthy of a hanging victim. He holds the plastic handle of the Swiffer in one hand and taps it across the other, raising a small cloud of dust up into the air.

"What about her?" he demands. "What's she done?"

"She hasn't done anything," I say, hoping it's true.

Another tap. Another cloud of dust. It settles on the shoulders of Lysander's suit, like dandruff from on high.

"We're looking for her," I say. "We were hoping she's around here somewhere."

"If she was here, do you think I'd be doing this? Not my job to shine up the showroom. She's been around precious little these last few weeks." His smoldering gaze levels on me. "Ever since you showed up in town, in fact. Now. I'm a busy man. Got two bodies waiting to process downstairs, and here I am up here, polishing coffins. She ain't here. So unless you've got something else to say—"

"Where's Craig?" I ask, surveying the space around me. I don't buy the idea of Lysander dusting coffins, not if there's another staff member to be bossed around.

He laughs, short and ugly. "You think I'd let Craig in the showroom? He'd scare off the customers. Good worker, but hot damn, not so good in the looks department."

"I didn't think your customers would scare so easy." I swing around to face him. His bulldog face is still set in stubborn lines of irritation and anger.

"Families are mighty particular who they deal with. Craig is purely night shift material. Trust me on that." He brushes the dust off his shoulders. "If you see Sophronia, tell her to get herself back here and help out, or she can start paying me rent."

"I don't know that we will see her," I tell him. "Or that you'll see her either. That's the thing. She's...having some difficulty."

"Suppose you tell me what you mean by that."

"Do you know who Ravenna is?"

He looks genuinely surprised by the question. "Rav who? What sort of name is that? And Sophie had better not have gone off anywhere. She lives here free, the least she can do is help out a little." His eyes narrow, his jaw juts forward even further. "There's more. What happened? What would make her run off all of a sudden, like you say?"

Matt opens his mouth, but Lysander brushes him off with a hand gesture. "Not you, you're a blatherer. Her." He stalks toward me and plants himself right in the confrontational zone. His eyes are a muddy shade of brown. Low brow, jutting jaw, thick lips. Sophronia has none of his genetic structure. Eyes, bones, hair. She's tall, slim, green-eyed, her hair jet black.

"You. Talk."

"Sophie must look like her mother," I say.

"Get out." His voice offers the prospect of violence.

I watch his hands, his eyes, hoping he'll smack me with the Swiffer so I have an excuse to smack him back.

"I was just wondering whether your daughter's special gifts come from you or her mother. Such things usually have a genetic component." I offer him my most infuriating smile.

"Her *mother* abandoned us both when she was eight. We don't talk about her."

"Abandoned you. Or fled. Or worse. Look, Lysander, I don't like you much, but I will be honest. How much do you know about Sophie's special abilities?"

"Avoiding work, you mean? Or playing dress-up with dead people? Oh, yes, I've caught her at that little game more than once. Listen, maybe the two of you have nothing better to do with your time than to stand around gawping, but those bodies in my basement aren't getting any fresher. Are we done?"

"I was wondering," Matt says, "whether Sophronia has any siblings."

His voice sounds strange, and I shoot him a glance. He's

fixated on the mirror gloss of the black coffin, his pupils so large his brown eyes look black, his face softened, as if in sleep.

Lysander drops the duster, both hands clenching into fists. "What's it to you? Get out."

I elbow Matt in the ribs, and he snaps to with a visible startle just in time to duck as Lysander takes a swing at him. Lysander is furious and a bull of a man, but it only takes Matt about three casual moves to lay him out on the floor, curled into a ball and gasping to get a breath.

"If Sophronia should come home, you might be wary," I tell him, for her sake, not his. "I suspect you know that her skills go beyond playing dress-up with the dead. I don't see that you've given her much reason to spare you if she should happen to go on a rampage."

His face turns purple, between the oxygen deprivation and fear. We leave him on the floor, flopping like a stranded fish.

Craig is waiting for us by the front door. "Where is she?" he asks.

"We were hoping you could tell us."

He shakes his head. His good eye, so perfectly beautiful in the wreck of his burned face, stays focused on me. "She's in trouble. I'm worried."

"If you've got any information that would help us find her, now is the time to spit it out."

He knows something. I can tell that from his posture, the way his gaze slides away, but he doesn't answer.

"Who's Ravenna?" Matt asks.

"Ravenna?" Craig shakes his head. "I don't know about any Ravenna. But—Sophronia has been getting letters. Unsigned."

"What kind of letters?"

"She'll hate me forever if I tell you."

We wait, letting him weigh all the options. His back straightens. His shoulders square. He digs into his pocket and pulls out a folded envelope.

"I took one from her room. I was thinking maybe I could help her."

"You did the right thing." I pull a type-written sheet out of the envelope. My blood chills as I scan the contents.

"She had more like this?"

He nods. "They're gone. I looked."

I pass the letter to Matt, watching the horror dawn on his face. I can only imagine the effect of a missive like this on a girl like Sophronia.

Pulling out my cell, I dial Jake.

"Is Jill still alive?"

"So far. Why?"

"Don't leave her alone. Details to follow."

Craig waits, quietly. It's impossible to read the expression on his face, but I don't think he's surprised.

"Can we see her room?"

He nods, and leads us through the hallways and to a staircase that takes us up to the family living space on the second floor. It's cluttered, but clean. In the kitchen, a pot half full of congealing soup appears to be the remains of Lysander's dinner. There's one bowl and one spoon in the sink. Craig leads us through a living room with a couple of bookcases, a TV, a coffee table, and unremarkable furniture.

Sophronia's room looks more like a cell in a nunnery than something belonging to a teenage girl. The walls are painted white and the only decoration is a poster print of something Egyptian involving the jackal-headed god of the dead.

There is a twin bed, neatly made up with a white coverlet.

Judging by the dog hair, a folded blanket at the foot of the bed is the sleeping place for Morpheus. A neatly arranged bookcase contains a mix of fantasy novels and textbooks on Egyptology, mythology, and anatomy. There's a closet containing only clothes and a couple of pairs of shoes. The only other item of furniture is a student desk. Nothing of interest in the drawers. The top is clear of everything except for one of those Himalayan salt lamps.

"Her backpack is missing," Craig says. "Her favorite jacket. And her copy of *The Book of the Dead.*"

He flushes under the look I give him. "Somebody needs to keep an eye on her. Lysander doesn't."

I suspect there's more to his motivations than that, but I let it pass. I scribble my number on a piece of paper from her desk. "Look, Craig, if she comes back, call me."

He nods, but not with any conviction.

"Call me, and stay out of her way."

At which, unexpectedly, he laughs. "What can she possibly do to hurt a guy like me?'

Oh, grasshopper, I think. You believe you are suffering already. You have no idea.

JAKE IS WAITING for us outside the hospital, a lit cigarette between two fingers. He's drawn tight as a wire about to snap.

"No change. Did you find Sophie?"

"Her van's there, she's not. Looks like she came home for some of her stuff and then left. Lysander hasn't seen her; neither has Craig."

Jake drops the cigarette to the pavement, half smoked, and

grinds it out with his heel. "Let me guess. Lysander didn't have a clue. Will he let us know if she comes home?"

Matt and I exchange a glance and Jake sighs, elaborately. "What did you do?"

"Matt asked a question. Lysander tried to answer with his fists. The result was a learning opportunity."

"Does he need a hospital?"

"What do you take me for?" Matt asks. The silence is just long enough for us all to remember that he is more or less responsible for the deaths of two good men.

"I didn't say *you* did anything. Thought Maureen might have shot him."

"Very funny," I tell him. "The question that got Lysander all riled up was about other children. Whether Sophie is an only child."

"Ahhh, you struck a nerve with that one." Jake pulls a pack of Camels out of his pocket, starts to tap one out into his hand. Stops. Puts it back. "I never did see why Jaz married Lysander."

"He might have been good looking once."

"He was on the football team," Jake says. "All the girls loved him, couldn't seem to see that mean streak. I guess he kept it buried better back then. If I'm honest, maybe he loved Jaz too. He was—softer—the first year they were married. How did you think to ask about kids?"

I glance at Matt. "I've been wondering the same thing."

"Just a hunch." He stands with his back to us, staring at the houses across the street.

"Huh," I say, remembering the weirdness in his eyes just before he asked the question. But Jake goes on, and his answer requires my attention.

"Jaz and Lysander had a baby, one year to the day after

they got married. It died. Crib death, far as anybody could tell. Jaz changed some after that. Still sweet, but always had a look on her face that made you want to cry. Lysander reverted to rage. It's what he knows. It's like he took that baby's death as a personal insult. Got himself arrested a time or two over the next year for various assault charges. Bar fights. That sort of thing. Gossip said they were trying to have another baby. Doctor visits. A specialist in Spokane. Special meds. And then Jaz was pregnant again, and nine months later there was Sophronia."

"You'd think he'd have an extra-special love for a child that hard to conceive."

Jake passes a hand over his head and massages the back of his neck. "You'd think. Even when she was a baby, though, before he could have been put off by any indication of her being special, he didn't seem to want anything to do with her. You'd never see him holding her. If anything, he got meaner. That's when Jaz started showing up with black eyes and bruises and every lame excuse in the book as to how she came by them."

"And then she disappeared."

He nods. "And then she disappeared. Sophie was already a weird kid. Those huge green eyes, always staring off at things nobody could see. An imaginative child, her teachers called her, but you got this sense that her imaginary friends weren't so imaginary. She was unsettling."

"And now she's a lot more unsettling."

"Around the time she turned thirteen she started hanging out at the hospital when somebody was about to die. It was uncanny. She didn't go into the ICU or the ER so much; she'd just quietly slip into a room in the adult care unit. When the nurse would come in later, she'd be sitting there, holding the patient's hand, and they would have passed. Some of them started calling her Angel of Death, always behind her back. Those were the kind ones."

"Psychopomp," Matt says.

"What the hell is a psychopomp?" Jake asks.

"A soul guide. Someone who leads the soul to the doors of the afterworld and helps them go through."

That's what I'd thought, soon after I met her. But that was before I watched her suck the soul right out of a body—somebody who needed to die, mind you, that was intent on killing all the rest of us. But still. Psychopomps don't have that kind of power.

Jake reads it in my face. "So, what happens if a guide decides not to wait for souls to cross? Or to rush them along a little?"

When neither Matt nor I answer, he continues: "What's wrong with Jill is nothing the doctors are going to fix, I take it. And if she dies, then Soph—" He can't finish, but he doesn't need to. We're all thinking the same thing.

"Sophronia's not going to come back here," Matt says, still staring out into the dark. "And she's not going back to Lysander."

Jake looks from Matt to me. "There's more. What are you not telling me?"

Reluctantly, I hand him the letter. I can't stand still to watch him read and start pacing, grateful for the way the pain in my leg wakes up my brain.

Sophronia:

What an unusual name for a girl, but then, I hazard a guess that you are an unusual girl. Is this so? Have you felt that you don't fit in with the rest of the twittering flock?

I don't know what they've told you of the circumstances of your birth, but I will be direct. You are not fully human. Yes, you were conceived of a union between two human beings, and delivered of a human mother in a hospital, but I contributed to your DNA. And my genetic makeup being what it is, I can only guess what you are experiencing, isolated and trapped among lesser beings as you are.

I must ask.

Have you killed yet? By this, I do not mean helping a soul cross over. That's bread and butter to those of our kind. Have you actually tasted a soul? Maybe kept some of it for yourself? I'm sure the humans have indoctrinated you with all sorts of notions about right and wrong, but they do not apply. Embrace your origins. Go where your desires take you.

I am sorry I have not been able to be there with you, to watch you grow. When you are ready, come find me...

"Oh, hell," Jake says, when he's done. "Do you think this is that Ravenna person who texted her? I'll run this for fingerprints, but I'm pretty sure we won't find any beyond Maureen's and mine."

"And Sophronia's. And Craig's."

"Craig?" Jake sounds startled. "What's he got to do with this?"

"He gave us the letter."

"We have got to find Ravenna," Jake says, which is all fine and good, but I've got no more idea of how to do that than how to find the World Tree Girl. I can only think of one place to start. Jake will protest, on ethical grounds, so I attempt to spare him.

I yawn and stretch. "Well, I'm headed home. Long day and all that."

"I'll drive you," Jake says. "Matt can stand watch for a bit."

There's not going to be any point objecting, so I get into Jake's car.

"You know if you find anything, it won't be admissible in court," he says, about halfway up to the Manor.

"What are you talking about?"

"Oh, come on Maureen. Don't play games with me."

"Manor rules say I'm permitted to search a resident's belongings at need."

"Jill is hardly a resident."

"She's residing at the Manor, something she insisted on. Come on, Jake. What I find might save her life."

"But that's not why you're looking."

"No, I'm looking because we are damn short of leads on Dason, the World Tree Girl, or what's going on with Sophronia. Jill is the only thread I can tug at right now."

"You don't think maybe she just came home to get her father's ashes?" he asks. I give him a killing look and he very nearly smiles. "I'd think you might have some affection for Phil's daughter."

"I barely know her. She wants to take the Manor from me."

"And that's the cause of your hostility?"

I don't answer, and he lets it lie.

SEVENTEEN

All is peaceful when we return to the Manor. The temperature has returned to normal. No flickering electricity. A few of the residents are out and about, apparently free of harassment from invisible sources.

"Are the spirits resting up for another attack?" Jake asks, as I unlock the door to the suite Jill occupied last night.

"I have no idea. Ghosts are Sophie's speciality."

Jill's room is a disaster zone. Clothes are strewn across the bed and hanging over the backs of chairs. Cosmetics are scattered all over the bathroom vanity. Her suitcase is open on the bed.

Jake exudes professional disapproval, but doesn't stop me as I sort Jill's possessions into piles on the bed, taking mental notes of exactly where each one was located. I'll put it all back when I'm done and she'll never know I searched her stuff.

"You think there's more luggage somewhere?" Jake asks, echoing my own thoughts.

"Matt brought up her stuff." We exchange a measured look. Matt is a valuable addition to our team, but neither one of us quite trust him.

"I'll check out her rental car myself," Jake says, with a gusty sigh. "If we can find the keys."

I hold up a cashmere sweater with a designer tag sewn in, thinking about her expensive handbag and the money her father left her.

"I wonder what she really wants with the Manor?" I ponder out loud. It can't be about money. Maybe she really is questing for her dead father's love, and sees him willing the Manor to me as yet another betrayal on his part.

There's certainly nothing in her belongings to indicate that she's either a secret agent or a villain. Her passport is unexceptional. Her clothing is fashionable and expensive. No listening devices or snooping devices or anything remotely unusual except for a small key, which might fit a locker or a padlock.

Jake, forgetting his scruples, examines the suitcase for a false bottom or a secret compartment, and I take advantage of his distraction to slip the little key into my pocket.

Frankly, I'm disappointed in Jill. I expected she'd have at least some kind of contraband, but all that turns up is six bottles of booze—less than 4 ounces each, stashed in an easy access compartment. Vodka. Four are empty.

"Can you get a lab to test these?" I ask.

He glares at me. "We have not searched her belongings and do not know about this. Even if we did, she hasn't committed any crime."

"Fine. I'll hold on to them then." I sniff an empty bottle. Then a full one. Nothing.

"Are we done?" Jake queries.

We are. I let him walk me out of Jill's suite and across the hall to my own.

"I'm not exactly in need of a male protector," I tell him, when he waits for me to work through my complex series of locks.

"Humor me," he says, then frowns as the door opens and Morpheus comes bounding out, demanding to be petted.

"Sophie really has run off somewhere, then, hasn't she? She'd never just leave the dog." He rubs the creature's ears. Morpheus whines, his tail thumping. "I'll take him out for you. Be right back."

I'm grateful to him for walking the dog, since all I really want to do is collapse in a chair and rest my aching body. Instead I busy myself with precautions—securing the door to the secret staircase with a salt barrier and a silver cross.

Anubis sleeps peacefully on the back of my ruined couch, a sign that no wandering spirits are hanging out in my suite right now. When Morpheus bounds back into the room, excited from his little outing, the cat hisses and slaps at him but goes promptly back to sleep.

"I'll be back for a council of war first thing tomorrow," Jake says from the doorway. "Sleep well."

As I lock my door behind him, I'm conscious of a fatigue so deep I don't bother to take off my clothes before falling into bed. Even so, the last emotion I'm aware of, as sleep claims me, is regret that Jake's warm body isn't in the bed at my side.

—————

THE HOURS I spend in bed are too few and too restless. Untangling myself both from my sheets and a twisting, panoramic dream in which I'm searching for something lost and long buried, I head for the kitchenette on autopilot, stubbing my toe and staring at the coffee maker for a good thirty seconds before I remember what happened to the carafe.

Which leads me to all the problems needing to be solved: Phil's ashes. Jill in the ICU. Sophie missing and presumed responsible. My suite still a wilderness of boxes and misplaced furniture. My ruined couch. The World Tree Girl, Dason, and the Medusa on the loose.

Fortunately, I thrive on crises and there are plenty here to keep me occupied. Anubis is still asleep at the foot of the bed, curled up into a ball with his nose buried in his tail. Morpheus is another issue. He whines and goes to the door, giving me a soulful look.

Dogs. So damn needy. I should have had the foresight to send him home with G, the middle schooler, or pawn him off on Matt or Jake. I throw on a clean pair of jeans and a T-shirt, jam a ball cap on my head, and make for the kitchen, the dog at my heels.

It's only 5:36 a.m. and I expect Matt to be still sleeping, but the smell of coffee meets me halfway down the hall. He's leaning on the counter, unshaven, uncombed, looking more like a fallen angel than a Greek god.

Without a word, he pours me a mug and hands it over.

My leg aches with a vengeance, as does the tight place in my side, and I perch on the edge of a stool, the mug cradled between my two hands, breathing in the life giving aroma.

The dog whines, urgently. "I'll take him," Matt says. "Come on, boy."

When he reappears a few minutes later, a much happier Morpheus trotting down the hall ahead of him with his tongue hanging out, Jake is with him. "Couldn't sleep," he says, pouring himself a mug of coffee and doctoring it with cream.

I've never seen the sheriff anything other than clean shaven, and the shadow looks good on him.

"What's on the docket?" Matt asks, waiting until I signal an acceptable level of caffeination by making eye contact.

The dog flops onto the floor and lays his head on my foot. I eye him dubiously, wishing he'd choose another human.

"What do we do about that kid?" Matt asks.

"G? I doubt you'll have a problem there," Jake says. "Her mom's an addict, not unwilling to raise a kid but incapable. Her dad loves her okay, but she takes care of him, not the other way around. She's exactly the type to buy into a secret society and die before she betrays it."

"Let's hope it doesn't come to that."

They both startle, as if I've said something drastic, rather than a reminder of the truth and what we're doing here.

"I don't like her involved," Jake says.

"She involved herself," I say, moving on. There's nothing to be done about G at this point. Besides, I suspect she has gifts of her own and she'll be better served learning how to use them than by hanging out with people who pretend they don't exist.

"We need to hit social media today and see what the buzz is. I'll check Dason's feeds and hack into Sophie's. Jake, can you do searches for the World Tree Girl? Throw some tattoo pics out there, see if anybody knows the artist?"

Jake nods assent.

"Matt—"

"I'll be contacting the Unit." He catches my expression and half smiles. "You're going to have to trust me on this one, Maureen. I'm not giving away anything about Soph, but if they can tell me something that will help us find her, then I have to try."

He's absolutely right, but it worries me. I had felt the need to reach out to Abel, too, when he went missing. He ended up dead and I'm not entirely sure my phone call didn't cause that chain of events. Guilt never solved anything, though, and I push it aside and get to my feet.

"Good luck. Let's get to it."

I don't even mention the mess down in the lab. I figure the ashes of my dead former lover and his possibly wrathful spirit are my responsibility. Still, even though things have settled down and I receive no further ghostly messages, I procrastinate dealing with Phil, telling myself it's not my first priority.

My other efforts lead nowhere. There's nothing of interest on social media. Sophronia doesn't have an online presence at all, which is odd for a girl of her age. Dason was careful and circumspect on his feeds. Facebook and Instagram yield cat pictures and motivational quotes. I can't trace his computer to the Underground Weird website where we first saw the photos of the World Tree Girl.

As for the moving boxes and the clutter that arrived with my ex, the task of opening and sorting through the items feels almost as overwhelming as dealing with the basement.

A phone call saves me.

"I need to show you something."

"Mac. Good morning to you, too."

"Come on down. Wear something warm."

I look out my balcony window to see the Harley in the parking lot, straddled by Mac in full motorcycle leathers. He waves up at me.

The weather does not look promising. Gray sky touches the

horizon. There's fresh snow on the higher elevations in the distance. I've never much liked the cold, and the damnable hardware in my leg would make a ride in this weather a misery.

But I'm not about to turn down a lead, cold, warm, or otherwise. I scrawl a quick note for Jake and tape it inside Dason's laptop and then put the whole thing back under my mattress. If Mac turns out to be a bad guy and I disappear, Jake will find it and know where to start looking.

My favorite knife—the one that Jill stabbed me with so many years ago—is in my ankle sheath. I have another looped around my belt, along with Phil's special flashlight. My gun goes into one pocket of my winter coat, ammo into the other.

When I arrive in the parking lot Mac hands me a helmet and waits while I strap it on, not offering a hand or even looking in my direction while I struggle to get my stiff leg up and over the seat and settle myself.

The engine roars into life, the big beast of a bike vibrating with power, and we're off.

Cold is an insipid word. It has absolutely no weight in the face of the biting, hungry force that envelops us as Mac shifts into ever higher gears and the bike picks up speed. In a matter of moments my face goes from pins and needles to numb. My body is shielded by Mac's and retains a reasonable amount of heat, but the metal plate in my leg feels like an instrument of torture, freezing my flesh from the bone on out.

The pain is more than balanced by a rush of pleasure at the wild freedom of the open road, the roar of the engine, the insanity of riding a bike in this kind of weather, and the sharp edge of danger. By the time Mac turns off the highway onto a dirt trail that winds up into the trees, I'm riding an adrenaline high that would sell for a small fortune if it could be bottled.

When the bike stops and Mac kills the engine, I can still feel it throbbing beneath me. A rushing fills my ears—there's a river nearby. Maybe a waterfall. My leg is nearly numb, but it obligingly swings over the bike and holds me when I lurch to my feet. I flex the fingers of my gun hand, which I had taken care to protect inside my pocket, and take off the helmet.

I edge away from Mac toward a clearing surrounded by a perfect circle of towering red pines. The trees here have a presence. Silent. Waiting. I venture over to run fingertips over a large, flat stone. It doesn't dawn on me that I'm standing dead center of a sacred circle, broken only where the rough track breaks through a gap in the trees, until Mac swings off the bike and blocks the opening.

I feel the circle snap shut. A raven flaps his way overhead and alights on Mac's shoulder.

Always a large man, Mac looms in this place. His bronzed skin looks darker, his hair blacker, and there's something primal and untamed in his eyes. My fingers tighten around the gun in my pocket.

"Why did you bring me here?" I ask.

"It's pretty, no?"

Looking around at the sentinel trees and the stone that looks like it could have done past service as an altar, pretty is not a word that comes to mind. Majestic. Eerie. Awe-inspiring. Deadly. These are words I might use. I have a highly unfamiliar desire to drop to my knees on the cold earth and bow before some unnamed deity. This is not a place for words or idle chitchat.

Mac and the trees and the altar are waiting for something. I have questions, but I can see he won't answer if I ask, or give anything away.

My eyes go back to the stone. No lichens cling to it, no moss. A vein of quartz runs down the center. I let my fingers trail across it, registering a layer of grit.

"She died here," Mac says.

"Who?" I ask, playing dumb.

He doesn't need to tell me. My imagination gives me a clear image of the World Tree Girl—so young, little more than a child—laid out here, the stone ready to receive her blood. My belly heats into a simmering rage.

"What kind of ritual was it that required the death of a child?"

Still Mac is silent.

"What's your connection with the Medusa?"

His poker face registers nothing.

"What is it with coroners in this county? Is there some sort of murderer's club you have to be part of before you can serve in the role? If you know she died here, either you participated in the killing, or covered it up. And now you've brought me back to the scene of the crime. Maybe to commit another."

The gun in my hand feels extraordinarily heavy, colder than it should, despite the warmth of my pocket.

"If you're planning to shoot me," he cautions, "I'd advise against it. This place would not take kindly to the spilling of my blood."

"But would happily drink up mine. I get it."

Given a choice between a clearing that thinks for itself and a score of vamps or werewolves or even another one of those intestine-hungry slugs that damn near killed me, I'd opt for the critters. Nasty as those suckers are, at least you can see them and fight.

Every hair on my body is standing upright, and the full-on

chill I feel has nothing to do with the weather. I've been a fool. By the time Jake finds my note, I'll be nothing but a statistic.

"Didn't know the local tribes were into blood magic." I make my voice obnoxious, rude, trying to provoke him into some action I can fight against.

"They're not," he replies, evenly. "The secret of this place was passed to me from my mother and her mother before her. My Irish mother," he adds.

"Mac is short for Cormac," I say, light dawning. "Druidic magic."

He inclines his head. "No one in my family has spilled blood here. What the earth and trees choose to do—well, that's not for me to dictate."

I'm silent, processing all of the ramifications of this revelation.

"Who are you, really?" Mac demands. "What's your affiliation?"

There's an unusual weight to his words. The pressure to answer is compelling. My mouth opens without my consent and I snap it shut again, almost catching my tongue. The words tremble at the edge of speaking, pushing for utterance.

"I would advise that you speak only the truth," he says.

"And the consequences if I don't?"

I feel the earth through the soles of my shoes, alive, sensing me, tasting. I weigh my words carefully before I let them cross my lips. "You already know my name. My affiliation, as you put it, is none of your business. And now one for you. What did it cost to buy your silence?"

"I had nothing to do with her death," he answers. "I don't know who—or what—killed her, or why it was done here."

"Does Jake know? That she died here?"

The thought that her death would have been reported to the sheriff's department, that Jake has been hiding information from me, feels like lead in my belly.

Mac doesn't answer my question. "Whatever act caused her death sullies this place," he says, after a long silence. A wind moves through the tree tops at his words, and they seem to lean in, pressing on me, passing their judgment.

"Why bring me here?" I ask.

"To judge the truth of you."

"The truth of *me*? Let me tell you what I think happened. The girl was found here, dead, killed by the Medusa. It came to your attention. How, I don't know. Who comes out to a place like this? But she was found. You did your duty. Called law enforcement, sent the body off to Spokane for forensics. And then one day a stranger came to you—maybe two of them, together. They told you to forget ever seeing the body. They warned it would be better for everybody. How is the public going to react to stories of a bloodless body laid out on a stone altar in the middle of the forest?"

"How do you know this?" His voice is low, more lethal than shouting could ever be.

"Because I've done that job, been that person. Hush up all the paranormal events, make people believe all supernatural juju is just for movies. Let everybody think the poor suckers who actually saw something are crazy. Eliminate the evidence. I'm guessing there's not even a police report. Do the parents know she's been found?"

"So you were with this special FBI group," Mac says, evading my questions. "But no longer. Why?"

I hunt for words, saying as little as I can, hoping it's enough to gain his cooperation while still keeping him partly in the dark.

"Because I know something they don't want me to know, connected to the paranormal I believe killed this girl. They want me silenced. They sent a hit man after me."

"So that's what all of that fuss was about up at the Manor. I never did believe the story that went out. And your goal?"

"To stop this paranormal from killing again. I need to know the identity of the girl who was killed."

He seems to be considering my request, but instead of telling me something helpful, he says, "My Irish grandmother had the sight. The day she died, she called me to her house to tell me a dream. It was important, she said. A dream of what will be, affecting not just me but many others."

His voice takes on a lilting cadence.

"'Sit and listen,' she told me. 'In my dream, you are responsible for a hen house.'"

"I laughed. I was young and stupid. "You have a great dream about me and it's that I own chickens?" I asked her.

"'I did not say you owned these chickens,' she said. 'You were responsible for them. There is a deep difference in this, and one you must understand. In the dream, you go inside this hen house to gather the eggs, as you do every day. Only on this day, all of the chickens are dead. They lie on their backs with their feet up in the air, stiff, stark. Not a mark is on them. There is no blood. No feathers are scattered as when a hen runs away in fear. A red fox sits at the center, watching you. She is not afraid, as a fox should be. She does not offer to harm you, but neither does she run from you. Be wary. Know her when she comes. Danger comes with her.'"

"That was the dream. My grandmother died later that day.

I grieved for her, but still I scoffed at this dream. The twistings of a sick woman's mind. Delirium. Chickens and foxes. All foolishness, until I began dreaming the dream myself. Always the same. I believe *you* are the red fox, Maureen Keslyn. And what I brought you here to know is this: Does the danger follow you, or are you the danger? And now I will ask you again. What are you doing here? What is your mission?"

I want to joke and deflect. To tell him I'm more of a silver fox by now than a red one. But he has shared with me a true dreaming, and there is no answer to that besides my full truth. And that truth is not a thing I know myself. So I answer with a question.

"Did you know that another girl has gone missing? Sophronia. The undertaker's daughter."

Mac sighs, deeply, and the air softens around me. "Sophronia is the reason I brought you here, but how can I tell you what little I know until I know if I can trust you?"

And to this, I have to answer, willing or not.

"I have guilt in this," I tell him. "Mine is a sin of silence when I should have spoken, a long time ago. If I had done things differently, maybe the World Tree Girl would still be alive. Or not. Maybe if I'd spoken I would have died then to no purpose. But I need to right what I can. I need to stop the killing. That's my goal. My mission, as you put it."

Mac considers my words. "My silence was not bought," he says. "I gave it freely. I judged the girl's death to be from forces not human. What business does law enforcement have with a paranormal killer? What court of justice is there for this? Should more people die? Should there be stories in the news, and reporters discovering and profaning this secret place? I thought of burying her in the woods, not saying a word to anybody. But I couldn't do that. Her family would be grieving her disappearance, wondering what happened to her.

"So, yes. I moved her body and lied about where it was found. I sent her to Spokane for an autopsy. She had no ID on her, so I couldn't notify next of kin. Before I had a chance to do an identity search, two agents showed up. They flashed FBI badges, told me this was a matter of national security and my silence was key. They asked for all my notes on this girl. They sat at my computer and cleaned out all related files. What they said made sense to me, and they promised that they had means to track the killer."

"They aren't investigating, Mac," I tell him. "They want to cover it up. And yes, they want to track the killer, but I doubt they'll destroy her."

"You think," he says.

"I know."

I give him time to digest my words, to weigh the the truth of them, and then go on.

"The two who came to see you may have been in good faith. But they won't know what is being planned up the chain. Did you examine the girl's body? See a copy of the autopsy report?"

He shakes his head. "I did not do a full examination. I saw that she was pale beyond reason. No lividity. Not a mark on her that was a clear cause of death. And then I sent her to Spokane and that was the end."

I take a small step toward him, pressing against the invisible boundary. "Those agents are dangerous, Mac. If I tell you all I know, it could mean your death."

"My hen house," he says, with a sudden grin. "My risk. Speak the truth."

And so I tell him my suspicions about why Dason was killed. And I tell him about the secret government lab where paranormal testing of all kinds took place. About the paranormal-human genetic experiments conducted at the Manor when it was the Home for Unwed Mothers.

"They implanted genetic paranormal material into the babies while still in the womb. The resulting babies that survived were transported to the Paranormal Project Lab. It was supposedly decommissioned, but if that happened, not all of their monstrosities were destroyed. One of the most dangerous creatures they created was a thing named the Medusa. She was invisible, and she killed by absorbing blood from a living body and replacing it with jelly. It's a horrible death."

I shudder, remembering the feeling of that cold jelly filling my veins, my laboring heart trying to pump that sludge, the agony of trying to breathe. At the last minute the creature backed away. I don't know why, my best guess being she was repelled by the fragments of a silver bullet that remain embedded in my flesh.

"You okay?" Mac asks.

I shake off the memory, and go on. "The Medusa found her way here, to the Manor. Who knows why? Visiting her birth place? Dr. Sorenson, the woman responsible, followed her or accompanied her. She died at the Manor."

"Who died? This Dr. Sorenson, or the creature?"

"The doctor. We thought we'd killed the Medusa. But the manner in which the World Tree girl died makes me question if the Medusa survived. I will tell you this—if there are more of these creatures than one out there, so help us God."

"What's a runaway kid doing way up here, anyway? How

did she get here?" Mac says. "Few know of this place—none who would be complicit in murdering a girl. Sacrifices haven't happened here since well before my time, and even then, they were never human." He steps forward, opening the gap, and immediately I feel the pressure ease as the circle is broken.

"Maybe she was drawn by the magic of this place. Who knows? A better question is this. Do you have a gun, Mac?"

"I'm more of a knife man."

"Get a gun. Keep your eyes open. Don't trust anybody. Whatever happened here, the people who want to keep it quiet are deadly."

"Your truth is a gift," he says, "even if not freely given."

"My truth may mean your death."

"In which case, it will be a good day to die." His lips pull back from his teeth in a smile that makes me hope he considers himself my friend and not my enemy. "How is Sophronia tied into this? Do you think that monster took her, too?"

I can't tell him what I really think. "I don't suppose you know somebody named Ravenna?"

His eyes narrow. "What's that old bird got to do with any of this?"

Hope flares up inside me. "You know her then?"

"I thought she'd be dead by now." He touches the tattoo of the bird on his jawline.

"She's a tattoo artist?"

"Was, I'd think. She was already old when I was sixteen and she did my raven. For free, she said. Sixteen is too stupid to know that nothing ever comes free."

"I don't suppose you know where to find her?"

He shakes his head. "A retirement home? If she's still alive, that is."

"Oh, she's alive, all right. Sent a message to Sophronia just before she disappeared."

His jaw tightens, an action that makes the raven flex its wings. "You know, that dead girl. A tattoo job like that is precisely the sort of thing Ravenna would do."

"Anything you can tell me might help."

"For starters, Ravenna's real name is Marietta Marcelina Livingston. She goes by Ravenna when she's telling fortunes or doing tattoos. Last I heard of her, she was in Seattle. But it has been twenty years at least."

"I'll find her."

"If she's done anything to harm the girls—either of them..."

The threat hangs in the air, unspoken and lethal. I shiver a little with something other than cold, grateful that Mac is on the same side as I am in this. He would make a formidable enemy.

EIGHTEEN

Jake is waiting in my suite, sitting at the table with Dason's laptop open in front of him. He has my note in his hand.

"I see you survived. Care to tell me why you think the coroner would want to do away with you?"

"Everybody wants to do away with me. I have that effect on people." I keep my tone light, but I leave the door open and don't move into the room. I'm regretting my decision to trust him with a set of keys. "Look, Jake, I'm tired and cold. I need to—"

"Freshen up? Rest? Powder your nose? Bullshit, Maureen. I know you better than that. You are keeping something from me."

I don't answer. The extent of what I'm keeping from him goes well beyond a casual omission. Given what I've just learned, this was likely a good call. The problem is that I had begun to trust Jake, and Mac's revelation has shattered my fragile faith.

"Never figured you for playing games," he says, and there's a roughness in his voice I haven't heard before, underscored by something that sounds a lot like disappointment.

"Mac took me to the scene of the crime," I say, keeping to the doorway.

"And which crime would that be? Are you coming in, or are you going to stand out in the hall all day?"

His gray eyes take on an expression that bodes ill for somebody, but he doesn't move, and his face remains impassive.

"I'm digesting the implications of the fact that our World Tree Girl was found in Shadow Valley County."

He gives me his shark look for a long minute and then walks away to the balcony and stands looking out. "Can I smoke?"

"Do you have cigarettes?"

"I told you I quit."

"You had some last night."

"I quit again."

I know he's buying time to think, but I could use a little time myself. "They're in the desk drawer. Help yourself."

He lights up and steps out onto the balcony. Cold, clean air flows into the room. I shiver, but it's a good shiver. My blood is waking up, brain and heart clearing. I follow him, leaving the door open behind me.

Jake leans both elbows on the railing, holding his cigarette between two fingers, not even glancing at me. I'm fine with that. I don't want the distraction of his face. The warm heft of him beside me is bad enough.

"If I tell you I knew nothing about the body," he says, after a long interval, "you're not going to believe me."

"Is it the truth?"

"Swear to God. Just trying to figure out how that got past me. Or which of my deputies might have been corrupted."

I fill my lungs with smoke and then let it trickle out between my lips. As always, the thought that I should quit is followed immediately by the knowledge that somebody's going to kill me before I have a chance to die of cancer or lung disease.

I want, more than I've wanted anything in a long time, to believe Jake is telling me the truth. Trust feels good, but it's a hard-won commodity.

"You never considered the possibility that I didn't know," Jake says after an uncomfortable silence. "Jumped right into the belief that I sat there and lied to you. Not about some little detail, but about the actual crime scene of a murdered kid."

"Don't throw this back on me," I retort. "You're the sheriff, and you're not some fat, lazy slob who lets his people do all the work while he hangs out in a bar. You want me to believe that you really didn't know that a murder occurred in your territory? Come on, Jake. Get real."

Silence stretches between us and I let it get to me. "They can be very convincing, the feds. All sorts of reasons to keep your mouth shut, from the good of the community to your own safety—"

He laughs, a bitter, sharp sound in the cold. "I've done it once, right? Let them shut me up. Why wouldn't I do it again? People never really change."

His anger doesn't bother me, but that laugh does something to my insides, like the twist of a knife. I want to put my hand on his arm, touch him somewhere, anywhere, and tell him—something—that will make things right between us. Instead, I just stand there, one hand on the railing, so cold my fingers are beginning to go numb.

"So where was she killed?" Jake asks, after a long moment. His voice is all cop again.

"Out the north highway. Through the Knife Creek settlement and up the back of the mountain."

"That's Ferry County, Maureen. I wouldn't have been called in."

"But Mac—"

"Mac is temporarily working both counties. Filling in until the next election."

I crush out my cigarette on the railing, torn between relief and guilt. "Damn it, Jake. I never even thought of that."

I owe him an apology for suspecting his complicity in hushing up the World Tree Girl investigation. Instead, I gift him with a confession of my own sins. "You're right about me keeping things from you."

"Do tell." His voice is dry, but his lip quirks and a spark of humor warms his eyes.

"Only a couple of things. Well, three. One, I had a message on my laptop I think was from Phil. Two, the spirits sent a message last night through Val. Three, Mac knows, or at least knew, Ravenna. She's a tattoo artist. Did his raven when he was sixteen."

"Well," he says. "So much for teamwork."

I feel sick and sad in a way that I don't understand. I have a sudden urge to fling myself into Jake's arms and weep like a child.

"You're shivering," he says. "Let's go in."

I follow him back into my suite, closing the door behind me. It's still colder in here than it ought to be and I wonder whether Phil is haunting me, and if so whether he's alone.

Jake opens Dason's laptop. "Here's another thing you forgot to tell me. You said it had been wiped clean."

I stare at the screen for a moment of confused silence. Photographs of five people stare back at me.

"This is new," I say. "I swear."

"Do you know any of these people?"

"Not a one. Maybe Phil sent those, too."

"You really think the dead are sending you messages through the computer?" Jake straddles a chair and leans forward to study the photos.

"Somebody is. I went through that laptop repeatedly and never found a thing. Photos can't just pop up on their own."

"I don't see a pattern here, do you?" Jake asks.

I sit down to study the pictures. Two are candids—one male, one female, both probably in their thirties. The woman is rock climbing, grinning into the camera. Blonde hair, blue eyes, nothing extraordinary about her. The male stands on a city street corner and seems unaware he is being photographed. Suit and tie, briefcase, clean shaven and dark haired. Your typical business man, and not somebody you'd look at twice.

Following this is a pair of yearbook photos. Again, one male, one female. The male has eyes that are strikingly olive green in a dark-complexioned face, tightly curled black hair, a white flash of teeth. The girl is almond-eyed, with a port-wine birthmark on her right cheek.

The last photo is clearly a mug shot. A male, so thin his cheekbones look like they might cut through his skin. He has a sharp and restless expression and his eyes shout defiance.

"We need hard copies. There's a printer in one of these

boxes." I survey the room with frustration. Since I wasn't here when the boxes were brought in, and I wasn't the one who packed them in the first place, I have no idea where anything is.

Jake moves to examine the boxes. "Aha. Here is one that is marked COMPUTER ACCESSORIES. Is a printer an accessory?"

"Beats me. Let's look."

Sure enough, the box contains my trusty color printer, the necessary cables, and even some photo paper.

We print the pictures, one to a page, enlarged, so we can get a better look, but there's still nothing that makes it obvious why we want them.

I mull the problem. "When I was in the Unit we had facial recognition software. Would have made this a whole lot easier."

"Gonna have to work with what we've got." He clears off the top of my table and lays out the photos, moving them around into different combinations, still looking for a pattern.

I open my tablet and start searching for Ravenna, a.k.a. Marietta.

"Is it possible," Jake asks, very, very carefully, "that it isn't Phil communicating with you? Maybe it's something else, deliberately misleading you, or leading you into danger. You're not—"

"I'm not what?"

I'm surprised to notice my fists are clenched. Anger blazes in my chest and I'm warm for the first time in this long day. The need to break something, throw something, or shoot somebody is a pressure in my body that threatens to break me apart. I can't sit another minute.

My leg has other ideas and spasms while I'm getting to my

feet. The chair tips and clatters to the floor as I lean forward with a hiss to support my weight on the table.

No mercy from Jake, not that I want any. "Maybe you are letting your grief interfere with your thinking."

"That's a cheap shot. I have perfectly good reasons for everything. You're just reacting because I didn't tell you—"

"Him, you trusted. The rest of us, not at all. So you want him back. Normal grief process, Maureen, except there's too much riding on this. Danger to everybody in this Manor and in this town. You can't be the lone ranger on this one."

"I'm not—"

To my horror my voice breaks, and tears well up and spill over before I can blink them back.

Jake's too smart to say anything, or to try to capitalize on the moment by offering pats and consolation. He doesn't flaunt a smug look either, or say, "I told you so." Which makes me hate him a little.

"I think you should go now."

"I'm not going anywhere."

"Jake—"

He waits, his eyes boring holes through all my layers of protection and finding the center where everything hurts. The tears continue to flow, and it's all I can do to stand up straight, hands clenched so tight the fingernails are digging into my palms.

And then, before I know what I'm doing, I cross the space between us. Not to seek shelter and comfort, but to kiss him. Hamlet was wrong about the heyday in the blood—turns out it's far from tame. I feel a quick sympathy for Hamlet's queen mother as Jake pulls me against the hardness of his body and smothers my mouth with his own. I wouldn't care if he was a murderer so long as he goes on kissing me this way.

When we surface for air, we're both breathing hard. We break apart, not touching, our eyes locked with the same intensity our lips were a minute ago. Every nerve ending in my body seems to be lit up. My brain is definitely not working. There's a reason why I wasn't going to do this, many reasons, none of which seem valid anymore.

When I hear the knocking, I figure it's somebody at the door. They can wait, whoever they are. Only the knocking doesn't stop and when I manage to orient my swimming head, I realize it's coming from the closet.

Rap tap. Rappety tap tap.

"Ignore that." I rest my hands on Jake's chest, feeling his heart beat against my palms, inhaling the clean smell of him, memorizing it for later. His hands, in turn, light on the small of my back and run up toward my shoulders.

"Do you think that's wise?" His lips are against my ear and then my neck.

I gasp a little, weak in the knees. "No."

Jake's lips continue their downward course. His fingers fumble with buttons and then he's kissing my collarbone, moving down...

"Jesus, Maureen. What happened here?"

It's not my breasts he's looking at.

The thuds from the closet door are getting more insistent. A cold wind swirls around us and lifts the packing foam out of an open box, carrying it back around and pelting Jake in the face. He shields his eyes with his arm and the wind dies, the bits of foam drifting harmlessly to the ground.

I take a breath, and then another, using the moment to do my buttons back up and take a step back.

"That scar is damnably close to your heart."

"Knife. It missed."

"And the knife wielder? Dead? Behind bars? Knock knock knocking on your closet door?"

I don't want to answer him. For a million reasons. But I'm not going down that road again, so I tell him the truth.

"In the hospital and unconscious, last I heard."

Breath hisses out between his teeth. "Jill." He paces away from me, breathing hard with an emotion that isn't passion. When he turns around, his face glows with anger. "That's another small detail you neglected to tell me."

"She missed the first time. I'm not likely to give her another opportunity."

"Damn it, Maureen. You think she's here to finish the job?"

"When she first got here, that's what I thought. Now I'm not so sure. She seems a little lost. Grieving."

"You realize that this now also makes you a suspect in assault. Murder, if she dies. You have motive. Opportunity." Jake begins to swear, effectively and fluently.

The rapping on the closet door starts up again, louder now.

Jake takes a deep breath. "Let me make sure I understand this. A woman shows up in your apartment who once stabbed you within an inch of your heart and you let her take up residence in the Manor right across the hall from you."

"I wanted to keep an eye on her. And let's not forget that you felt sorry for her and took her side."

"I didn't know she'd tried to kill you!"

"Thirty years ago! She was only sixteen, for God's sake. We haven't seen each other since."

"And that makes everything okay, I suppose."

My heart has settled down. My knees are steady. No danger of tears and no misbehaving heyday either. This is good, but I'll admit to a slight feeling of having been robbed. I sit back down at the table and open the laptop.

"You are an infuriating woman," Jake says. "I'm not objective when it comes to you. I'll be sending one of the deputies around to take a statement."

"That will have to wait. I've just located a Marietta Livingston. I think we need to pay her a visit."

NINETEEN

As the name suggests, Riverview RV Park overlooks the river. In fact, it boasts a splendid view, and the Park portion of the name isn't as ironic as it usually is in these places. Huge maple trees spread their branches protectively over many of the trailers. Flower beds promise a riot of color, come spring. The lots are far enough apart to give at least an illusion of space and privacy.

Most of them are empty this time of year, the snowbirds having wisely packed up and headed south to places like California and Arizona, but Ravenna still inhabits a fifth wheel parked in lot number 25. Unlike the other mobile units, there is no welcome mat, no cutesy wooden sign, no spinning lawn ornaments. She's made the concession of unhitching the Ford 4x4 that pulls the trailer, but it's parked in the driveway lined up perfectly, so all she needs to do is roll a foot in reverse and hitch back up. Perfect setup for a woman who might want to leave in a hurry.

Matt and Jake and I go as a team. No more solo acts. No more secrets. Opting for obscurity, we drive over in Matt's rattletrap pickup.

A plump, white-haired, rosy-cheeked woman answers the door in response to Jake's knock. She looks like a Disney grandmother. Her right hand grasps a cane, the knobby, arthritic knuckles whitening with the pressure as she leans her weight on it.

"I'm Sheriff Jake Callahan," Jake says. "I'd like to speak with you about a missing child."

She peers up at him, squinting, cupping one hand behind her ear. "I'm sorry, my eyes aren't what they used to be, and I'm a little hard of hearing."

"Sheriff Jake Callahan," he says again, louder. "It's about a missing girl. Would you like to see my badge?"

"If it isn't too much bother. One never knows these days. I heard a story about some thieves buying UPS uniforms off some Internet place called eBay the other day. Can you imagine? I'm sure you are who you say you are, but one can't be too careful."

Jake hands her his identification. She pulls out a pair of reading glasses and sets them on her nose, holding the card right up close. She takes so long about it that if we were a gang of ruffians intent on mischief, we could have killed her three times over before she gets through.

"That's what it says, all right. That you are Sheriff Callahan. Let me have a look at you."

He starts to bend closer to her but straightens, coughing, when my elbow catches him in the ribs. Just because she's old and bent doesn't mean she's not dangerous, and Jake needs a little reminder.

Ravenna doesn't seem to notice. "Blind as a bat, I am, these days. Well, come in, come in. I don't know who these people are, Sheriff, but if they are in your company, I'm sure I couldn't be safer."

Jake ducks his head to get through the low doorway and brushes past her.

"Oh dear," she says, peering across her yard, eyes shaded with one hand. "Janice and Elsie are staring at us. There will be gossip all over the park by dinner time."

"Sorry about that." Matt gifts her his most charming smile as he steps up into the trailer. "We left the cruiser behind so as not to raise too much interest with the neighbors, but you can't quite disguise a man in uniform."

"So sweet and considerate. And you are such a beautiful young man, too." She reaches up to pat his cheek, but before she can touch him, I pretend to catch my foot on the threshold and stumble forward. Matt grabs me before I hit the floor and I lean on him, heavily, breathing hard.

"Are you all right?" Jake asks.

"Fine. Fine." I paste on a smile of patient suffering, release Matt's arm, take a step, and let my leg collapse. Matt catches me again, this time not letting go.

"You'd better sit," Ravenna says. "Did you twist your ankle?"

"I must have done. My bones are getting fragile I guess. This getting older is such a difficult thing."

The interlude has given me time to look around the tiny sitting room. There's a low bench, big enough for two, and a comfortable chair. A basket of knitting sits beside the chair, with a pair of knitting needles poking out of what might be either a baby blanket or an old-fashioned shawl. There are nails on the walls for two pictures, but nothing is hanging there. No knickknacks. The kitchen is pristine. A coffee pot is gurgling. Fresh baked chocolate chip cookies are cooling on a rack and a mouthwatering aroma of butter, sugar, and chocolate combines with the smell of coffee.

No extra cups or dishes. No indication of visitors.

Matt helps me to the bench and I draw him down beside me, keeping one hand on his arm, looking as small and frail as I can manage. Marietta closes the door and turns to survey the three of us.

"Coffee? Milk? Cookies? I've just finished a batch of chocolate chip."

I shake my head, resisting the temptation. "Ah, for the days when I could eat without getting fat. One cookie, and I'll be dieting for a month."

Matt's mouth opens and I dig my fingernails into his arm. He whimpers instead of speaking.

"We don't want to trouble you," Jake says, "and we haven't really got time for refreshments. Or the appetite for them, either. Understandably we are all quite worried."

"Oh, yes. The missing girl. Dear me, how sad." She shuffles across the room, leaning heavily on the cane, gets herself turned around with painful deliberation, and lowers herself into the remaining empty chair with a sigh that wafts up from her toenails. "I don't see how I can help, but I will be happy to do anything I can."

I open my handbag and pull out a tissue, dabbing at non-existent tears with one hand, holding the open bag with the other. My .38 is in the holster at the small of my back, where it belongs, but I've got a tiny .22 nestled right beside the package of tissues. Not my favorite weapon, but handy at close range.

"She's been having such a difficult time," I say, between sniffles. "The other girls at school have been unkind. And her father is emotionally unavailable. She just melted down and ran off."

"Poor thing," Ravenna clucks. "How old? A teen? Such a difficult age. But are you quite sure she's run away? And how can I help you?"

"We thought she might have come to you," Jake says.

She gapes at him. "Why in heaven's name would you think that?"

"There are special circumstances." He shows her the text message on Sophie's phone.

"I'm sorry, I can't read that," she says. "Let me get my glasses."

"I don't believe you need your glasses for this, Ravenna."

My fingers dip into my purse and close around the handle of the little gun. Matt's arm, where it presses against mine, is taut as a steel wire.

"Who?" Her voice is tremulous. There's a slight palsy of her hands that makes the phone tremble as she peers at it with a lost expression on her face. "I'm terribly sorry. I would love to help you. Who is this Ravenna person? Are you thinking I know her, then?"

"It's very important that we find Sophronia. Another girl was murdered, not long ago."

"But, Sheriff, I don't know this girl. I couldn't have sent her this message. I don't know how to use this technology. Texting, they call it, yes?"

"Could I maybe have a look around?" Jake asks.

"Pardon? You'll have to speak up."

"Can I have your permission to look around?" he shouts.

Marietta's hand goes to her heart. "Oh, my goodness. You suspect me of harboring a runaway. Or a fugitive. This is not the sort of house that is good for hiding."

"Still," Jake says, with a pleasant smile.

"Very well then," she says. "I can't imagine how you think I am involved in this. I am so confused."

Jake gets up and takes a look around, which truly only takes a minute. There is a bathroom and one small bedroom and that is all.

"Dearie," Marietta says to Matt in a breathless voice, her hand still pressed to her chest, "would you fetch me the pill bottle on the kitchen windowsill? And a glass of water, please. I —" She lapses into harsh breathing.

Matt complies, at least taking the precaution of glancing at the label before handing the bottle to her.

Hands shaking, she taps out a pill and swallows it with a gulp of water.

"If there was anything I could do to help, anything at all, you know I would do so."

My patience is exhausted and I shift to more direct tactics. "You can stop lying, and tell us the truth."

"I have no idea what you are talking about."

"Mac, the coroner, recognized Ravenna as your nom de plume for your tattoo business, and gave us Marietta. So we know that part."

"Oh, my goodness." Her forehead creases in bewilderment. "Mac? I don't think I know any Mac. And I hope I'm not offending anybody if I say I've always thought tattoos were ugly, unconsidered things. How they do look when people grow old and their skin begins to sag, you know?"

An involuntary image of the naked girl on Chuck's bloated

belly speaks truth to her words. The old woman looks so fragile, so sincere, so grandmotherly that I'm tempted to believe we've somehow found the wrong Marietta Livingston.

Jake holds strong. "Mac is seldom mistaken about anything."

She shakes her head. "I used to draw and paint a little. Learned from the television. You know that artist who taught you how—what was his name? The man with the happy trees? He's dead now, I understand. All the good people are, present company excluded of course. Oh dear. What was I talking about? My mind does wander so." Her right hand, also wandering, strays up from her lap to pat her cottony white hair.

"Tattoos," I tell her. "Your work. In Mac's case, a raven tattooed on the jaw of a sixteen-year-old boy."

"Young woman"—she fixes me with a severe and reprimanding gaze—"if I were capable of tattooing people, which my affliction of Parkinson's disease renders out of the question, I would certainly not be sticking needles into a child too young to understand the consequences."

"This was a number of years ago. Perhaps Parkinson's was not a problem then." I hand her a photograph of the World Tree Girl. "This one is much more recent."

She gasps, the rosy color fading from her cheeks. "How terrible," she says. "Who would do such a thing? And to a child?"

It's not clear whether she's talking about the tattoos or the fact that the girl is dead. Either way, she turns the picture upside down on the coffee table, her face firming into strong resolve. "I shall have nightmares about this picture and I can't imagine why you are going around showing it to people. Sheriff, I'm going to have to ask you to take these people away. I can ask that, can't I? You have no search warrant and nothing against me."

"I have this." Jake turns the picture back over and lays another down beside it. "Your work, Ravenna. And not so long ago. I can get a warrant. Do I need to do that? Your space is not good for hiding runaways, but a tattoo kit would be easier to tuck away under a bed, in a closet."

The old woman closes her eyes, her face crumpling in what looks like genuine grief. "She's truly dead, then?"

Nobody answers.

For a long moment she sits there, her face hidden by her hands. Then she takes a deep breath. "Are you here to arrest me?"

"For what?" Jake asks.

"Tattooing a minor. That's it, isn't it? She wanted them so badly."

On a whim, I lay a picture of Sophronia down beside the World Tree Girl. "And this one? She also wanted them so badly?"

Ravenna touches the picture with an index finger and sighs. "Well then. I guess the gig is up."

Her hands steady. Her spine straightens. When she looks at me, her eyes are clear and direct, and her voice no longer quavers when she asks, "Who are you people and what is your interest in all this? And don't give me some twaddle about being grieving relatives. Give me the truth."

What is it with everybody and this truth thing of late? I keep my mouth shut, for once, and let Jake do the introductions. "Maureen owns Shadow Valley Manor. Matt runs the food services there. Sophronia doesn't exactly fit in well with the kids her age and we've all struck up an odd friendship."

"Which has nothing to do with the pictures of a dead girl who is not this missing Sophronia who I may or may not know."

No problem with her hearing now.

"You might as well tell her the truth, Jake." I pull out my FBI consultant ID. She doesn't need to know that it's no longer valid. "Matt and I are with a special victims unit. We are looking into this child's murder. So far, we haven't even been able to make an identification of the body."

Ravenna takes out the spectacles and rubs them with a cleaning cloth, perches them on her nose, and surveys us all, but the grandmotherly air no longer fits. "The dead girl's name is Aline Montgomery, or at least that is the name she gave me. I met her in Seattle. No, I don't know the names of her parents or where they live, or the girl's birthday or social security number or anything useful for finding them."

"It takes a long time and a high pain tolerance to achieve a full body tattoo like that," Jake says. "How old was she when you got started?"

Ravenna answers him with silence.

Matt leans forward. "We're not here to get you in trouble. We just want to find the killer."

She sighs and her eyes focus on distance. "You're not going to arrest me?"

"Not for tattoos," Jake says.

"Fair enough. Let me show you something." She reaches over to open a drawer.

I grab my pistol out of my open purse. Matt's hand goes to his hip, Jake's to his service belt.

When Ravenna turns back, holding something wrapped in a silk handkerchief, so old the fabric is thin as cobweb in places, all three of us are holding weapons.

Her eyes widen, and then she laughs. "I'm flattered, but I'm unarmed, as you can see." Removing the bit of silk, she reveals a deck of cards. Tarot, I think, in the brief instant before her hands begin to move. The deck becomes a living thing, the cards flowing fluidly back and forth in an unbroken stream.

"Cut the deck," she says, offering the cards to Matt.

I reach for them. "I'll do it." The cards are over-sized, the edges worn feather-thin with use. I split the stack and Ravenna lays out a spread.

"Oh dear," she says. She didn't so much as flinch when she turned to see three guns aimed at her. Now her face pales to a shade of gray that makes me think of the morgue, and her hand wanders back to her heart.

This is no ordinary Ryder's tarot, maybe not tarot at all. The colors are jewel-bright, the forms stylized, like art during the Renaissance. Only a few of the cards bear a resemblance to the familiar.

One is clearly the Death card: A woman in a flowing black robe sits astride a skeletal horse. In one hand she grasps a scythe, in the other she holds a chalice emitting beams of golden light. All around the horse, human forms cower in terror. I've been told that the Death card in tarot doesn't necessarily mean death and isn't a bad card, speaking only of endings and natural cycles.

This card blows all of that out of the water.

It's accompanied by another one I recognize, altered as it is: a towering castle on a cliff, struck by lightning. Smoke rises up from the towers and turrets. Stones tumble into the sea. Human forms dive out the windows, as if something within the castle makes a death on the sharp stones far below a welcome ending. The Tower, also a symbol of a sudden, unexpected dissolution of old things. I've never liked that damn card. It's showed up in both the readings I've had done, once shortly before my ill-fated venture to the experimental lab with Phil that ended up in a lifetime of secrets and a parting of our ways, the other before the paranormal slug did damage to my body that will never fully be repaired.

The rest of the layout means nothing to me, but does nothing to allay my fears.

One portrays a shipwreck deep beneath the sea. Sharks swim through the wreckage. A crab holds a gold coin in one claw. The colors are dark and ominous. Another portrays an individual so richly robed in brocaded scarlet, gold, and purple it's impossible to make out whether the individual is male or female. In one hand it holds an hourglass, turned so that it is empty, all of the sand run out. The other holds a mask to hide the face.

The next card depicts a gigantic male form, human but distorted, sporting long curling horns and holding strings that make a marionette dance. The last shows a graveyard under a gibbous moon, lurid red light shining on graves that are opening to release their dead.

"I don't understand," Jake says, ever the pragmatist. Matt says nothing.

I understand more than I care to.

Ravenna handles the cards by the edges, gingerly, as if they burn her. Her forehead is furrowed in worry lines. "I don't like this. At all."

"What does it mean?"

"I'd have to guess. I hesitate to say until I've thought about it more."

"While you're thinking," Jake suggests, "maybe you could

tell us about how you came to tattoo Sophronia. And the other girl."

She draws a visible breath and lets it out with a *whoosh* that lifts the edges of the Tower card and skitters it across the others.

"Not good," she mutters. "Fine. I will tell you what I know. What the cards tell us may yet be altered.

"This girl—the one you call Sophie—yes, I know her. But I did not send her that message. I have given her only the one tattoo—that of Anubis. The cards told me she would come to me, and which tattoo would be right for her. The Death card, as you see. And a card of new beginnings." She shuffles through the deck and turns over a card that features a single blossom open on a tree heavy with buds.

"This card"—her finger taps the tree—"was also in the spread for Aline."

"And what other card for Aline?" I ask, leaning over to see better.

Again the gnarled hands fly through the deck, producing, as if by magic, a card that portrays an old-time sailing vessel. Men are climbing the rigging and leaning far out to look at something on the rocks. Several of them have taken a header into the sea; another is launching himself over the bow. The object of their attention sits on the rocks, not even looking in their direction.

"A mermaid?" Jake asks, incredulous. "You've got to be kidding."

"A Siren," Matt corrects, picking up the card and sliding it back and forth across his palm. His tilts his head to one side, as if he's picked up a distant sound and is trying to figure out what it is.

"Tell us about Aline." Jake's voice is dry and professional. I know his moods by now. Enough with mysteries, he wants some good old-fashioned facts he can sink his teeth into. I want more than facts. I want something I can fight. I'd been hoping Ravenna would turn out to be a black-hearted paranormal in need of killing, but no such luck. The woman doesn't seem to be evil, although her eyes are unsettling and I don't like the way she looks at me and smiles, as if she's privy to some secret information about me that she's not sharing.

She sobers again, quickly, and the girl's name crosses her lips like an invocation. "Aline. Such a beautiful child. But so lost. So perilous."

"Less poetry," I tell her, "more story."

"You are a bloodthirsty soul, Maureen Keslyn. I will tell this story, but I will tell it in my own way. He knows why." She gestures at Matt, who still has that distant expression on his face. There's a line down the center of his forehead now, as if he's trying to see far off into the distance.

"Three years ago, Aline found me. I had set up a business telling fortunes as well as doing tattoos. Nance, my assistant, kept turning over the same run of cards—the Moon, all the Aces, the Tower, the Devil. She wasn't a true reader and she hated it when the cards started to talk. She'd try to assert her will, to silence them, poking them back into the deck, cheating, but they'd jump out at her, fall out onto the table, leap onto the floor. When Aline came in and asked to have her fortune told, the child drew them out of the deck herself and laid them out on the table.

"'You must start with a question,' Nance had told her, the way I taught her to say it. Unlike most of the seekers who come in, Aline didn't ask whether she could keep the question to herself. She looked up, huge blue eyes crystal clear to the depths, and said, 'Do I have a soul?'

"The heartbreak, the longing in her voice went straight to my heart. I didn't even wait for Nance to come get me. The girl needed a real reader, someone who could understand, so I sat down to talk, heart to heart.

"She asked me the same question she'd asked the cards. 'Do I have a soul, do you think?' And then she asked, 'What am I?'

"And I had to tell her I didn't know. She was a smart girl, though. The cards scared her. 'Is this me? All this fear and death?'

"'The cards talk in riddles,' I told her. 'Sometimes they tell parts of secrets. I think what they are saying is that you are something new, shaking up the order of things. Whatever you are can go two ways—creating great beauty or causing heartache.'

"'But there is so much death.'

"I couldn't lie to her.

"I wanted to give Aline something. A gift. A symbol with meaning. The Ape is an incorporation of the Egyptian god, Thoth, a mediator between the darkness and the light. I gave her Thoth."

"It's a long way from one small ape to a full body tattoo," says Jake, who isn't mollified at all by her rendering of sympathy for a bewildered child. If anything, his tone is harsher, more acerbic.

"I meant only to give her the Ape. She was underage, yes, but it would be a talisman for her, and she seemed to need one. You judge me, all of you. I see what lies behind your eyes. You think I took advantage of innocent children, went behind their parents' backs, marked them for life before they knew who they

were or what they would be. How could they know? No adult
to guide them. And both of these girls, drawn away from the
balance to the dark, could become a terrible force of evil in the
world. Have you not seen this? I see the fear when you speak of
this Sophronia. Something has turned her—she is running wild
and loose and you are afraid of what she can and will do."

"Finish with Aline," Jake says, and the old woman
continues her tale.

"I gave Aline the Ape. A month later she came back to see
me. Terrified, embarrassed, ashamed. She had a skin problem.
She didn't want to show her parents or the doctor. She was so
distressed I agreed to look. The skin around her navel had
changed. It was smoother, almost rubbery, and it shone in the
light. She begged me, pleaded, with tears, that I do something
to cover it. She was on the swim team at school. The girls in the
locker room would notice.

"'They will also notice a tattoo,' I told her. She shrugged
that off. A tattoo would be cool with the other kids. Her parents
would never need to know.

"I had a sinking feeling that this was only the beginning.
She was just reaching puberty, and with the change of her
body, so would come the physical manifestation of her...other-
ness. In case, just in case this should be so, I began the tree. Just
the roots, for starters. A little green grass and a flower for color.
The vine for beauty. She came back the next weekend, begging
for more.

"I asked about her parents, and how they would react. She
smiled at me, the most beautiful and terrifying smile imagin-
able. 'They already think I'm the devil's child. What difference
does it make?'

"'Go away,' I told her. 'You've had two tattoos completely

free. What do you think this is, a charity house?' I was cruel. She frightened me.

"A light went out in her eyes and I felt as if I'd killed something. All that week I went through my days with the taste of ashes in my mouth. But the next weekend she was back.

"'Please,' she said. And then she pulled a wad of tangled bills out of her pocket and set them on the table. 'It's all I've got, but I can get more. I'm old enough to babysit, if anybody will let me.'

"The way she said that last, and the smudge of a bruise on her cheek, aroused my suspicions. I picked up the money and straightened it all to lie flat, to give me time to think. Fifty dollars. Not even enough to pay for the Ape, not that I wanted her money. 'People are always looking for a babysitter,' I told her.

"'Not from a demon spawn like me,' she muttered.

"'Who calls you that?' I demanded.

"She didn't answer, but she wouldn't look at me, either. 'Are they beating you, child?'

"'What if they were?'

"'We could get you some help.'

"She made a terrible, heart-wrenching sound, halfway between a laugh and a sob. Have you ever heard a child make a sound like that? Yes. You have, Sheriff. I see it in your eyes. 'There is no real help for me,' she said. 'Please. More ink. The skin thing is spreading.'

"And so I added the rest of the tree trunk, making it strong and brave, pushing up from the center of her toward her heart, her brain. She was young, but she understood the significance of it. After that she came back often. Both of us became caught up in the art of it and she began to request little things. Birds, squirrels, flowers."

"And you're sure you have no clue as to her parents?" Jake persists. "Last name, address, any identification at all?"

Ravenna sighs and leans back in the chair. "Too late now to help or harm," she says, speaking more to herself than to us. She plays with the cards. I watch, half mesmerized. It's as if they have a life of their own. She pulls out a card, looks at it, puts it back into the deck. With slow, deliberate motions, she wraps them back up in silk and tucks them into their wooden box.

Without another word, she hefts herself to her feet and walks out of the room, without the cane this time, but as if every step exacts a price. She draws a slider as she passes into the bedroom, and I can hear her rustling around on the other side. She's gone long enough for the three of us to start to fidget. Jake and Matt search every visible inch of the room with their eyes. I get up and start moving things around.

"Maureen, you can't—" Jake breaks off, knowing that I can and will. Matt says nothing. Something weird is going on with him. He's got the look of a deer in the headlights, dazed and mystified, like that look he had in the coffin room, only more so. I'll worry about that later. Right now, I've got a tiny window of opportunity I don't intend to waste.

The first set of cabinet doors, when opened, reveals well-stocked bookshelves. Ravenna's tastes run to romance, heavy on the erotic side, but she has some literary tomes and some esoteric and strange books that draw my interest: an old copy of Budge's translation of *The Book of the Dead*; *Ovid and the Metamorphoses*, in Greek; a small, cheaply bound volume titled *Mythology and Genetics*. Either she is a collector, or has an IQ that is a point of interest.

A small handgun, a .22, loaded and with a bullet in the chamber, nestles in a drawer with a pair of scissors, a flashlight, spare batteries, and other odds and ends. The antique wooden trunk against the wall is half full of clothing, but there is one cloth-wrapped bundle, round and heavy, that feels interesting.

I unwrap it and sigh with disappointment.

Just a gazing ball. It's as big as my head, cobalt blue, and reflects everything in the room around me. I've got no use for fortune-tellers. Paranormal is one thing. Spirits might know things going on around us that we can't see, given their invisibility, but even they can't travel into the future.

The ball is a beautiful thing, though, and I hold it up to the light to see it better.

A hissing intake of breath from Matt freezes me, the ball held aloft.

"Put that thing away." He's lost the dreamy look.

I open my mouth to tell him it's just garden decoration, but at that instant the door cracks open at the end of the hallway and I drop it back into the chest and close the lid.

"Well, did you find anything interesting while I was gone?" Ravenna asks. "I assure you I have a license for the gun."

"It's not the gun that interests me."

She gives me a knowing look, lips quirked in the hint of a smile, and hands a small, plastic rectangle to Jake.

"School ID. Aline dropped it once. I meant to give it back to her, but that was the last time I saw her."

Ravenna sinks into a chair, as if her little trek down the hall has been completely exhausting. "When you meet her parents, brutalize them a little, would you, please? They did not treat her right."

I nod at her, a silent promise that there will be retribution. "If Sophronia should come looking for you..."

"Bless your heart, my lamb, I have no intention of staying here any longer. Oh, I know what you're thinking. Maybe I can hold her. Maybe I can explain something, offer her comfort. One does not explain things to an emotional teenager. This girl has a moral compass. She will have to make her own decision. If she lives long enough to do so."

"What exactly does that mean?"

"You really must be going if you hope to catch a plane. If I'm right, you've got just enough time to make it to the airport. Don't drive. I see you considering that. Trust me. Bad idea."

With that, she shoos us on out the door and I hear a dead-bolt as she locks up behind us.

"Do we trust her?" Jake asks, once we're back in Matt's pickup.

"About as far as we can throw her," I answer.

Matt says nothing. He moves like a robot on autopilot, as if his body is with us, but his brain is elsewhere. He starts the truck, shifts into gear.

"Matt?"

No answer. I jostle his arm with my elbow. "Matt!"

"Hmm?"

"Pull over."

He looks at me then, as if surprised to notice I'm there, even though I'm smashed in beside him with my shoulder pressing into his ribs. "Why?"

"Just do it. Pull over."

I wait until he's parked to turn off the ignition and take the keys. Both men stare at me like I'm the one that's crazy. "Now, Matt, start talking."

"I don't—"

"Don't bullshit me. You've been acting weird ever since we walked into Lysander's showroom. Either you can explain yourself, or I'm going to believe that you've been hijacked and put you in protective custody. Which is it?"

"Maybe it's personal."

"And maybe somebody's driving your body. Out with it."

"She's right," Jake says. "This team thing seems to require full disclosure."

Matt's jaw clenches. A little white dent appears in the side of his nose. "I told you, I thought I saw something at the funeral home."

"What kind of thing?"

"Something that—wasn't there. I kept catching glimpses out of the corner of my eyes. Things moving. But whatever it was, I couldn't see it in the room, only in the reflection from the coffin. Maybe there are paranormals that reflect but you can't see? The opposite of vampires." He looks at me, hope in his eyes, but I shake my head. If there's a creature like that, I've never heard tell of it.

Matt sighs, accepting the inevitable. "And then, with the crystal ball, the images were clear. I didn't see much, before you put it away."

"What did you see, Matt?"

"A series of dead bodies. All of them bloodless." His voice sounds raw, like there are rocks in his throat. His hands on the steering wheel are white at the knuckles.

Jake looks from Matt to me and back again. "Help me out here. Does that mean these people are all dead? Or are we talking something like—Scrooge and the spirits?"

His voice sounds distant; I'm focused in on Matt. Maybe

he's young and inexperienced, but he's still FBI. It's going to take more than an unexpected vision of some dead bodies to rattle him this badly.

"What else?"

He doesn't answer me.

"Matt!"

"Sophie," he says.

Jake's color is almost as bad as Matt's. Men. Never can keep their heads in a crisis when someone they love is in trouble. He swallows. "Sophie killed them?"

Despite my lack of faith in seeing stones and visions, Matt's face in that moment chills me to the marrow of my bones. He shakes his head.

"Sophie was one of the dead."

TWENTY

I end up flying to Seattle alone.

Jake, always the stickler for the rules, says there will be trouble if he strays outside of his jurisdiction. Besides, somebody needs to keep an eye on Jill and keep looking for Sophie closer to home. Matt stays to keep an eye on the Manor.

Both of them worry about me going off alone, but I don't let that bother me. It will only be a couple of days. I pack an overnight bag and spend the driving time to the Spokane airport mulling over what we know, what we don't know, and creating theories to follow up with the investigation.

Aline's parents are among the unknowns. Maxine and Jim Montgomery have done an admirable job of keeping their lives off the public record. My Internet snooping, assisted by the spyware programs I've borrowed and modified from the FBI, has rendered very little information.

Aline was their only child, born at the Swedish Medical Center. In the year before her birth, a fertility consult was canceled a week in advance. The chart note said: *patient happy to report pregnancy.*

There was nothing remarkable about Aline's birth. Her health, as well as that of her parents, has since been unmarked by anything more dramatic than the occasional sprained ankle or flu bug. She was vaccinated on the usual schedule. They've attended a quiet, old-fashioned Baptist church that keeps to itself and has no electronic records. Neither of them has ever been arrested.

Farmers Insurance covers their modest home, one vehicle, a four-door 2006 Impala—and of much greater interest—a yacht, purchased within the last two months.

Aline's school record is unexceptional. She has maintained As and Bs and had no disciplinary problems.

THE GPS in my rental car guides me to a modest house, one of six identical models all crammed in so close you could pass a cup of borrowed sugar to the neighbor, window to window. No frills. No flowers. Beige drapes.

I navigate four steps up onto a concrete porch. A sheaf of dried corn leans up against the metal railing, anchored at the base by three knobby gourds. A hand-lettered sign taped to the door says, "No solicitors, please."

The doorbell chimes with a straight from the factory *ding-dong*. I check out the neighborhood while I wait for a response. The neighbor to the right still has Halloween cat decals on the windows. The neighbor to the left decorates with empty six packs, lined up neatly. Across the street the houses are quiet. No kids playing, nobody out washing cars or doing yard work or even getting in the car to go to work.

The Montgomerys don't answer the door. I ring again, then knock, but I'm pretty sure the house is empty.

Just as I'm debating the relative merits of letting myself in through the back door or going back to wait in the rental car, a man emerges from the Halloween cat house, whistling and jingling car keys. Neighbors are trouble when you're contemplating a little friendly lock picking, and I immediately don a hopeful expression and ring the bell again, as if I've just arrived.

The whistling stops, although the key jingling continues. "You looking for the Montgomerys?"

His age is somewhere between sixteen and twenty. He's wearing lace-up boots and one of those beards that has, for some obscure reason, become fashionable lately. A backpack hangs over his left shoulder, and his left hand rests in the pocket of a long coat, spacious enough to conceal any number of weapons. Car keys dangle from his right hand.

I feel naked without my gun, left behind due to airport TSA.

"They're not here," he says, oh so helpfully.

"I don't understand." I shoot for bewildered and weary. "I called ahead. They knew I was coming."

A crease mars his perfect young forehead and the keys jingle louder. "I have to be somewhere, and my folks are out. Otherwise you could wait over at my house."

Either he's a nice young man, worried about my well-being, or he's a smooth-talking psychopath.

"Oh, no, I wouldn't want to trouble you. I do wonder where they've gone. Is Aline at school?"

"You haven't heard then."

"Heard what?"

"Aline vanished a couple of months ago. Not a trace of her since."

I put the back of my hand up to my mouth as though to stifle a sob, and lean against the railing, overcome by shock. "Oh my God. This is terrible! Last time I saw her she was just a wee bit of a thing. What happened? Was she kidnapped?"

"My opinion is she ran away. Who could blame her?" He realizes, too late, that he doesn't know who he's talking to. "No offense," he adds, quickly. "Who did you say you are?"

"They always were strict with her," I say, taking a guess.

"Strict is the understatement of the year." He has good intentions, but the threat of an emotional outburst makes him restless. The keys jingle louder as he tosses them up in the air, catches them, and descends to the bottom of the stairs. When he turns back, his face is open and unmasked.

"They probably aren't grieving much. Aline was a great kid. They didn't see that."

"Young man, how can you say such things?"

He shrugs. "Like I said. I didn't mean to offend. If you want to find Jim and Maxine, I'd suggest the Shilshole Marina. They're probably down there working on the boat."

I ring the doorbell again, looking over my shoulder to watch my informant unlock a bicycle and ride away. Only then do I make my way back down the steps and head out in search of the marina.

———

I HATE THE OCEAN. Call this the sound or a bay, or whatever you want, but it's still ocean. The vastness of the water, the alien smell of salt, the hundreds of moored boats with their sails all furled, the squawking seagulls—all of it has the effect of making me feel small, mortal, and uncomfortably alone. The best antidote to such emotions is putting my brain to work, so I study the layout, methodically turning a bewildering chaos of boats into order.

Really, it's nothing more than a giant parking lot, if you turn the boats into cars and the water into asphalt. Each pier is conveniently labeled. Each boat has a numbered slip. I know that Maxine and Jim are at Pier C, slip number 80. Not so conveniently, the ramps down to the piers are gated and locked.

Fortunately for me, a man is headed up the ramp in my direction.

He's fortyish, bare-headed, a couple of days' worth of unshaven. He carries a canvas gym bag slung over one shoulder and whistles an off-key tune. When he sees me, he makes easy eye contact and grins, but lets the gate slam shut behind him instead of holding it open for me.

"Lose your fob?"

I pat my pockets as if looking for this mythical item. "I feel so stupid. I'm new to this. I left it on the table at the house."

"Are you far?"

"Not so much. But I took a GoCar, and somebody nabbed it before I'd made it a hundred feet." I make a point of looking as old and frail as I can manage.

His eyes flicker from me to the gate. "I haven't seen you around."

"I just bought the boat. I was so excited to come down and try my sea legs I forgot the damn fob."

"I could give you the grand tour," he offers. "Which slip?"

"Oh, I couldn't trouble you with that. You're on your way someplace."

"Just up to the showers," he says, but he shifts his weight and the fingers of his free hand tap a tattoo against his thigh.

"Oh, I wouldn't think of stopping you. I don't suppose you could let me through?"

He hesitates, then shrugs, and touches a key fob to an electronic panel. The gate clicks and he opens it for me.

"People take the gates seriously," he says. "Try to remember the fob."

"Got it. Thank you so much. God bless." I start down the ramp, letting my limp become exaggerated and not looking back to see if he is watching me. Fortunately, my cover story lets me look a little uncertain, watching the pier numbers, reading the names on the boats. Straight ahead is sky and what looks like a forest of tangled masts to my land-bound eyes. A wind springs up and sets a clanking and rattling into motion.

I find Maxine and Jim on the deck of a boat larger than any of the others on Pier C, moored at the far end. Maxine is polishing windows with a spray bottle of Windex and a roll of paper towels. Jim has a can of paint and is carefully painting letters on the side of the bow. Both of them are wearing blue jeans and matching sweatshirts, with the lettering KESTREL on the back and a screen print of a soaring bird superimposed over an old-time sailing vessel. The effect is that of a giant flying creature attacking something that is more sail than ship.

Jim is balding, middle height, a little rotund, the sort of man my eyes tend to slide over without fully registering his presence. Maxine makes up for any of his self-effacing qualities. Flat belly, breasts that don't even register under the bulky sweatshirt, square hips. Her hair is tied back in a ponytail so tight it raises her eyebrows and gives her a perpetually questioning look.

"Yes," she says, looking down at me. In her hands, the bottle of window spray looks like a weapon, as if she might begin squirting me if threatened. "You want something."

Most people would turn this into a question. Not Maxine. No subtle beginnings here, no discussion of the weather. Not even the opening of asking what I'm doing on the dock and how I managed to get past the gate. Do I have a boat? Do I belong here? Which is fine by me. I can do without the preliminary chitchat.

"I'm here about your daughter."

Her expression, already unwelcoming, shifts to hostile. "I don't have a daughter." She turns her back on me and goes back to scrubbing windows.

Jim freezes, the paintbrush poised halfway between the paint can and the boat. Black paint drips onto the slip. His mouth opens, sucking in air. He looks like a runner at the end of a long race, replenishing oxygen reserves.

"But you had a daughter. Aline. Sixteen years old last month."

Maxine's gaze scours me from head to toe. Nothing of softness in any inch of her. "We're busy here."

"I understand she disappeared. What—a month ago, two?"

Jim is still having trouble with his breathing. His face looks haggard, jowls hanging loose under hollowed cheeks.

"I don't know what you're talking about," Maxine says.

My eyes rove over the boat. There's a rectangle of black right where Jim has started painting. It is of a slightly different shade than the rest of the boat.

"I see you've changed the name. Good for you."

"I don't—"

"The Kestrel. I like it."

"Jim, don't you say a word. Look, whoever you are—"

"How much did they pay you?"

That's what does it. Jim drops the brush. Maxine swings around and stomps across the deck. "Go. Away. Now."

"Enough to buy the boat, I'd guess. Maybe a new car. You should have held out for a house while you were at it. Or is that still in the works?"

Jim leans against the boat as though he's about to topple.

"Are you a reporter?" He wipes his mouth with the back of his hand. "They promised there would be no reporters."

"Don't you dare judge us!" Maxine spits like an angry cat. "We deserve some compensation after what we've been through."

"Max," Jim says. "Don't."

His voice might as well be the buzzing of a fly. "Everybody wants to go on about the poor child, as if she's the one suffering. What about us? What about the heartbreak and the expense?"

"Maxine. Stop it." Jim's voice is stronger now, his spine straightened. She turns to look at him and he blows it all by whispering, "Please."

"Oh, you always were soft on her. You know as well as I do the girl has been heading in this direction from the day we brought her home from the hospital. If she hadn't gotten herself murdered, she'd have wound up in prison. Sooner or later."

As soon as the words leave her mouth, she covers it with her hand but it's too late to call them back.

"I'm right then," I tell her. "You do know."

"They said there was a serial killer and Aline was a casualty. That we needed to pretend she was still missing, or we would hinder the case. You're right about the money. But she was a child. Our child." Jim's voice breaks and he smears his palm over his eyes.

"If you were half the man you think you are, maybe she'd have turned out different." Maxine's voice is a knife, wielded with the skill of long years of combat.

I see the hit strike home, but it's an old wound. Jim is a man with no blood left to lose. He sighs. "Always my fault."

"We should have bowed to God's will. But no, you had to bypass that. A child, a child. Give me a child. Well, you got a child all right. I hope you're happy."

Jim's face flushes. He draws in a visible breath. And between that breath and the next, a transformation happens. Same balding head and unremarkable features. Same rounded belly and sagging jeans. But the weak jawline firms. His muscles tighten and energize.

"Not another word about Aline from you," he says. His voice is a command.

Maxine startles and nearly drops her window spray. "How dare you?" Her face flushes with anger, but for the first time she is asking, not telling.

"I loved her. She was a bright, beautiful child. You drove her away with your blathering and nagging and constant criticism. I was a party to that. I let you do it. My sin, to carry with me into death and possibly hell. But no more."

He pulls his Kestrel sweatshirt off over his head and drops it onto the deck.

"Put that back on. You'll get a chill."

He laughs, a bitter, coruscating sound. "And how would that matter to you?"

"I'll be the one taking care of you when you're sick. Fetching tea. Doing laundry. Making chicken noodle soup."

"Good news. You're off the hook. If I die from a chill, you won't be around to tell me how it's my fault."

They stare at each other. He's as surprised as she is at what he's said.

"Jim. Come up here. Don't be ridiculous." There's fear in her voice now, but if he can hear it, he's long past caring.

"Goodbye, Maxine." He nods at me, touching his hand to his forehead in a casual salute. "No idea what you came for, but I thank you all the same."

Maxine follows him with her eyes until he's out of sight, and then continues to stand there, looking at nothing, as if he's going to suddenly reappear on her horizon. When he doesn't, her arms drift toward the ground, not by intention but as if gravity has overpowered her will. The paper towel roll hits the deck.

She stares at it, as if wondering how it got there, and then finally looks at me. Her assurance is cracked right down the middle. "You're still here."

I clear my throat. "Your daughter—"

"I don't have a daughter." But the words are automatic. No energy behind them.

"My granddaughter has gone missing. I know—"

"You don't know anything. How about this? I didn't really want a child. That's my secret. When we failed to get pregnant, I was fine with that. God's will, I said. It happens. But the Bible also says, obey your husband. And where did that get me?"

The chance to play martyred wife. That's what it got her. I can see it clearly. Dutiful, dedicated, and all the while toxic and corrosive toward both him and the child.

"Men," I say, voice weighted with meaning. She doesn't take my offered bait.

"I don't need him." Her voice is flat. She seems oblivious to the tears streaking silently down her cheeks. Without brushing them away, she bends, picks up her paper towels, and goes back to her windows. I've been dismissed.

TWENTY-ONE

I could sure use a cup of coffee, and there's a little café right on the corner by the Marina. Two teenage girls stand in line at the register, both busy with their phones while they wait for a businessman to pay for his order. The single barista behind the counter is focused and busy. There are only two other people in a small, well-lit room. One faces me, with a newspaper spread out over the table in front of him, both hands on the table, circling his coffee.

The other has his back turned to the door and is doing nothing. A cup sits untouched on the table in front of him. I keep an eye on him while moving through the line and ordering my coffee, then slide into the seat across the table.

"What are you going to do?"

Jim's head comes up and his eyes focus as though he's been a hundred miles away.

The slouch in his shoulders is habit, not defeat, I'm happy to see. A spark still burns in his eyes. He studies me, takes a sip of his neglected coffee, and makes a face. "I don't even like this stuff."

I raise my eyebrows in a question and he half laughs, rubbing the side of his jaw with the palm of his right hand.

"Maxine won't ever let me have coffee. Bad for the heart, she says."

"So you begin with a small act of rebellion."

I mean it kindly, but the grief washes over him like a tidal wave. His face crumples, his shoulders slump. "Too little. Too late," is all he says.

"You can help me find another missing girl, maybe. It won't bring yours back, but might save somebody else the same grief."

He plants the palms of both hands square on the table, and I think for a minute he's going to push his chair back and leave. Instead, he takes a breath and looks me directly in the eyes for the first time since I've met him.

"Ask whatever. I'll answer what I can."

"What I need to know is about Aline's conception."

If I'd fired a round point blank into his belly, it might have hurt him less. He recoils physically, but then again, straightens and meets my gaze. He's tougher than he looks, this man. He's tried himself at his own tribunal, and letting me grill him is the punishment he's decreed upon himself.

"This would be easier over whiskey." He takes another swallow of coffee, grimaces, then centers the cup between his hands before he speaks.

"We tried for two years after Maxine decided we should have a baby. I'm not sure if she ever really wanted a child. It was just something people do, and once she'd decided on a pregnancy, God help her she was going to have that baby. Every month, when she realized I'd failed to impregnate her, she would walk around for a week trailing clouds of resentment and unfailingly doing what she saw as her duty as a Christian wife: Healthy meals. Clean house."

He stops and sits for a minute, just staring. I can already see how this would have played out with a woman like Maxine. I could save us both the pain of half of this narrative, but the poison needs an out and I wait for him to go on. Jim adjusts the cup about three degrees to the left and resumes: "She took to monitoring her body temperature and crossing off days on the calendar. I came to watch the growing series of slashes with dread, prepared to do just about anything to avoid the night each month where she'd vanish into the bathroom with a thermometer and come out naked to announce it was time for me to do my duty and give her a child.

"I—well, sometimes I wasn't able. I took to spending evenings out in the bar and coming home late and drunk. Not that this helped. She secured a stash of Viagra. But we still didn't have a child."

"Clearly something changed." I swallow the last of my coffee with regret and set the cup down beside his.

"Doctors. We started with our family practice provider. He ordered up basic tests. Hers all came back normal. I had a low sperm count, and poor sperm motility. That made her happy, that the problem was a deficiency on my part. She was pleasant for a couple of weeks and I thought maybe we'd move on. We could adopt a child. Or even do artificial insemination. No such luck. Maxine's interpretation of the Bible and God's will was that she must be fertilized by my sperm, and my sperm alone, and that this must be done by the usual means.

"So there was a regimen of vitamins. No hot showers. Boxer shorts instead of briefs. Chelation therapy in case I was harboring heavy metal toxicity. No more alcohol. Another year went by. I did everything she said—it was easier than fighting. Except for the drinking. I was turning into an alcoholic, ruining my liver despite all the healthy living in the rest of my life. Still no baby.

"One day I came home from work and she was waiting for me, all dressed up and ready to go out. She'd made me a sandwich and hustled me out the door, explaining once we were already in the car and driving that she'd found a fertility expert who had agreed to make us part of a research experiment.

"When we got there, it turned out that the 'we' was a bit of a stretch. *I* could be part of a research experiment. They would inject my testicles with some secret mojo and voila! Superpowered sperm that could not fail to swim with speed and determination to their goal. I was against it. I asked for time to think.

"But the good doctor and my wife were both firmly allied against me. It was now or never. There was a timing issue with the medication. Tomorrow would be too late. Two hours from now would be too late. No, I wouldn't be told what was in it. This was a double-blind study, to rule out the possibility of placebo effect. The doctor was very convincing about this. 'Sex is very much a matter of psychology,' she said, 'as is conception. Focus on the science of this will distract.'

"What the hell? I figured if this didn't work, Maxine would have to back off and leave me alone. My only condition was that she not be allowed in the treatment room. Last thing I needed was her looking on while somebody stuck needles in my balls. I felt emasculated enough already.

"The actual procedure wasn't as bad as I expected. An injection of local anesthetic, and then nothing. We were provided a room, immediately after, with access to porn, medications, penis pumps, or whatever we needed to facilitate an encounter.

"Aline was conceived in a sterile room out of a loveless marriage with some sort of super-charged sperm. It's amazing she turned out as normal as she did."

I cough. "Your wife called her a devil's child," I remind him.

He crumples. His face goes into his hands and his shoulders shake as he weeps. The teenage girls at the table across from us look up from their phones and then quickly avert their eyes. The barista appears not to notice.

The spasm passes quickly. He wipes his eyes, smoothes his hair, as if the act of shedding tears has somehow rumpled it, and answers with a quiet dignity: "The worst of my sins is that I didn't leave years ago and take Aline with me. She was a sweet child. Bright. Beautiful. Loving."

He hesitates.

"But?"

"She had a way about her. Too persuasive, even as a tiny tot. No tantrums for her. If she wanted something she had this way of—persuading you. Before you knew it, you were giving her what she'd asked for, even while you were berating yourself for being a pushover. It caused some trouble at school."

"Like?"

"Like, she'd end up with dessert from other kids' lunches. Or come home with somebody else's toy. We'd have parents calling, demanding that she return some item or other. Maxine punished her repeatedly, to no avail. I would talk to her, bewildered, because she never struck me as a selfish child. And she would tell me that she didn't mean to. If she wanted something, it just sort of happened. Elementary school wasn't too bad, but when she turned thirteen and the boys started showing interest, all hell broke loose."

"Maxine would never have approved of budding sexuality." I could picture it. The beautiful young girl, the hormonal boys, the jealous classmates.

"The boys were crazy for her. She could have whichever one she wanted, effortlessly. Something wasn't right, I don't know. I still just thought it was because she was such a pretty and charming little thing..." Again his voice trails away. He crosses his arms over his chest and I know I've hit the place of true resistance.

"And then something changed your mind."

He looks at me, his face firmed into a shape that would have made his life a lot easier if he'd figured out how to take a stand as a younger man. This is not a good time for him to develop a spine. I need him to talk to me. But instead of bullying him, I lean forward on my elbows and say just one word:

"Please."

He nods. Runs his hand over his hair again.

"She loved the water. And I don't mean *like*, I mean *loved*. Even as a baby, she would scream when we took her out of the tub. As soon as she discovered swimming, she would beg to go to the pool. We went boating with some friends one day. They have a daughter, same age as Aline. The two had always been friends, but apparently there was a boy they both wanted. I never did get the whole story. They got into a row. The other girl slapped Aline, called her a bitch. Both of them were in tears.

"Maxine turns around and says, 'How many times have I told you not to act like a whore?'

"Aline stopped crying. She sort of shrank into herself. And then she went over the side of the boat. I knew she could swim and I kept waiting for her to come up, but she didn't.

"It seemed like forever before I pitched over the side and went under looking for her. I'm not much of a swimmer and didn't get far. The other man came in after me, both of us diving down, looking for a glimpse of her.

"Long after we were sure she had drowned, she surfaced. Perfectly fine. Wasn't even gasping for breath. I've told myself all kinds of stories about that. Maybe she was under the boat in some pocket of air. Or the water was cold enough that she didn't need oxygen. Or that the time just seemed like forever but was only a minute."

Ravenna's cards come into my mind. The Siren on the rocks, the foundering ship.

"How long was it?"

"Forty-five minutes, Maxine says. I don't see how that could be. I'm sure she's exaggerating. But—it was time enough for me to be shivering with cold. Out of breath. Exhausted. And Aline looked like she'd just stepped out of a warm shower after a good night's sleep."

"What was the doctor's name?" I ask, holding myself where I am in my seat, not leaning forward to convey the intensity of interest I have in his answer.

He blinks at me, as if I'm speaking in a foreign tongue. "Which doctor?"

"The fertility specialist."

"God. It's been seventeen years."

"It's important."

His gaze sharpens, and he's the one who leans forward in his chair.

"Why?"

"Because this other girl who is missing was also the product of a secret, experimental fertility treatment. If I know the doctor, I might be able to track some records that would help me find her."

He drums his fingers on the table, thinking, but he shakes his head. "I can't help you."

"Male or female? Age? Anything that might help."

"She was Indian. Pakistani, maybe, but she wore western clothes. Thick accent. Dark hair and eyes."

"Are you sure?" I'd been hoping his evil scientist-doctor had been Alice Sorenson. What a tidy little package that would have been—the creator of the Medusa doing a little research on the side. Now I have to contend with the reality that there's another mad scientist running around out there doing paranormal-human experiments.

"I don't recall her name, but I remember her face well enough."

"Do you remember where the office was? Anything?"

"That I can tell you. Not the exact address, but the location." He pulls a small notebook and pen out of his pocket and draws me a map, planting an **X** on one side of the street. A moment of hesitation, and then his eyes brighten. "Maybe this will help."

He writes the word GENESIS in capital letters, next to the **X**. "That's what it was called. The clinic where she worked."

Genesis.

One of the words the spirits transmitted through Val. Also, an allusion to the beginning of human history and the story of a woman delving into mysteries not meant for her.

I consult the rough map and fold it into my pocket. "Thank you. This is very helpful. What will you do, now?"

He shrugs. "Maxine can have the boat. She can have the house. I'm thinking I'll get away for a bit, take a trip. And then, maybe, a different job. Doing something helpful."

I'm glad the hush money is going to some good effect. "Look, Jim—talking to me about this might not go over well with the people who paid you to keep it quiet."

In response to his expression of alarm, I hold up my hand and go on: "Don't worry about how I know. Here's what I suggest. Get your share of the money out of the bank. Get on a plane. Go somewhere far away and stay there for a few months. Maybe a year. Get a whole new start."

Before he can answer I'm up out of my chair and heading for the door. What he does with the advice is up to him. I'm all the way out to the car when a thought hits me like a ton of bricks.

I barge back into the café and catch Jim in the act of putting on his coat, one sleeve on, the other still hanging over the back of his chair. He blinks up at me.

"What?"

"Letter? Picture? Both?"

"I don't know what you're talking about."

"The fertility treatment was a research project. They followed up. How often?"

"Once a year. What—"

"And you sent them reports. Letters, pictures?"

"Both."

"What did you do when she ran away?"

"Maxine sent letters for awhile, making stuff up. They

wrote and asked for pictures. She kept 'forgetting' to send them."

"I need to ask you for one of those letters." My brain is spinning. Return address, probably not. Postmark, maybe. Fingerprints, if someone was careless.

He shakes his head. "Always the screwup," he says, and laughs as if something is heartbreakingly funny.

I want to slap him, make him focus. I grit my teeth and clench my fists.

He sobers as rapidly as he dissolved into laughter. "I'm afraid you're out of luck. I burned them. After they told me she was dead. I burned every single one."

TWENTY-TWO

I call Jake from the airport and fill him in.

"Genesis Project? Did you find it?" he asks.

"There is now a Vegan restaurant at the former clinic location. Preliminary Google search turned up nothing."

Jake sighs. "Figures. That would have been too easy. I'll go have a friendly little chat with Lysander."

"Any sign of Sophie?"

"No trace," he says. "We've been watching Ravenna's place. News of the day is that Jill's awake."

"How is she?"

"Bright-eyed and bushy tailed, like a kid after a nice long nap. They want to keep her one more day for observation and then discharge her."

I consider the ramifications of this. "So the discharge plan is back to the Manor then? Or are you still worried I might try to eliminate her?"

He sighs, heavily. "Protocol, Maureen. I never really thought—"

"Then you should have. Is she pressing charges?"

"She claims she tripped and fell. So, no. When can you be here?"

"Flight leaves in an hour."

He's quiet, calculating the length of flight and drive. "Hook up to in-flight wireless. I'll update you."

"Will do. Ask Lysander about letters. Aline's parents received requests for regular updates on her development."

IN-FLIGHT WIRELESS, as it turns out, is useful for more than just staying tuned for bulletins from Jake. The flight is a short hop, but I use my time well. Google yields nothing about Genesis, of course, not that I expected there would be a website advertising black market fertility experiments. But other easy access sites, such as online yearbooks, are fascinating. By the time my plane lands, I'm revved up and champing at the bit to get on with my investigation.

Unfortunately, the weather is not cooperative. The plane descends through snow swirling so thick I can't see the terminal from the runway. Much as I love my Jag, it's not exactly equipped for winter driving. The hundred miles of two-lane highway to Shadow Valley will be treacherous.

It doesn't help that even the short flight crammed into the middle seat is enough to set my leg on fire. Between that and the effort required to navigate my traveling companions and the ramp while dragging my carry-on behind me, my mood is black by the time I hit the main concourse.

When I run smack into a large man blocking my way, I start snarling before I even look up and see that it's Mac.

"Let me take that," he says, reaching for the handle of my bag.

"I can manage, thank you. What are you doing here?"

Mac's face remains impassive. "Jake sent me to give you a ride home. Said that despite your belief in your own super powers, the Jag was not the best tool for the job and he needs you intact and timely." He registers my expression and raises his hands. "Don't shoot the messenger."

Behind me somebody says, "Excuse me, but would you mind?" The words are polite. The tone is not.

The mood I'm in, it feels good to stay right where I am, annoying other passengers.

"And how am I supposed to get my car home?"

"We'll fetch it when the roads are clear. Besides, I have something you need to see."

"Again?"

"This is a matter of a certain hen house and a red fox." His face is unreadable, but there's a new grimness around his eyes.

I start moving, a little slower than necessary for the benefit of the impatient passengers behind me.

"Do tell me you didn't come on the Harley."

He laughs. "Nope. I'm acceptably equipped with an enclosed vehicle. You'll see."

We cross the skybridge into the parking garage. Mac's vehicle—a serviceable Jeep Cherokee, dented on the front fender, but equipped with studded tires, four-wheel drive, and a deer guard—is parked wonderfully close to the elevator. I make him stop by my Jag so I can recover a couple of critical items from glove box and trunk. I'm not going anywhere else unarmed.

Once we've cleared the parking lot, I start with the questions. "Who, what, when, where... All the details."

"There's been another murder."

"So that's why Jake really sent you."

"He doesn't know."

Even for me, this is a stretch. I'm willing to bend, break, and repurpose the rules, but some channels are there for a reason.

"Whatever you tell me, I'm going to fill him in." Either I trust Jake, or I don't, no more halfway.

"Your call." Mac hands cash to the parking attendant, then eases out of the garage. "On another note, while I was waiting for your flight, I swung by the address we had for Dason in Spokane."

"Find anything interesting?"

"A brand-new set of renters and a landlady who swears she never heard of him."

"Wonder how much they paid her? All right. Nothing to be found there. So we're going to look at a body, then?"

He shakes his head. "There is no body."

"Are you being cryptic on purpose? Or can you not help yourself?"

The car in front of us, going way too fast, fishtails and nearly slides across the centerline. Mac swears and feathers the brakes, just managing to avoid a collision. "Idiot."

He turns onto Sunset highway, avoiding the freeway and most of Division, but traffic is still slow, and conditions are even worse when we clear city limits .

Visibility is minimal, what with snow coming down from

the clouds and blowing around on the road, which needs to be plowed. I try to call Jake, but he doesn't answer. Neither does Matt. I leave them both messages, but I don't like the silence.

By the time Mac turns off the highway to an unmarked road just inside the Shadow Valley County line, my nerves feel like a whole classroom of middle schoolers is dragging fingernails across a chalkboard.

Here, under the shelter of forest on either side of what I assume is a road, since all I can see is a blank white flatness between trees, the snow floats down in leisurely flakes, no longer swirled by the wind. Mac slows to put the Jeep in four-wheel drive and speaks for the first time in an hour.

"Not too far from here. Up past Skeleton Lake."

"That sounds promising."

"Likely named after a dead deer or some such. It's a popular fishing hole."

"Not in this weather, one assumes."

"Are you kidding? This is perfect fishing weather." He laughs, relaxing a little, obviously back in his own element.

"So you're taking me to a murder scene, but there's no body."

"Yep."

"And the murderer?"

"Presumed long gone."

"Hmmm." The haze of fatigue that's been sucking me in for hours lifts with a burst of adrenaline. I take the opportunity to load my revolver. Lead in the first two chambers, then silver, then my own special amalgam. Extra rounds in a pouch. All in order.

I've also retrieved a knife and Phil's modified flashlight

from my car, so I'm set, unless we're off to see the Medusa, in which case I'm my own best weapon.

My thoughts are interrupted by a lurch and sway and some creative cursing from Mac as we turn off what I already think of as a track to an even narrower road. Branches scrape the sides of the Jeep. The tires spin and we lose traction climbing a hill, and I have visions of trying to drag my aching leg through the snow. Mac shifts into low gear and tries again, and this time the Jeep makes the climb. The trees open up into a small clearing, and he parks next to a pickup that has seen better days.

At the far edge of the clearing there is a cabin. The logs are weathered to silver gray. A plume of smoke rises from a stovepipe chimney, and firewood is stacked neatly on a covered porch. A narrow trail leads to a small lake about fifty feet farther on, with a dock so rickety I'd hesitate to set foot on it. All else is trees. Pine, fir, and cedar, mostly. A couple of naked vine maples.

Mac knocks at the cabin door, which is opened promptly by a gnome of a human that could be either male or female.

"Aunt Leo," Mac says, bending to kiss a cheek that is more wrinkles than not.

Aunt Leo wears a flannel shirt and patched blue jeans held up by a pair of strawberry red suspenders. She's under five feet tall, with wispy gray hair in a shoulder-length braid and a triangular face. A wall of heat, bearing the odor of wood smoke, wet wool, and bacon slams into me, overpowering, but not unpleasant.

She turns her head sideways to peer up at us out of bright black eyes. "Cormac. 'Bout time you showed up. Who is this, then?"

She does not invite us in, standing square in the middle of the doorway and looking maledictions at me.

"This is Maureen. She might be able to explain things. Can we come in?"

"No explaining needed, as far as I'm concerned, but suit yourselves." She steps aside to let us enter.

The interior of the cabin is small and dark, lit by only one light bulb, dangling from the low ceiling by a wire. A woodstove at the center is the source of the heat. A cot presses up against one wall. Wet wool socks hang on a dryer close to the fire. A pot simmers on an old green stove next to a low table holding a pitcher and wash basin.

There are only two wooden chairs. Leo drops into one of them with a little grunt and looks me over from head to toe.

"You trust her, then?" she asks Mac.

"I do."

"What did you tell her?"

"That there has been a murder. The rest is yours to tell. Or not."

"I wouldn't say a murder," she says, "Although certainly a mystery. Come here, then, you." I obey the summons, standing in front of her while she makes an assessment. Her eyes check me over from head to toe and then she actually snuffles like a dog, though how she can smell anything beyond the olfactory overload already going on in this cabin I can't imagine.

"This good-for-nothing told you there was a murder?"

"Yes."

"But not who, or how?"

"True."

"Give me your hand."

I give her my left, reserving my gun hand in case it's

needed. She holds it palm up, tracing the lines with one finger. I've got no patience with palm reading, any more than I do with crystal ball gazing. The future will be what it will be. Trying to avoid some coming catastrophe is probably what leads to the disaster in the first place. But I contain myself and let her do her thing.

"Patience and trust, not your virtues," she says, dropping my hand. "And yet here you are. You have a great desire to know something." Her eyes are impenetrable. "Many secrets you keep, many secrets you are after. All right then. I have a story to tell you. Sit."

Mac carries the other chair over for me and I lower myself into it, knowing that Leo's sharp eyes don't miss the stiffness or the involuntary hitch in my breath as the leg spasms. She would never allow such weakness as pain to slow her down, I'm certain, but she makes no comment and waits for me to settle before she begins talking.

"One week ago, my nephew Vince comes to stay. He doesn't tell me so, but when he shows up, I know he's got himself on the wrong side of the law again. Why else does he come to the woods to sleep on the floor beside the fire of an old woman? Not out of love, you can be sure, although I'm the one who raised him." She fishes a can of tobacco out of her pocket and inserts a pinch into her cheek.

"He doesn't tell and I don't ask. Soon enough he'll run back to the city and they'll catch him. Not the first time he's been locked up—won't be the last. Usually, he only hides out here for a day or two. This time, it's five days and counting. I'm getting antsy, worrying my food stores aren't going to last until the monthly shopping. I figure he's really got himself mixed up in something bad this time and wonder should I call the cops and have them come pick him up? I send him down to the pond to go fishing, get him out of my hair so I can make that phone call, maybe make himself useful while we're waiting for the law to come for him. And then, before I have a chance to even dial the phone, the spirit of the lake wakes up and takes the decision out of my hands."

She nods her head once, decidedly, as if she has made a clear and important point, and then rummages in a paper shopping bag beside her chair and comes up with a ball of yarn, knitting needles, and what looks like a sweater with arm holes in all the wrong places.

"Winter gets cold," she says, by way of explanation as the needles begin to click. The minutes tick by in time with her stitches and I open my mouth to ask a question, stopped by a slight gesture from Mac.

Leo appears to be focused on her knitting, but catches him in her peripheral vision and shakes her head. "Always with the questions and the signals. Like I don't see what you're up to. Both of you want to know more about the Lake Spirit, and Mac over there thinks I've gone bonkers."

"How many years you lived out here now?" Mac asks. "And no sightings of this mysterious Lake Spirit before now? Excuse me if I'm skeptical."

"Just because she never showed herself before doesn't mean she hasn't always been there." She glances up at me, her sharp eyes not missing a thing. "And you, inquisitive Miss that you are, want to know what she looked like. Well, I will tell you that. Young, she looked, despite the fact she must be timeless. Smooth and slim and shapely, she was. She rose up out of the water, naked as a baby from the womb, her skin all covered in symbols and patterns. Vince drops his fishing pole at sight of her, goggling. Should have got down on his knees to her—maybe she'd have spared him.

"But no, he whistles at her. Catcalls. That was Vince for you. She stands there in the shallows, her feet in the water, all come-hither eyes. And he goes to her. Makes a grab at her breasts and she lets him. Something about that finally clues him in and he starts screaming and stumbles backward, but by then she's got her arms around him, her mouth latched onto his. He's still struggling, but he can't scream anymore and she starts backing into the water. One step at a time, dragging him with her."

She stops there, going back to her knitting, a faint crease between her eyebrows.

"There's something more you don't want to say."

She finishes a row. Inspects her stitches. Makes the turn. Starts knitting again before she finally answers: "Even I think I'm a little bit crazy. From here it seemed to me like she wrapped him up inside her own body just before she pulled him under, like the two became one. They went down without a ripple. Two days ago, that was, and I've walked the perimeter of the lake twice over and never seen hide nor hair of a body. That's how I know it was the Lake Spirit because nothing else makes sense."

"And you have told no one? Not his parents, not anybody other than Mac?"

She makes a chuffing noise, like a steam kettle. "The boy's parents are either dead or as good as. Haven't heard from them since his mother dropped him on my porch twelve years ago. Nine years old he was, a rat-faced bag of bones, mistreated and neglected. Nothing I tried to do could set him right. If he ate a deer all by himself every day of the week, that one would never gain a pound. His heart was the same. He sucked up my love like milk from a bottle and never gave back a drop. I guess now he never will."

Her voice doesn't change, and she doesn't miss a stitch, but her eyes brighten and silent tears roll down her cheeks. I give her all the time I have to spare her right now—a moment for her grief.

"I'd like to show you a photograph." I open the manila envelope I've brought in with me. "Is this your nephew?"

I show her the mug shot of the rat-faced man who showed up on Dason's laptop.

"That's him, sure and certain, right down to his favorite outfit," she answers, cheeks and eyes already dry again. "How did you come by this?"

"Another mystery," I tell her. I pass it to Mac, who hasn't yet seen the five laptop photos of different people.

"And the Lake Spirit—did she look anything like this?" I hand Leo the picture of the World Tree Girl. She takes it from me and holds it close up to her eyes, poring over it as if it holds the secrets of the universe. To her, maybe it does.

"Explain." She levels a commanding stare at me.

"It's best I don't," I tell her, getting to my feet. "There are people who would kill you and dump you in the lake without thinking twice if they knew what you have seen. Mac will explain, later, when we've got things under control."

"Secrets mean more than my life just now," she says. "Tell me."

I hesitate, looking from one to the other, but the truth is that they're both already in up to their eyeballs.

"Her name is Aline. Aline Montgomery. She was recently

killed in Shadow Valley County. Mac here saw the body. She's actually from Seattle."

Leo looks at Mac, questioning, and he nods. "I found her, but then she vanished. Whatever the thing is that killed her, there are people who want to hush it up. I begin to see why."

"So it was a ghost that killed my Vince?"

"Not exactly. Listen, Leo—was there anything unusual about Vince's birth?"

Her fingers slow as she considers my question. "Perfectly normal, as far as I know. If you can call it normal for a woman to carry a baby and keep on shooting up methamphetamine. That boy was born addicted."

"You're sure?"

"About the normal birth? Five hours of labor is what she told me. He was just a bit of a thing, under five pounds. But what do you expect from a meth whore?"

"Leo," Mac says, very quietly, "Sherri was your daughter."

"And you want me to speak gently of the dead? Believe you me, that is as gentle as it's going to get. Her getting herself pregnant and pawning a damaged child off on me." The pace of the knitting accelerates, her toe tapping on the wooden floor.

The house of cards I've been assembling to link Aline with Vince and Sophie no longer makes sense. No scientist, collecting data about genetically altered DNA, would choose an unstable drug addict as a test subject. But it's the only angle I have, so I show her the rest of the pictures. "Have you ever seen any of these people?"

"I don't get out much. Town for supplies. That's about it."

"Vince didn't bring any of them here?"

She snorts. "If he had, I'd have run them off with a shotgun."

"Any idea where else he might have gone besides here?"

"Jail. Don't know of anything else."

I look up at Mac, hoping he has something else to offer, but I can tell from his face he's got nothing, and is busy trying to figure out where I'm going with my line of inquiry. Which is fair, since I haven't filled him in on the whole Genesis Project. Time to bring him into the loop.

"Does the name Genesis mean anything to you?"

"Like the Bible you mean?" Leo asks. "God created them male and female and said, go on and multiply. Bad idea, I've always thought. But then, he's God and I'm mortal, so what do I know?"

Dead ends wherever I turn. The Medusa—if my guess is right and it is the Medusa who killed both Aline and Vince—can't be just randomly wandering the countryside, killing on impulse. These have to be targeted victims. And if they are targeted, then there must be a common denominator. What do a teenage runaway with a love for water and a rat-faced jailbird have in common, if it isn't for the Genesis factor?

But I'm hitting a wall with Leo. Either she doesn't know anything, or she's not talking. If that's the case, maybe Mac can get to her later.

"Didn't picture you for a Biblical type," she says now, her expression as guarded as can be. "I don't take to missionaries, coming around, trying to convert folk. I saw the Lake Spirit, plain as plain, and I'd thank you not to be putting doubts in my head."

Leo shoves her knitting back into the bag and stands up, making it clear that I am no longer welcome.

I manage to get myself back to my feet, grateful for the solid wooden arms of the chair. "I'm not fond of missionaries myself.

You believe whatever you want and I won't try to change your mind," I tell her. "If you think of anything, would you let Mac know? Also—if something shows up at your door looking like Vince, don't let it in. In fact, I'd recommend a line of salt right across the doorsill as soon as we leave."

"Don't you worry none about me. I'll be just fine. You drive safe now, you hear?"

Mac gives her a quick hug. "Don't talk about this, Leo. To anybody else."

"Who would I tell? They'd lock me up, certain sure. That, or put me down on my knees and pray my memories away."

She precedes us to the door, light and spry as a child despite her years, and stands in the doorway watching us, despite the snow blowing in around her.

Leo's voice calls after us. "Just thought of a thing. Don't know if this will be any help to you, but the boy had a phone on him."

"Was it on him when he was killed?" I picture the phone at the bottom of the pond, another dead-end lead.

"No, no. Hang on. I've got it here." She disappears into the cabin and comes back a moment later with a smartphone. I make a move to come back into the warm to have a look, but she bars the door with her small body and waves me away. "You just keep that. Any friend he keeps in there isn't anybody I'll want to talk to. I had thoughts of throwing it into the lake behind him."

With that, the door closes, leaving me shivering on the porch. Mac is brushing snow off the Jeep. By the time he opens his door and gets in, accompanied by a flurry of snow, I'm engaged in trying to break the password Vince used to lock his screen.

TWENTY-THREE

"What the hell is Genesis?" Mac asks, navigating the treacherous driveway.

"Some kind of research project for enhancing fertility. Aline's and Sophie's parents participated."

"Vincent's mother was a poor candidate for fertility research."

"True. Which disrupts the theory I've been putting together."

"If it helps at all," Mac says, "Vince's father was married at the time Vince was born—and not to Vince's mother. As far as I know, he had no other children."

"Hmmm. So maybe he received fertility treatment and spilled his special seed on unsanctioned ground. Can't imagine his marriage ended well."

"You'd suppose right. Heard a family rumor that she tried to forgive him until she met the baby, and then it was all up. Vince was born mean and ugly." Mac gives me a side glance. "I suppose you're curious about my connection to someone like Leo."

"I'm more curious about your connection to someone like Vince."

"Spent as little time with him as possible. As for Leo—I'm not even sure, to tell you the truth. Some sort of third-cousin-twice-removed on my dad's side of the family. She's been a living legend since I was a little kid."

"What else do you know about Vince's dad? His history? What kind of guy he was?"

"Besides whether he was the kind of guy who gets a fertility treatment and then hires himself a hooker instead of going home to his wife? Honestly don't know. He didn't have much to do with Vince, and I only met him a couple of times."

"Do you know where he is now? Could we talk to him?"

"Dead. Ran off the road and into a tree about, oh, five years ago now. Vince was in jail at the time, so we can't blame him for that, at least."

I tap my fingers on the door. "House all packed up and sold, I suppose. No papers or documents anywhere. Next of kin?"

"Vince. The ex-wife was clean out of the picture by then. I heard it all got auctioned and went to yard sale. If you're looking for documents, those would be long gone."

"Where was this, though? His father's home?"

"You think that...thing will go there?"

"I don't know what it will do. If it does go there, I suspect it will look exactly like Vince. What I'm trying to figure out is why the Medusa targeted him and Aline. Why come all the way out here after Vince? How would it know Aline was way out there in the woods—and why was she out there?"

"Aunt Leo's about half crazy. Might be she's just imagining all of this."

"Crazy or not, she described Aline perfectly."

I don't like what I'm thinking. At all. The Medusa was already too damned dangerous and intelligent last time I encountered it. If it can take on the appearance of its victims and maybe some of their special attributes, that's like adding nuclear capabilities to an already lethal weapon.

By the time Mac drops me off in the Manor parking lot, I'm frustrated and on edge. Whatever the password is on Vince's phone, it wasn't something obvious like his birthday. I'm going to have to hook it up to my computer and run a password hacking program.

Insult to injury, something is off-kilter at the Manor. Before I can get my door open, Cathy barrels out of the building, face like a thundercloud. She should still be on shift, but she's in her car with the engine running before I'm able to intercept her.

"Need help?" Mac asks.

"No, I've got this. Thanks for the ride." He lifts my bag out of the back seat for me anyway, salutes, and heads on out.

When I knock on Cathy's window, she doesn't turn her head, just sits with both hands gripping the steering wheel, hair screening her face. I can guess by the set of her shoulders that she's crying and I knock harder.

Without looking at me, she finally presses the button to lower the window.

"What's happened?"

At last she looks up at me. I'm right about the tears, but it's outrage that lies behind them, not grief.

"Like you don't know. Nice job, pawning your dirty work off on somebody else."

"Cathy—"

But she rolls up the window and starts backing up, pissed enough to run over me if I get in her way. I let her go and walk into the Manor, where the chaos continues.

A little clump of residents stands in the hallway across from the office, voices raised, hands gesticulating energetically. I'm about to ask, when my question is answered for me.

Jill bounces out of the office. She's dressed in nursing scrubs, albeit they're the high-end variety in slightly shimmery fabric, black with pink trim. Her hair is twisted up in a bun that would be more appropriate to a benefit dinner than a retirement home, and her makeup job is no doubt meant to be prim and professional, but still looks exotic and Parisian.

She makes shooing motions at the seniors with her hands. "I've told you, this is not an appropriate place for you to loiter. Please go to the games room or—"

All four of them turn to face her—oldster solidarity. Dan, articulate as always, acts as spokesperson. "Young woman, we've earned the right to loiter by reason of years of hard time. You, on the other hand, have not earned the right to wear that uniform."

I'm almost sorry to break up the party. The old timers seem to thrive on the occasional shake-up. But I don't have time to observe the little drama play out. There are serious issues afoot. So I barrel into the fray.

"What's going on? What did you do to Cathy? Shouldn't you be tucked up in bed, having chills or seizures or something?"

"I fired her," Jill says. "And—"

"You did what?"

She raises her voice, enunciating each word as though I'm deaf. "I. Let. Her. Go. She was incompetent and—"

"And you're supposed to be in the hospital until tomorrow. Did the doctor change his mind?"

Her eyes shift away from me.

"Right. You left against medical advice."

"I feel fine."

"You're brain damaged. And you waltz in here and dare to start firing staff and giving orders?" All my half-formed intentions of tolerating her for Phil's sake have evaporated in the instant of actual contact.

Jill makes her voice overly reasonable. "I have a number of issues I want to address with you. How about you come into the office?" The emphasis on office has a possessive quality. From out here in the hall I see evidence that she's been rearranging things in there. Clearly, I need to see what she's been up to, but since that's where she wants me to go, I carry on down the hall.

The residents clear a path to let me through.

I hear Jill's ridiculous heels tapping along behind me. "Maureen, come back here. I need to talk to you."

"Hey, Maureen. Glad you're back." Dan gives a little military salute as I pass him, which warms my heart in a completely unexpected fashion. I grin at him and he grins back and actually winks.

There's another clump of gossipers farther down the hall-way, and an entire gathering in the games room that has taken on the look of a formal meeting. Ginny presides at the front of the room, with Julia as her second.

"I make a motion..."

"Seconded..."

I stand at the doorway and catch Ginny's eye. She doesn't

smile, but she nods at me and glares at Jill, so I leave her to whatever it is she's trying to stir up and keep walking. "God, Jill, you can't have been here for more than a couple of hours. How did you manage to get them so riled up?" I can't help a faint tinge of admiration.

"You abandoned them," she says, behind my left shoulder, "without leadership. So I took over."

"They aren't children, Jill. They are fully functional adults. Cathy has my cell phone number and knew to contact me with any questions or concerns."

"My attorney says—"

"I don't give a damn what your attorney says." I punch the buttons for the elevator and turn on her, looking her up and down from the top of her shiny head to the soles of her French-heeled shoes. "You certainly made a rapid recovery."

"Look, I've changed my mind. I'm not trying to take the Manor away from you, I just want to share it. We can run it together!"

She follows me into the elevator. "That Sophronia girl—"

"Is missing. Thanks to you."

My anger has reached a danger level and it's all I can do to keep my hands off all of my weapons. The elevator stops. Jill holds the door, but makes no move to exit. "Come on, Maureen. Let me help you run the Manor and I won't tell anybody."

"Tell them what, exactly?"

"About the secret passage. About Sophronia's special talents."

"Blackmail, now? Oh, Phil would be so proud." I tug my suitcase across the uneven gap into the hallway. "No teeth in that, Jillian. G has probably already spread the word. It's expecting a lot for a kid to keep her mouth shut."

Jill follows me down the hallway. I insert keys in all five locks, wishing there was only one instead of many.

"You went through my things," Jill accuses. "Don't try to deny it."

I turn in my open door and smile at her. Her cat-with-the-cream expression fades to something close to fear and I speak to her, very gently. "My dear, don't push me too far. I hold my hand because of Phil, but as you say—he's dead now. I suggest that you watch your step." And with that, I close my door and shut her out.

MY FIRST TASK, immediately after hooking Vince's phone up to my code-breaking software, is to call Cathy and cajole her into coming back to work. It costs me half an hour and a dollar an hour raise, plus the promise that Jill will not be permitted to speak to her. I left Morpheus in Matt's care, so at least he's not demanding attention, but Anubis winds around my ankles, meowing as if he's actually missed me.

Cats being what they are, I figure he's likely wanting food, even though I left him giant bowls of food and water. The litter box does need attention, and I've just finished scooping when Jake arrives.

"What's kicked over the Manor anthill?" he asks, bolting the door behind him. "Residents scurrying all over hell and gone."

"Jill."

"I thought she was at the hospital."

"You and me both. Walked right out, she tells me. How did it go with Lysander?"

"You were right," Jake says. "Lysander's been getting letters from Genesis all along. Swears he didn't ever answer a single one of them, and shredded them all on arrival. None of their business, and all that."

He drops a file folder on the table. "It's pretty clear both Sophie and the World Tree Girl have some sort of connection to this Genesis Project. I found this in Sophie's room."

"Lysander let you search? Without a warrant?"

"I phrased it as a missing person problem, adding in my suspicions that it might be time to look more closely into the disappearance of his wife."

He opens the file and withdraws a sheet of paper. "Found this under the mattress."

It's a letter. On the top left there's a Genesis logo. Out of the **G** grows a wide branching tree. Serpentine vines wind through the rest of the letters, and the **i** is dotted by a tiny red apple. There's a PO Box for the return address.

Dear Miss Alexander,

I have attempted repeatedly to make contact with you through your father, but he has not responded. As you are now of legal age, I am writing directly to you.

Not knowing what your parents may have told you of the circumstances of your birth, I will first explain.

Your mother being unable to conceive and carry a child to term, your parents presented at the Genesis Project for fertility treatment. Both agreed to a new experimental technology designed to enhance Lysander's sperm. Happily, the experiment was a success. Your mother conceived, and you were born healthy.

One of the conditions of participation in this study was that the research team would continue to monitor your growth and development. Your mother complied with this until that time when she stopped responding. Your father has ignored all requests for contact or information.

As you are now legally an adult, it falls to you to meet with me to complete the survey and allow me to gather data about your health. As there could be unintended and unanticipated side effects to the experimental technology, it is essential to your health that you present for a physical examination.

I must impress upon you the need for caution if you are sexually active. Procreation could be dangerous for you. Please contact me at once, using the phone number listed below.

If you do not comply voluntarily, I'm afraid that we must come to find you.

Sincerely,

Eve

I read and re-read, my body temperature dropping as if another spirit storm is brewing.

"So, she could just as easily have responded to this, as to the text message from Ravenna."

He nods. "I ran the letter by Lysander. He swears the logo is the same. Before you ask, I called the number and got an auto-recorded computer-generated voice: 'Leave your name and number. We'll get back to you.' Not helpful. I also had a trace put on the number and there's no record. Probably a disposable cell."

"This logo—"

"I saw that too. Remarkably similar to the World Tree Girl's tattoos. Matt is on stakeout at Ravenna's."

Unease twists in my belly. "I tried to call him. He's not answering."

"Cell service is spotty down there. Always has been. Now. What are you not telling me?"

I fill him in on Vince, watching my words wind him up like one of those old-time toys from my childhood. By the time I'm done, he's up and pacing, or trying to, given the boxes still making an obstacle course out of my suite.

"So, we have a death, or a disappearance, and our coroner and you have already interviewed the reporting party and scoped out the scene of the crime—"

"Possible scene of the crime. Leo might just be crazy."

"—without word one to law enforcement! Just because there may be paranormal elements involved doesn't mean you can cut out the law altogether!"

I let him rant, comparing my photos of Aline's tattoos with the Genesis logo. The concept of the World Tree is not uncommon, but the similarities are notable. One of the branches growing out of Aline's world tree even bears a tiny red apple.

Jake has apparently asked a question and is waiting for an answer.

"What?"

"You're not even listening to me."

"You were being predictable. Would you rather I don't tell you anything in the future? I thought not. If you're unhappy with Mac, tell him so. Not me. What I might offer as something useful would be a look at the place Vince's father lived. Maybe tracking down his ex-wife and seeing what she knows."

"I thought you said Vince is dead. What would I be looking for?"

I'm reluctant to give voice to the dull fear lurking in the back of my brain, as if speaking it will give it more power.

Which is just stupid. Still, it seems like speaking the thought turns it from conjecture into fact. I start with a question.

"When the Medusa killed Alice, before it disintegrated, what did it look like to you?"

He stares at me and then his gaze flicks upward, remembering. "I thought, at the time, that it looked like a child, almost as if it went to Alice for comfort."

"And after that? After Alice was consumed?"

He sees it. His jaw tightens; the color drains from his face. "It looked like Alice."

"Right. And what Leo saw come up out of the lake looked like Aline."

Jake sinks into the chair across from me. "I don't think I like what you're implying."

"I don't like it, either. But if it can take on the shape of whatever it has killed, then we need to be on the lookout for something that looks like Vince."

He sits there for a long moment, thinking.

"I'll put out an APB. But—if they find a thing that looks like Vince and try to arrest it—"

"Say he's armed and dangerous. Wearing an explosive device. Make something up."

"I know how you feel about the FBI and the special unit— but would this be something they should know? Should we have Matt pass it on?"

I weigh the pros and cons of this decision for a long moment. "You're thinking in order to protect civilians?"

"That's what I'm thinking."

"I don't know, Jake. Six of one, half a dozen of another. You might save a cop, but we might lose Sophie."

He absorbs this, then shrugs. "Moot point just now since

we can't reach Matt. I'll put out the search bulletin and then hang out at Vince's daddy's old house myself. Anything else?"

"Other than Jill back at the Manor and creating havoc? Nothing." It's not a lie, exactly. Just a shading of the truth.

Five minutes after he's out the door, though, the password for Vince's phone cracks. I'm in. There are a couple of text messages that look like petty drug deals. One from a girl showing him a graphic image of what he stands to gain should he come to her house and bring her a little hit for free.

And then a text message that says: *Come to me. You need to check in.*

This looks very much like the text on Sophie's phone. I try to get into Vince's head from the little I know of him, then send a reply: **They r watching me. Hard 2 get away.**

The response is immediate: *Make sure you're not followed.*

Very interesting. I type in: **River rode. Pull out btwn park and Radio Springs. 1 hr.**

Again, an immediate reply: *Just come to the usual place.*

My way or high way. Gotta go. Somebody's watching.

I wait, but nothing follows this last message. Hopefully that means my quarry is already en route to the rendezvous site. If I'm going to get there on time, I need to move. When Jake's cell rings once and goes directly to voicemail, I'm relieved. I can move faster alone. Besides, I'm spoiling for a fight and his scruples would only get in the way.

TWENTY-FOUR

The only problem with flying solo is that my wheels are still in Spokane. Fortunately, I have the keys to Jill's rental. It's not much better in snow than my Jag, and I very nearly slide off the road and into the ditch when I hit the first corner. After that I drive at a snail's pace, and when I finally arrive at my destination, there's already a vehicle parked in the turnout. It's an SUV. Black. I memorize the license plate, texting it to Jake from Vince's phone. If I vanish, at least maybe he'll know where to start looking.

My windows are tinted, letting me observe my quarry without being seen

As the door of the SUV opens, I draw my gun and loosen my knife, ready for anything. The woman who emerges and walks over to my van is the last person in town I'd been expecting.

"Open up, dear," she says, kindly, knocking on the window. "It's about time we had a chat."

I don't see evidence of a weapon and roll down my window.

"Mrs. Hemsley. Can I call you Eve? Does the good pastor know where you are?"

She startles when she sees that it's me, not Vince, but recovers rapidly. "Do tell me what this is all about," she says. "I haven't much time. There's choir practice tonight, and I need to take a casserole to the Flinders. And poor Geneva is drinking herself into oblivion over Dason's death."

"The length of this conversation depends entirely on you," I tell her.

"But that doesn't make any sense." She smiles sweetly, as if I'm seven and she's bent on demonstrating that she's the boss of me. I'm not here for a pissing match, so I try to morph into a softer woman, using Ed's new squeeze as a model. I soften my voice, relax my muscles into the seat, allow myself to shiver a little.

"You might as well get in. It's warmer in here."

"Oh, I don't think—"

"I do think. Walk around to the passenger door, and get in. Don't try anything."

She presses a hand to her chest and tries to look faint. "Why are you pointing that gun at me? I don't understand."

"Just get in."

Apparently my tone convinces her I mean business. A last moment of hesitation, and she complies. "What is this all about then?" she asks, as she settles into the passenger seat.

"Seems like I should be asking the questions. Why did you want to meet with Vince?"

"That poor boy, on the path to destruction. I've been trying to bring him to salvation. He's been recalcitrant."

"I can imagine. What do you know about Sophronia?"

"What about her?"

"She's missing."

"Did she finally run away from Lysander?" Eve Hemsley asks. "Can't say that I blame her. Poor, motherless girl. It's not true what they say about her, you know."

"And what do they say?"

"Oh, you know. That people die when she is around them, that she's some sort of witch. She has a compassionate heart and is drawn to comfort those who are ill. When you spend a lot of time with the sick and old, the probability of death is highly increased, of course."

"And you believe she's not a witch?"

Eve laughs, indulgently. "Now you're playing with me. Surely you don't believe in fairy tales."

I don't believe in fairy tales, which is what she's giving me. But the witches of my acquaintance don't have sharp noses and warts, and they don't have magical powers in the way the world thinks of magic. They are powerful women, and some delve into the dark.

I jump to another question. "So, why would Vince want to meet you in an out-of-the-way place like this, I wonder?"

"Why would *you* want to meet me here?" she counters. "I can't imagine what you want to talk about."

"I want to talk about Vince."

"What's he done now?"

"He's dead."

My words hit her like a sack of bricks. She sinks back against the seat, as if under a heavy weight. "How? When?" Her eyes gravitate to my revolver. "Did you kill him?"

That, I don't answer. The more off balance she is at the

moment, the better. "Tell me why you wanted to talk to him, so much that you'd agree to meet him here."

"As I said. Prayer. Repentance." She's recovered quickly, her eyes alert and watchful. "It's my job as a pastor's wife."

"And are you always so mysterious with your former parishioners? 'Meet me at the usual place, it's time to check in'? Hardly sounds like prayer meeting."

Her hand strays for the door handle and I press the gun barrel into her ribs and offer up a friendly smile. "We're not done."

"What do you want?"

"The truth. I want to find Sophronia."

She's good. Her features and her hands give away nothing. But her breathing quickens, just enough.

"Where's Jake?" she asks. "If Vince is dead and you're looking for Sophronia, why isn't the sheriff talking to me?"

"Oh, I'm quite sure the two of you will have a conversation soon enough. He's busy. We're working together on this." I show her my FBI card and wait for all the implications to register.

"How well did you know Alice Sorenson?" I ask.

"Who?" She visibly startles for the first time, eyes widening. Recovery is quick, but it's too late.

"Ten years you've lived in Shadow Valley, is that about right? Came to town just before Sophronia's mother vanished. Did she disappear before or after your arrival?"

She stiffens. "If you are insinuating—"

"I haven't begun to insinuate. What was your relationship with Alice Sorenson?"

"I don't know what you are talking about."

I hand her the letter that Jake found in Sophie's room.

"Look familiar? Signed Eve, which is interesting. I looked up your marriage license—documents are so delightfully easy to find. Your given name before you became Evelyn Hemsley was Eve Hightower. Eve went to Harvard Medical School. And she collaborated with Alice Sorenson on a thesis involving the manipulation of DNA. Alice went on to work for the government in paranormal research. Eve got an MD and specialized as an obstetrician. I'm guessing that Genesis was a collaborative project between the two of you. I don't have proof yet, but give me a few days, I'll find it. Meanwhile, your test cases are dying like flies and I'd like to stop that."

"You have no proof of any of this."

"Other than the text messages between your phone and Vince's, and the fact that the cell number given on certain letters with the Genesis letterhead happens to be the same number he's been texting."

For a long time she's quiet, thinking through her options, staring out the window. Finally, she draws a deep breath.

"The letter to the girl was a mistake. I see that now. But her father refused to answer his, or respond to phone inquiries. I tried to observe from a distance, but the subject wasn't interested in religion—"

"Sophronia. She has a name. She's not Research Subject Number Four, or whatever they named her."

"Number One-Oh-Three," she says, correcting me.

"God."

"Most of them died as juveniles. Birth defects. Cellular incompatibilities. It was—unpleasant—for the parents."

"And a barrel of laughs for the kids, I'm sure."

"Test subjects," she says. "Not kids. Especially those ones."

"Are you sure about that? What if they had souls?"

"They didn't," she says, her voice clear with conviction. "Trust me. These newer models, like Sophronia, have done quite well. Vince is older, and marginal—"

"And dead. Did you kill him?"

"No! Of course not. It was important to get data. So few of the test subjects had survived into adolescence. But I couldn't risk speaking with the subjects directly."

"So you sent a letter to Sophronia—who has all the emotions of any teenage girl, by the way, and maybe a few extra besides—explaining that her parents are not her parents and she's a freak of nature you're trying to study. Is that about it?"

"When you express it that way, you make me sound heartless. It's all in the interest of Science and—"

"So when the research is done, you're killing them off? Is that it?" I hand her a picture of Aline, dead on the autopsy table. "She was a child."

"No! No, killing them was never the plan. At least not now. Not yet. We want to keep them alive long enough to reproduce, to see if the genetic material—"

I hold up my hand to stop her. "Just be quiet. Now. Or I'll forget that I have reasons for you to be alive and do a mercy killing. Tell me where to find the others."

"I don't know."

"How about this person? And this?" I show her the photographs of the pictures from Dason's laptop.

Her hand wanders toward her purse and I reach over and take it from her, searching through it with my free hand, cursing women and their habits the whole time. The gun is buried beneath a packet of tissues, a little bag of cough drops, lipstick, travel size hairspray, a wallet, several sets of keys, and a phone.

"A gun really isn't very useful if you have to mine for it," I tell her, fishing it out. "Do you have a permit?"

"Of course. Pastor Hemsley suggested I carry that. For self-defense, you know, but I could never shoot somebody, for heaven's sake."

"Do you really call him that all the time? He calls you Mrs., you call him Pastor?"

"Of course," she says, with dignity. "He's a man of God."

"And you're a mad scientist and a spy. Poor man. Does he know? Is he in on it, too?"

"No. No, of course not."

"Do you have any other weapons?" A quick pat down turns up nothing further, but I don't trust her for a minute. "Look. You don't want to give away the location of your few surviving test subjects. I get that. What I want to know, besides Sophronia's whereabouts, is who is killing these people. This girl was only sixteen. A little Siren in her genetic makeup, I believe. And Vince—"

Her breath catches, an involuntary reaction.

"What was his thing?"

"He was a—mistake."

"Let me guess. His father took what you billed as a fertility treatment and spilled his altered sperm on a drug-addicted prostitute. I'm surprised you allowed the child to live, at all."

She doesn't confirm my guess, but doesn't deny it, either. I want to put my hands on her shoulders and shake her until her teeth rattle in her head. "After he was born, you couldn't use your position as the pastor's wife to help him to something better than a crazy old aunt who can barely take care of herself? Food, shelter, I don't know—an education?"

"Observation only," she says, primly. "Any intervention

changes the results. Even observation changes the results, like physics particles under the microscope."

"Didn't look like observation only at Dason's house. That looked a lot like damage control. Did you kill him yourself?"

"I was at the house for Geneva. I'm the pastor's wife. It's expected that I comfort the grieving, that I be there in their time of trouble. Geneva doesn't have anybody. I did not kill Dason."

"So you're part of the cleanup team."

I try to picture her killing Dason, blood spattering onto her perfect hair, the bandbox clothing.

She makes a clucking sound, like a broody hen sitting on a hatch of eggs, and shakes her head so that her earrings jingle, very gently. "Tragic. I can't imagine why somebody would kill any of them."

"Because somebody knows. Either that, or because the researcher has decided it's time to stop the project and destroy the evidence."

"Oh, surely not! All that time and effort gone to waste?"

"Not to mention pain and suffering and loss of human life. You meant to say that, right?"

I've shaken her. Her hands grip each other in her lap, neatly folded Sunday school hands, except that the fingers are blotchy and the knuckles white.

"How many are in the project? This person? This one?" I go through the photos again, sorting them into piles on the seat between us. The two dead on one side, the others, including Sophronia, on the other. "I want to warn them. Give them a chance."

She hesitates.

"You're not in this alone. You have to confer with your team. Is that it? How about I confer for you. Give me names."

You'd think I'd suggested holding a satanic ritual in the church from the look she gives me. "Oh, I couldn't. That information is highly confidential."

"Fine. Maybe your husband knows. Is he home now, or out visiting somebody on their sickbed?" I pick up my phone and start pressing numbers. Her hand snakes out and clutches my wrist.

"Don't. Please."

Finally—a real emotion in her voice. Her eyes are direct now, holding my gaze, pleading. "Don't tell him. He's a good man. Don't hurt him."

Whatever the good pastor's wife does, he'll be blamed for it. If she's murdered somebody, he'll have to resign. And if he actually loves her, a possibility that has just now occurred to me, the rest of this will all be difficult as well.

Unless he's in it, of course.

"I told you the truth," Eve insists. "I don't know who is killing them."

"How about you let me figure that out? It's what I do. Honestly, I'm surprised you haven't been targeted and shot."

"I've had a good cover."

"And you can stay in cover, if you help me now. Understand?"

It takes her a minute, but the threat to her own safety finally cracks her. "The lipstick," she says.

I go back to her purse and fish out a tube marked "Autumn Rust." I handle it carefully. James Bond isn't just for movies, and a lipstick gun is a possibility. Or a bomb, with instructions to activate for self-destruction if discovered.

I open the lipstick carefully, not wanting to trigger anything, but it's not a weapon.

It's not lipstick either. The tube is empty, and inside I find a rolled slip of paper with a name and a cell phone number. I stare at it for a long moment, pieces coming together in my head.

"You won't tell the pastor?" she pleads.

"Not now. Not yet. If Sophie dies..."

I let the threat hang there, between us, knowing she'll take it seriously. The girl is her responsibility.

"What do you want me to do if Sophie calls me?"

"Let me know. You can reach me at the Manor."

Chances are good that if Sophie calls, she'll get me, since I'm keeping Eve's phone. I also pocket the lipstick, and on second thought, sling the whole purse over my shoulder. The damn thing weighs a ton.

"You can't have that," Eve protests.

"Time for you to go now. Get out. Go home to your husband and don't do anything stupid, like trying to leave town. We'll be watching you."

She opens the door and a cold wind swirls in. "Can I at least have my ID? Driver's license? Credit cards?"

"Have fun at choir practice."

I stay where I am, waiting until her SUV drives away. Then I call Jake and take another stab at reaching Matt. It's time all three of us catch up.

TWENTY-FIVE

A little preparation always pays for itself, and I'm willing to gamble that the extra time we've taken for set up will be worth it.

In usual circumstances, Jake is more patient than I am. In this case, his emotions are getting the better of him and it takes all my willpower to induce him to go along with my plan instead of sending out deputies to round up suspects for formal questioning at the station.

Now that the trap is set and there's nothing to do but wait, he paces the lab, one end to the other. "Do you think she'll show?"

"I can't imagine her turning down my invitation."

"What exactly did you tell her?"

"Very little. Ready, Matt?"

"Ten-4, Red Fox." He grins at me, and I grin back.

We've laid our little trap down in the lab. Phil's ashes are once again contained in the plastic potato salad container from the kitchen. We've scrubbed Jill's bloodstains off the floor. Apart from a few flickers of the electricity there's been no sign of spirit activity, and I can't help wondering what's going on with that.

The minutes tick by and even I'm feeling a little restless by the time we hear footsteps in the hall.

We hear her, before we can see her. "Maureen, I don't see why you are dragging me all the way down here. I've got things to do, and I'd think at your age you'd prefer somewhere more comfortable."

Jill stops short in the doorway when she sees that Jake is also here, but Matt is already behind her and relieving her of her purse and the knife at her hip.

Too easy. I'm sure she's got other weapons on her.

"Jake, can you hook her up?"

He shakes his head, stepping into his assigned role. "Insufficient cause. Nothing to be done in a legal capacity."

"Guess it's up to us then."

She tries to back out through the door, but Matt is quicker, slamming it shut and leaning against it. Her eyes take in the three of us, and it's Jake she appeals to.

"Are you going to let them do this—whatever it is?"

"They just want to talk, is all," he says. "I'd suggest you sit down and listen."

"Maureen said she had a message for me from my father."

"Trust me, he's here," I tell her. "Sit down. You have some explaining to do."

A muscle twitches in her right cheek. There's a tiny mascara smear under her left eye.

"You are paranoid and pathetic. What exactly do you

suspect me of?" She turns her gaze on Jake, trying to look piti-
ful. "Surely you can see that Maureen has lost it."

"Do sit down," Matt says, pulling out a chair for her. "We'd
be terribly distressed if you had another episode."

Jake's hand moves to his belt, resting just beside his service
weapon.

Jill's gaze flicks to Jake, then Matt, then back again.

I can see the calculation behind her eyes, and the moment
she realizes she can't fight all three of us. She sighs like a long-
suffering martyr and sinks into the chair, which Matt politely
shoves in close to the table.

"What is this all about?" she asks in a martyred tone.

"I've done a little research. Amazing what the Internet will
tell you. First, you lived with Phil. For about five years, I
believe. Kind of a far cry from the sob story you told me about
spending all that time in Juvie, but never mind the lie. I'm
pretty sure he taught you an interesting set of skills."

She doesn't answer. I sit down across from her. "What
happened with you and Sophronia?"

"The witch girl? You were there. She tried to kill me.
Sucked away half of my soul."

"You sure about that?" Matt asks. He's going to need to
learn to master his expressions if he's going to be in this game
for long; he has grief and anger written all over his face. As it is,
he's behind her, but she can still hear it in his voice.

I lean forward on my elbows. "What I can't figure out is
why she would want to hurt you. Never harmed a fly before
you showed up."

Jill snorts, a sound incongruent with her Parisian persona.
"To listen to the nurses at the hospital, she kills people all the

time. Gets away with it because she picks on the weak and the sick."

"And how did you come to be having this conversation with the nurses?" Jake growls.

All wide-eyed innocence, she responds, "They asked how I was injured. I had to tell them, *n'est-ce pas?*"

"How about the truth? What I saw was you engaged in a tug-of-war with your father's ashes. You won. You fell. You hit your head. Congratulations and here you go." I shove the plastic container toward her. She shoves it away.

"One wonders," Matt puts in, "why you want those ashes so badly in the first place."

"Because Phil is my father! My God, do none of you have any emotions?" She manufactures tears from somewhere, and a little quaver comes into her voice.

Behind her, Matt puts his hands to either side of her neck as if he'd like to strangle her. Jake's expression stays neutral. "You still haven't told us why Sophie would want to kill you."

"Does an Angel of Death need a reason? I could only speculate."

"Speculate away," he says.

"I thought I wasn't under arrest."

"You're not."

I open the container of ashes and push them toward her again. A faint, rotting smell drifts out, thanks to the contaminating blood. Jill turns up her nose and tries to shove her chair away from the table. With Matt solidly behind her, she's trapped.

"What, you don't want them now?"

"Let me go." For the first time, there's a taint of fear in her voice.

"When we're done with our chat." Jake pulls out the chair beside me, turns it, and straddles it so he can lean on the back. "Maybe," he adds.

"This is outrageous! I will call the cops just as soon—"

"Jake is the cops. And we're onto you. Tears, smiles, flirtation—none of those things are going to have any effect on us. Except maybe Matt. Can you withstand her charms, Matt?"

He rolls his eyes. "I think I can just manage."

"There you have it. So, tell us about Sophie."

"I can't tell you what I don't know! I had never seen her in my life before I met her in your suite. She threw a fit about me having Phil's ashes. You saw that, Maureen. You can't deny she's totally unreasonable about cremation."

"I'm a little unreasonable, too."

Jill adjusts herself in the chair and puts on her school-teacher voice: "My father's quick cremation had nothing to do with me. Your coroner, I believe. Whatever game you all are playing down here, it's time to end it."

"What about this? It came in that night, just before her little incident with you."

I hand her Sophie's phone, open to the text message.

She stares at the message just a beat too long. "I don't know any Ravenna. Probably one of her school friends or something, playing a joke, because who would ever name their kid that?" She slides the phone across the table and then, for no reason I can see, leaps half out of her chair, stopped by Matt's hands pressing her back.

"Ouch!" She swivels around to glare at him. "You pinched me. How dare you?"

Matt lifts his eyebrows. I shrug. Nothing touched her, at

least nothing visible. Matt's hands were where I could see them the entire time.

A cool breeze drifts across the table and flutters the papers there. So the spirits are here, after all. I'm surprised to find myself grateful, as though they are backup rather than threat.

Opening the laptop and switching on the projector, I flash the Genesis logo up on the wall. We've situated Jill where she can't help but stare at it, while we monitor her reactions.

"What is that supposed to be?"

I move on to an image of the letter sent to Sophie. While she reads, or pretends to read, I say, "I think you know perfectly well what Genesis is. In fact, I'm thinking you're part of it. Maybe you're the one who gave this letter to Sophronia in the first place."

"Your imagination is getting carried away with you again. Maybe you need to be evaluated. Dementia can begin quite young, I'm told."

"How about we call the number?"

"Be my guest."

Jake dials the number. My pocket starts ringing. "Shall I answer that?"

I pick up. "Hey Jake, is that you?"

He salutes with his phone and hangs up.

"I'm confused," Jill says.

"Join the club. There's confusion enough for everybody." I set the phone on the table. "This phone belongs to Pastor Hemsley's wife, a woman named Evelyn, and maybe known to you as Eve."

"Somebody connected to a project called Genesis," Jake growls.

Jill sighs. "Listen. Just because Phil was my father—genetically—it doesn't make me a spy or a scientist. I'm a publicist. Looks like an organization that would be at odds with publicity, don't you think?"

"Interesting thing about that," Jake says. "Because what likely would be useful is a molecular biology degree. A doctorate, no less. With a thesis on genetic manipulation. I don't suppose you know anybody with those qualifications?"

Before she can make up her mind whether to lie or tell the truth, I flash the 1998 Harvard class roster with her name and course of study.

"You'd have been a brand-new grad. Eager to prove yourself. So maybe the right people came along and offered you a job directly related to your area of expertise, and maybe you got involved because it was precisely the sort of thing your father was against."

"Would have, could have, maybe," she says, dismissively. "You're putting together random elements to make up a theoretical story. Great for a mystery novel, maybe, but real life doesn't work that way."

"Humor me." I bring up the pics of Aline. "If somebody was involved in such a project, say, and then the subjects started dying?"

"And?" she asks, moving her hands to her lap.

"I think you're involved."

"I think you're delusional."

"We have the letters from Genesis, you see. And we've talked to parents. So we know that two research subjects are dead and one is missing."

"A serial killer?" she asks.

"We were thinking it might be an inside job."

"That's ridiculous. If I were involved in a research project of some kind, *were* being the key word, I'd hardly kill off the subjects. That would be wasteful."

"Unless the study was over, of course," Jake says, conversationally. "And if the research study was illegal, or forbidden by the FBI or Homeland Security or some other watchdog, then destroying all the research notes, so to speak, might be in order."

"Or maybe somebody was onto you," I add. "Somebody like Phil, say, who wouldn't stop justice for his daughter, something he's proven in the past."

"You are all crazy. I have listened. Now I'm leaving."

"Not just yet. There's also a matter of this."

I flash a picture of the badly bound little book I'd found at Ravenna's. *Mythology and Genetics*. "This is a fascinating little research study, written by Hemsley et al. Do I need to tell you who et al. is?"

"So I contributed to a research paper written by a couple of boring old women. What does that have to do with anything?" Jill sounds petulant, and I know we've rattled her.

I nod at Matt, and he sets her purse on the table.

"Let's look at this, shall we? It must have gone to the hospital with you—a fortunate coincidence for you—since it wasn't in your room and I couldn't search it."

"I knew you went through my stuff!"

"Naturally." I rummage through the bag. "What have we here?"

She fidgets while I lay out the inventory: a switchblade, the kind that is illegal in the US; makeup; perfume; a wallet with credit cards and driving licenses from a number of US states, all with different identities; a passport; three rings of keys; a lock pick set; a tiny handgun.

"Tell us about your connection with Alice Sorenson and Eve Hemsley," Jake rumbles.

"I collaborated with them on their stupid little book. That's it."

"Are you sure?"

"Positive. Can I go now?"

"Oh, not quite yet. I think Alice is—was—the brains behind the Genesis Project," I say. "I don't think it was your father's death that brought you home at all. It was hers."

"I loved my father. I wanted to bury him beside my mother where he belongs. I was stupid enough to think maybe I could get close to you. That's the only reason I'm here, and I know absolutely nothing about any of this." She gestures at the wall where Aline's image floats suspended.

"Whether you loved your father is not the question. It's what you can tell us about the research subjects."

"I don't know what you're talking about."

"You'd be smart to cooperate." There's no way she can miss the warning in Jake's voice.

I start projecting the pictures that showed up on Dason's computer. "Do you know this person? How about this one?"

"I do not know any of these people. This is about keeping me from inheriting the Manor, isn't it? I thought—maybe—Phil would be a bond between us, but you don't want any more to do with me than you did when I was sixteen. Fine. You win." She starts stuffing her belongings back into her purse. "I'll go to a hotel immediately."

Matt, at a signal from me, steps away from her chair and out of the room, leaving the door open behind him.

"Spare me the guilt trip." I hold up the lipstick I took from Eve. "Do you know what this is?"

Her nose wrinkles. "Certainly not. That's a ghastly brand no right thinking woman would buy."

"I took it from Eve Hemsley."

"She always did have terrible taste."

"Here's the thing. It doesn't even have lipstick in it." I open the tube and pull out the phone number.

Jill stiffens.

I pat her shoulder. "I know. Keeping a number on you, even in a secret compartment, is a bad idea. But when it's a foreign number, one for a phone in France, maybe it's difficult to remember."

"So Eve had my number. Circumstantial evidence."

"Unfortunately true. Well, thanks for visiting with us," Jake says. "Sorry for the inconvenience."

"Don't forget to take Phil." I push the plastic container toward her.

She narrows her eyes at me, as if she'll be able to see my motives more clearly through a smaller visual field, then glances at Jake. She doesn't move toward the open door. "Can I have my weapons?"

"Don't look at me." Jake raises his hands in a gesture of innocence. "I have no legal right to search your purse. No warrant. No cause beyond a lot of circumstantial evidence."

She pushes herself slowly to her feet. Takes a step toward the door. Pauses. Looks back over her shoulder at me.

"If I was going to shoot you, Jill, it wouldn't be in the back. Not my way. I don't know about Jake, I've never seen him shoot anybody. Ever shoot anybody in the back, Jake?"

"Never yet."

Jill flips her hair over her shoulder. "I don't know what kind of game you're playing, Maureen, but I've had enough. I'll book my return ticket immediately." With that parting shot, she picks up the potato salad container and taps out of the room and toward the stairs. We give her a good head start and then follow.

By the time we get to the stairs, I'm cursing my bad leg for the millionth time this day. There's no way I can keep up, and I'm going to miss the fun. I motion to Jake to go on ahead. He gives me a salute and leaves me to focus on dragging myself up the stairs. About halfway up, a cold draft hits me from behind, powerful enough that I feel like I'm going to have lift off.

Either the spirits are following Phil, as Sophie said, or they have an interest in the outcome of the proceedings. Which leads me to think maybe I should have brought Val to join the show. Oh well. Best laid plans and all of that.

There will be time enough to lay the ghosts to rest when we've found Sophie and stopped the Medusa.

"I KNEW IT." Jill's voice, loud and furious, drifts down the staircase to me.

A male voice answers her, muffled and low.

Jill is not to be soothed. "I can't believe you fell for it! What did you tell them?"

Anubis comes thudding down the stairs toward me, ears laid back, looking like all the demons of hell are after him. He hits the incoming spirits and turns tail, with a howl, thundering back the way he came and vanishing through the doorway.

By the time I make it up through the closet and into my suite, he's nowhere in sight.

The action is taking place in my living room. Jill sits in my armchair, Jake looming over her in a way that implies she'd better stay there.

Matt stands behind Ravenna, who looks genuinely old and confused. "How was I to know? Matt here told me you'd decided to bring him and his team in, for the good of the study. Aline is dead, you know. So is Vince. Sophronia is missing. They are just children after all."

"They lied to you and you fell for it. How could you be so stupid?" Jill starts to rise from the chair. Jake puts a hand on her shoulder and she settles back, obviously seething.

Ravenna clucks and shakes her head. "Well now. I did want to help the children. But really..." She pauses, shivering. "Is there a door open? A window? It's chilly in here."

"Ravenna confessed her role in all this on our drive over," Matt says, filling me in. "She helps keep tabs on the kids. Lends a sympathetic ear. Shows up in their community around the time their abilities might start to surface. Makes contact over a little tattoo art."

"Are you ready to tell us where Sophronia is?" Jake demands. "We'd like her not to end up dead."

Or killing somebody else, I add silently. Of the two risks—Sophie dead or Sophie altered into a killing machine—I'm not entirely sure which would be the worst.

"I did not send that text," Ravenna insists. "I'm sorry. I have nothing to gain from lying to you at this point, do I? I did not send it."

"Where are the rest of the subjects? Tell us where to find them. Maybe we can save them. And your research."

Jill's jaw tenses. Her nostrils flare. "Don't you answer that."

That, for me, is as good as a confession.

Ravenna folds her hands into her lap. "Do I require an attorney?"

"This is not an official investigation," Jake says. "Although, it will be if it turns out Jill has been having these people murdered."

"Why would I do that? It makes no sense."

"To protect your research," I respond. "What does the hybrid DNA look like, anyway? I've been curious."

Her lips clamp down hard, holding back words that are threatening to burst out of her control.

"The FBI is involved," Matt says. "Coming along behind you, sweeping up the evidence. They may or may not kill your subjects, but you can bet they'll be taking the opportunity to look at your research."

I sink down onto a packing box, trying to ease my leg, which feels like the bones are on fire. "The way I figure it works is this: Ravenna, the listening ear, lures the subject out with offers of comfort and advice. Jill is waiting with the Medusa, who gets a soul feast as a reward."

Ravenna's eyes widen with horror, but I don't count that. We already know what a good actor she is.

Jill laughs. "And you think I killed Sophronia. Are we forgetting that I was in the hospital? Unconscious?"

"Probably faking," Jake says, in a voice thick with a menace that sends a little chill down my own spine, even though it's directed elsewhere. "I want to find Sophronia. I don't care what genetic code she's got. I've known her since she was a baby. She's a good kid. Tell me where she is."

"How should I know that?"

"Where are the rest of them?"

Jill clamps her lips together. "I don't have to talk to you."

It's the same defiant looks she wore the day she stabbed me.

"Oh my God," I say, as the light dawns. "You hate Phil. You're out for revenge."

"He called the cops on me. Chose one of his women over his own daughter." Her chest heaves with emotion, and her eyes burn with fury.

"You did try to kill me." I keep my own voice dry and even, despite a sickness in the pit of my stomach.

"He was my *father*." Her voice breaks on the word, and she goes with the emotion, crumpling into a damsel in distress and glancing up at the men from eyes luminous with unshed tears.

Jake has his sympathy look, the one where his eyes soften and his lower lip folds up a little over the upper. He's an old hand, though, he won't let emotions change anything. It's Matt I worry about. His Greek god face looks more chiseled than ever.

"You father's death made a convenient excuse," he says. "But that's not why you're here. It was Dr. Sorenson's death that brought you. That and the Manor. What's here that you want so desperately? I can't imagine you want to run this place any more than Maureen does. And yet here you are, contesting the will. Running off employees. Meanwhile, all your research subjects are being knocked off, one at a time."

"I think you're working with the Medusa," Jake says. "It fits."

"Aline died while I was still in France!" Jill protests. "Don't you try to pin this on me."

"How do you know when she died? I don't think we've mentioned that. Have we mentioned that, Maureen?"

"Pretty sure I haven't."

"That's it," Jill says. "Not another word until I have an attorney."

"Fair enough. You have the right to remain silent."

While Jake is spieling off Jill's rights and calling a deputy to come take her to jail, Ravenna draws me aside. "The cards are bad," she tells me. "Very bad. Sophronia, the one who is missing—there is great peril connected to her. Something much bigger than her death. I want to help."

"I don't suppose the cards tell you anything about where to find her?"

She shakes her head. "No. It's just the same cards over and over. I don't know the addresses of the test subjects, or even their names. I just go where I'm sent."

"Don't look at me," Jill says. "Attorney. That's the only word I'm saying."

Matt walks over to join us and takes one of Ravenna's hands in his. She startles, as if an electric current has passed between them, her eyes widening.

"Do you have the cards with you?" Matt asks her. "Show us again."

"All right." She sits down at the table and reaches for her handbag.

Matt takes it from her and smiles at her, charming and helpful. "Let me get those out for you."

He digs in her purse and then sets the card deck out on the table. Ravenna shuffles and cuts the deck, then lays out a spread. I recognize the cards, every last one of them. As she says, they are the same.

Matt sits down across from her, lining them up in a neat row. Death, the Tower, all the others. Last, his fingers touch the card showing the dead coming out of their graves. "I wonder..."

Both Ravenna and I look at him, waiting. "What if it denotes a place, rather than an event or a person? And the black robed woman on this card could be Sophie. We know what the Tower card is. But this graveyard..."

At his words, the hair on the back of my neck stands up. The temperature in the room drops dramatically so that we all shiver. My radio comes on, tuned just between stations to an ear-bleeding blend of static, rock, and sports commentary. I turn it off and unplug it, but the thing won't be silenced. The electric lights flare brighter and brighter until all the bulbs pop.

When a tap comes at the door, I assume at first it's spirit activity, but the tapping increases in volume and I finally go to open it. Val stands there. Her eyes are closed, and she moves into the room like a sleepwalker, seamlessly avoiding the collision course of packing boxes and random furniture. She goes straight to the potato salad container that holds Phil's ashes.

She picks this up and shoves it against my belly until I grab it, then exchanges her hold on it for a grip on one of my hands. She tugs, and I let her lead me as far as the door. Then I resist.

"I need to go to the graveyard."

She doesn't register that she's heard me. Her grip tightens on my hand. She pulls again, harder.

"You should see what she wants," Matt says.

"I don't know that we have time for side trips."

There is no way this little woman's hands can be so strong. The fingers clamped around mine are bone on bone. There will be bruises. An invisible breeze whirls around me. Again she pulls at me, and this time there's no resisting. Wherever the strength that moves her is coming from, it's beyond my power to refuse her.

"I'll go to the graveyard," Matt says. "Come as soon as you

can."

"Don't go alone," I call over my shoulder from the hallway. "You and Jake go together. Take the salt sprayer and the silver."

"No way are you going off by yourself," Jake protests, right behind me. "This is crazy. She's possessed."

"I think the spirits are trying to help."

"You think." He snorts. "Can't remember a single story of a possessed person doing anything good. This is why there are exorcisms."

"I don't think she's possessed exactly. She's a medium."

Val doesn't take me far before we stop. Right across the hallway, in fact, to the suite last occupied by Jill. She opens the door with her free hand and leads me in, Jake trailing behind.

"Jake," I say, turning my head to fix him with the most commanding glare I can manage. "Something is going down in the graveyard. And you need to see that Jill makes it to the jail."

"Something is going down right here," he says, stubborn as a mule. "I'm not leaving you alone with a whole bunch of ghosts."

We're shouting at each other to be heard over the increasing volume of the radio, now echoing down the hallway. I'm pretty sure the residents on the floors below can hear it. They'll be coming up to investigate.

"And what exactly are you going to do about it if the spirits do turn on me?" I ask him.

"Watch," he says. "At least I'll know whether to expect you back or not. Jill's cuffed. The deputy can handle her."

He closes and locks the door behind us. I have to admit I'm glad he's with me. My hand is starting to ache. The ashes are heavy in my other arm.

"You can let go now," I tell Val, or whoever it is that's

driving her. "We're coming."

She releases her grip and I flex my fingers, grateful nothing is broken, then shift my grip on Phil and check my weapons. I've still got Phil's flashlight at my belt. My gun. Not the salt sprayer, which is an oversight I'm going to regret.

Val opens the door to the closet, and then the secret door at the back and sets foot on the stairway.

"There's nothing down there," I argue, following anyway. "Storage. Hot water room. Spiders. Mice." Even as I say it, memory rocks me hard. My first encounter with the Medusa happened down in this basement. Blood drops disappearing before my eyes. That invisible clammy cold invading my hand, my arm, moving toward my heart.

What was she doing down here?

My heart remembers, too, picking up its pace and thudding against my ribs. When we hit the basement, it's all as I remember it: Storage area off to the right. The closed door to the room holding the boiler. The wall down the middle of the room, blocking us off from the secret passage that leads to the lab. The ordinary, public access staircase leading up into the Manor.

I stop at the center of the room, where the Medusa attacked me before, braced for another assault. Nothing happens, other than Jake bumping into me from behind and putting a steadying hand on my shoulder. He's warm and human and I'm grateful for his company.

"What now?" I ask.

The ghosts are not forthcoming. All is quiet. Val opens her eyes and blinks at me, then Jake. Unlike a sleepwalker, though, she doesn't look bewildered or frightened.

"Through a glass darkly," she says, her dark eyes intent on

my face.

Which is not helpful.

"White rabbit." She smacks the back of her hand against her forehead in frustration. "Through the Looking Glass. Backward. Outland. Australia."

There's no mirror in here. No windows. Nothing that is remotely connected to her words. I know that the words she can access are connected to an image in her brain, but it's like a demented game of charades to figure out what she's trying to say.

Jake, not having explored this part of the basement before, checks behind the closed door, walks around the room, shining a flashlight into corners. He sneezes at the dust he creates. "There's nothing down here," he says.

Val, muttering to herself, drifts over to the storage units. They are nothing more than wire cages, each padlocked for security and labeled with a number. Some are empty. A few are stuffed with boxes and unused furniture.

She stops in front of number four, puts her fingers through the wire, and rattles the door, turning to look at me. "White rabbit," she says again. "Down the rabbit hole."

"Are we late?" Jake asks. "Like the white rabbit in *Alice*...?"

Alice.

As soon as the name leaves his lips, it hangs in the air between us. Charged. Crackling with electricity. The two bare electric bulbs hanging from the ceiling brighten and dim. Jake and I exchange a look.

Alice Sorenson is dead, killed by her own brain child. But what she set in motion is not so easily stopped.

Val nods, rattling the wire again. "Down the rabbit hole," she repeats.

A padlock isn't much of a barrier. My lock pick set is in my pocket, as usual, and I make short work of it. As soon as the gate is open, Val makes a beeline to the back corner and puts her hands on a large box.

"You want that open?" I ask, following.

She shakes her head, vigorously, and tugs on the box. "I'll move it," Jake says, and she steps aside while he shifts things around until he can pull the heavy box back toward the entrance.

"Damn." Directly beneath where the box was sitting, a thin line marks out a trapdoor, just wide enough for an average human. This was here all the time, and I never knew. No time now to berate myself for not exploring this space further. Jake is already tugging on a small brass handle. The trapdoor opens, revealing a metal ladder descending into a dark shaft.

I shine my light down, but there's not much to be seen. The ladder ends about a hundred feet down. Maybe it's a dead end. Maybe there's another passageway at the bottom. Clearly, we're going to need to explore.

"Val, thank you. It's going to be dangerous from here, so you should go on back up."

I'm wasting my breath. Already she's started down. The ladder worries me. I've only got one hand to work with, since I'm still packing Phil's ashes. And my leg is not going to approve of this journey.

"Here," Jake says, "give me that." He doesn't insult me by suggesting that maybe I'm not up to this, or by offering to go first and catch me if I fall, so I hand over Phil.

Jake pulls a small LED flashlight out of his pocket and holds it between his teeth. Following his lead, I do likewise, and then lower myself into the passage.

TWENTY-SIX

The air smells stale and I wonder how long it's been since anybody else has been down here. I can't imagine Alice descending this ladder. She was an evil genius right to the end, but she was old and a little frail. Maybe there's a bomb shelter down below, given that the Manor began its existence as a Cold War military installation.

By the time I'm halfway down, I've stopped thinking. It requires all my focus just to force my rebellious leg into obedience and keep moving, one rung after another. My jaw aches from holding the flashlight. If Val can do it, so can I, is what I'm telling myself. She's eighty. She's had a stroke.

Still, by the time I step off the last rung onto solid ground, my legs are trembling like a California fault line and despite the constant spirit chill, my shirt is stuck to my back with sweat. There is nothing to say YOU'VE ARRIVED, though. No welcome mat, no visitor's information sign.

Jake and I shine our lights around and illuminate a small

room about twelve feet square. Bunk beds are built into three of the walls. The mattresses are missing. There's graffiti carved into the concrete over some of them.

JASPER WAS HERE.

USA FOREVER.

The fourth wall holds an elevator.

If I hate the elevator in the Manor, this one takes danger to a whole new level. The cage is, literally, a cage, fashioned out of green, industrial mesh. An electrical box on the wall next to it has only three buttons: Down, Up, and Alarm.

"Wonder if it still works," Jake says, pushing the Down button. The elevator groans, and begins a descent.

I turn my back on him and shine my light into every corner, hoping to see the outlines of a door, any door.

"Must be running off the Manor electricity," he says. "Hasn't been serviced in a while, I imagine, but it appears to still be working."

He's got that tone in his voice that men get around machinery, the same one a lot of women reserve for babies.

"Have you lost your mind?" I ask him. "That thing looks like every mining cage in every underground horror movie ever made."

"Good thing we're not in a horror movie."

The cables stop thrumming and Jake pushes the Up button, bringing the cage crawling back toward us.

"There has got to be another way to wherever we're going," I say to Val.

She shrugs. "Had we but world enough and time."

There are worse ways to die, I'm sure, than plummeting to your death in a steel mesh cage. Dying by inches in a nursing home is number one with a bullet. I step off solid ground and into the elevator.

Jake manually closes the door and locks it. There's a second button box inside, and Val pushes the Down button. The cage creaks into movement. As we descend, our flashlights flicker over red-lettered signs posted in the shaft.

1700

1680

1660

"Elevation markers," Jake says. "The Manor sits at 1700 feet, more or less."

This is one deep elevator shaft. If the thing crashes, we're dead. That I can deal with. If it stops working and it sticks halfway down, we're screwed. The likelihood that somebody will come looking for us is minimal.

1620 flashes past.

"Shadow Valley elevation," Jake says, which means this shaft was sunk all the way through the flank of Shadow Mountain and down past the town.

"One hell of a bomb shelter," I say, as we continue to descend.

We lurch to a stop with a grinding and creaking that makes me think my fear has been realized. But when I shine my light through the elevator door, I see another square room like the one above. Jake opens the doors and we step out.

This room has no bunk beds, but there are metal lockers along the wall. All have padlocks in place. While I'm curious to know what's stashed inside, Val has already moved beyond the circle of my flashlight. So I breathe, put a hand on the wall to steady myself, and set out after her.

"Hope you ate your Wheaties this morning," Jake says. "What do you think we've discovered, here?"

"Catacombs?"

He snorts. "Unlikely, though that would explain the throng of spirits."

I shine my flashlight upward, revealing electrical wiring and burnt-out fluorescent bulbs. "Only other thing I can think of is a Cold War fallout shelter, but why would there be anything this extensive under a town the size of Shadow Valley?"

By now my bad leg aches from hip to toe with a sort of deep throbbing that reminds me of the drums in Tolkien's mines of Moria. The muscles are barely responding to movement commands. My toe catches on a crack in the cement and Jake's hand immediately steadies me.

"Maybe there was a missile silo. Those things are more common than anybody thinks."

"In that case, shouldn't there have been a blast door? Because that trapdoor isn't going to cut it."

We walk for a long time in silence, both of us pursuing our own thoughts. Every few hundred feet new tunnels intersect to right and left. We walk for a good long stretch this time, before the narrow passage opens into another room.

This one is bigger, with room enough to set up cots for a couple of hundred people. Whether or not that was its original purpose, somebody is living here now. A sleeping bag and pillow are laid out neatly against one wall. There's a camp stove and a mess kit with a small pot and frying pan. A stack of books. Bottles of water. Some backpacker meals of the just-add-boiling water variety.

I sink down on the sleeping bag, not because my leg is

about to give out, but in order to get a closer look at the books. A couple of novels. A Bible. A well-worn copy of *The Book of the Dead*.

"Sophronia," I breathe.

"Will Robinson," Val adds.

"What?"

"Danger, Will Robinson," Jake echoes, in a robotic voice.

Val nods. "Will Robinson."

"What is the danger?" I run my hand over the sleeping bag. "Is Sophronia in danger? Or is she the danger?"

"White rabbit," Val says, moving off into the stretch of corridor so far unexplored.

Jake offers a hand up and I take it, not quite able to bite back the groan elicited by a sharp flare of pain.

"I'm not stupid enough to ask if you're okay," he says, not letting go of my hand. We traverse the room together, his strength steadying my body's tendency to lurch and stumble.

"I have a question for you," I tell him, after the pain settles into a steady state and I get a handle on it.

He doesn't answer, just raises his eyebrows in response.

"If Sophie has really gone over to the dark side..."

"Can I do what needs to be done?"His face and voice are grim. "Do you think it will come to that?"

"She was worried about it. After Betty. She talked about the power, the lure, of wanting a soul. Her fear that she was a monster because she'd killed."

"And then she got the letters. What do you think really happened with Jill?"

I shiver. Maybe it's my sweat-soaked shirt. Maybe not.

"Could have been something to do with that spirit storm. If she's sensitive to that kind of energy. It was intense. Or..."

I leave the thought hanging. Jake is strong, but the question that lies unspoken between us is a hard one. I play through the scenario over and over in my mind, and every time I pause before the killing shot.

Serves me right for getting attached. I know better. If I had to shoot Jake, for example, I would definitely hesitate. Even Matt, who I have so many reasons to mistrust, would be damnably difficult to kill.

After about an hour of brisk walking, Val takes a right turn into one of the intersecting tunnels. Almost immediately, we reach a spiral staircase, set into a stairwell. It curves upward about twenty feet where it stops abruptly at a ceiling.

I grasp Val's arm to hold her back as she sets her foot on the first step. "Wait. Where do you think we are?"

Jake whistles tunelessly, looking up, thinking. "The elevator shaft dropped us to just below Shadow Valley, if those elevation marks are right. And we've walked, I'd say, a couple of miles. My guess is we're under the town by now, or at least pretty darn close. If this was meant to be some sort of bomb shelter, it could make sense to be able to get back and forth to town."

My leg certainly feels like we've walked a couple of miles. I am not excited about climbing these stairs. "If that's a blast door, we're not getting through."

"Might just be a regular trapdoor," Jake whispers, although there's nobody in sight. The beam of his flashlight plays on the stairs and the ceiling above. "I'll go first and get it open."

He's right, of course. I'm only halfway up by the time he discovers a latch system, which he unhooks. When he pushes up against the ceiling, a trapdoor raises easily. Val is right behind him and he gives her a hand up, then reaches down for me.

By unspoken agreement, we all move like cat burglars, keeping low and not making any noise. Jake has switched off his light and the only illumination comes from the moon shining through a stained glass window above. We've surfaced into a rectangle big enough to hold a church choir, with wooden pews polished and dark with age.

It smells like every museum I've ever been in, a combination of furniture polish, mothballs, and old carpet. Shadow Valley doesn't have any museums, but it does have an old church that pretty nearly qualifies as a cathedral. It's a tourist stop, and people actually make a detour through town to come in and make ooohing and aaahing noises over the stained glass windows, the carved woodwork on the pews, and the statue of the Virgin Mary that presides over a set of battery-operated candles.

Good thing I'm not Catholic, because I'd have been cast out as a heretic long ago. I've never understood the attraction to the Holy Mother. Sure, she suffered. Horribly, I'm sure, but she's not the first mother ever to lose a child, nor will she be the last. Just because her son was divine, I figure it doesn't give her exclusive rights on the whole martyred saintliness business. Judas's mother probably suffered more, if you think about it.

We belly crawl forward to the railing, another insult to add to the grievances my body is going to hold against me for this day's work. My guesses are right. This is a choir loft. Most of the sanctuary is in shadow. There is just enough light to pick out some of the colors in the stained glass windows and to show me a solitary figure kneeling in front of the candles.

In the old days the candles were at least real. Now you

push a button and an LED comes on to signify your prayer for the dead. The kneeling worshipper was apparently not satisfied with the change, and has brought a candle of her own. Its flame shines clear and bright amidst the artificial light of the others. The girl's head is bowed, her face hidden, but I know that fall of long black hair.

We've found Sophronia.

Before I can decide whether to call out or to make a stealthy journey down the stairs and try to surprise her, she is joined by a man.

He stops in front of the statue and tilts his head upward, as if studying the Virgin's face and trying to arrive at a decision.

"If I ask her for a soul, would she give me one?" he asks, after a moment of silence.

The man's face is now directly in the light and I recognize it. Vince.

TWENTY-SEVEN

Vince is dead and has no business showing up in a church. Unless he isn't dead. Or unless this isn't Vince.

"What was that about a soul?" Sophronia asks.

"Joking," he says. There's something too flat about his voice, as if it never got the memo about intonation and pitch. "What about you? You were—praying. For what?"

He looks more rat than vampire, but he could still have the blood sucker gene. God only knows what creature they crossed him with. Despite all my fears about Sophie's life choices, I want her to morph into full-blown superhuman mode right now. Instead, she's never looked more human—lost and vulnerable, and heartbreakingly young.

"You didn't sound like you were joking," Sophronia says.

"Maybe I wasn't. It's not the sort of thing you can say to the average person."

"I'm not average."

A cold wind swirls around me, tugging at my hair, my

clothing, then sweeps down into the sanctuary. Val's eyes roll back in her head, and a soft moan escapes between parted lips.

"Damn," Jake curses. "Showtime. You ready?"

Ready or not, something needs to happen. We're too far away and we're too ill-equipped.

"Don't go down there," I try to tell him, but he's already moving, leaving me and Val to our own devices.

Blue light envelops Sophie. She brushes at it, as if it were a cloud of gnats or mosquitoes. "For the love of Thoth, can't you leave me alone? Even in a church?"

"Number One-Oh-Three," Vince says, in that same flat tone. "Parents, Lysander and Jaz. Experimental element, Soul Sucker." His face alight with curiosity, he takes another step toward her. His nostrils flare, and he makes a snuffling sound. "You've killed."

"Who are you?" she asks, recoiling, either from him or the cloud of spirits, or both. "What do you want?"

"Answers." He stretches out his arm and plunges it into the blue light, tipping his head back in ecstasy. "And souls. They are beautiful. So incredibly beautiful. How do they taste? Tell me."

"I don't eat them." Her voice is thin and strained.

"How can you resist? So many here for the taking."

"That's not how it works," she insists. "They cross. I help them cross. I don't—"

"But you've killed." He presses closer to her, both hands immersed in the blue light. "I know you have."

Blue fire coils around both of his arms. His body jolts, as though he's been struck by electricity. He laughs out loud.

Jake is close now, just behind Sophie. She's intent on the spirits and Vince and hasn't seen him yet. I have no idea what

Jake thinks he's going to do to intervene. I try to pick up my pace, but the ladder climbing has taken its toll and I feel like I'm trying to run in quicksand with a broken leg.

"What is going on here?" a new voice demands.

Between keeping my attention on Sophie and Vince and the difficulty of navigating the stairs, I've totally missed the entrance of yet another player.

Eve pauses halfway up the aisle. Her eyes dart from Sophie to Jake, to me on the stairs, and then focus on Vince.

"Oh, good," he says, turning away from Sophronia and taking a step toward Eve. "Our answers have arrived."

Even in the dim light I see her face change color. She staggers and almost falls. One hand goes to her heart, the other clutches a pew for support.

"I thought you were dead."

"Would you like that?"

"No, of course not." Her voice trembles at first, but she recovers, steadies. "This is fascinating. Are you the one who asked to meet me here? I thought it was Sophronia."

"I had a message to be here," Sophie says. "Why?"

"Answers. We deserve them, don't you think?" His face looks put together wrong. He walks as if his body is unfamiliar, a small hesitation with every step. I'd like to believe he's handicapped, maybe he's always walked this way, the modified DNA rerouting brain signals and causing motion malfunction, but that's the fairy-tale version. Barring that, I'd like to believe he's just come back from the dead. Much as I hate zombies, what we're facing here is much more sinister.

Vince lurches toward Eve.

"I want a soul," he demands. "Give me one."

"A soul is just a concept," Eve says. "Nobody knows for sure if there even is such a thing—"

"I know what a soul is. Alice had a soul. The Siren girl had one, too, but hers was different. And this girl—Number Three-Hundred-and-One—has more souls at her command than she knows what to do with."

His right cheek droops like melting wax, slipping down off the cheekbone. His lips seal together and lose their color, leaving a flat expanse of skin between nose and chin.

"Are you our maker then?" Sophronia's voice is clear and cold. "Responsible for what we are?"

"I had only a small part in it," Despite her obvious fear, there's a note of pride in Eve's voice.

Vince reaches up to his cheek, misses, and corrects his aim. A crease burrows into his forehead, followed by another. Wrinkles appear under his eyes. His hair lengthens, whitens.

"Stop it," he mutters. "Stop it, stop it, stop it. We are Vince now."

The hair shortens itself into a buzz cut, turns dark. The skin smoothes again into Vince's features, but the arms raised to press both hands against his temples are feminine, smooth, tattooed in full sleeves of twining branches.

Damn, but I need the salt sprayer and the silver. The only weapon I have is Phil's flashlight and it's nothing more than a deterrent.

"The girl who died, the one with the World Tree tattoos," Sophie says. "She was like me."

"Yes and no," Eve answers. "Part of one of the most exciting scientific breakthroughs of all times, yes. As you are. But her abilities were different."

"And you killed her." Bathed in the blue spirit light, her eyes glowing green, Sophronia doesn't look human anymore.

Eve is either braver than I expected, or else she doesn't yet understand what is happening here. Instead of running screaming for the nearest exit, she stops retreating and answers, with dignity: "I had nothing to do with her death. Why would I waste valuable research in that way?"

"Give me my soul," Vince threatens, "or maybe I will take yours."

"This is not Oz," Eve says, facing him, "and I am not a wizard. Either you have a soul, or you don't. You can't get one by stealing it."

A hole forms where his lips should be and a tongue pokes out, flickering, snakelike. Lips re-form and the tongue licks them, then retreats into the mouth. "Can't keep it, maybe. Can take it from you. And taste it. Taste souls and memories, yes."

"Memories have no taste," Eve objects.

The Vince thing advances toward her. She backs up again, stumbles, bumps into the end of the pew. Her gaze travels to me. "Help me," she says. "I did not create them. That was Alice."

Vince's face is melting again. This time he uses both hands to remold it. "A technicality. A lie. You had conversations. You had talks. You and mother. Plans. Give me a soul."

"I can't. There is no technology, no science—" She screams as his hands melt into her flesh. His lips cover hers, silencing her.

"Go ahead and shoot," I shout at Jake. I figure if we kill Eve with the bullet, at least it will be a more merciful death. He won't, though, he can't. He's a cop through and through, and she's a civilian. I don't have this limitation.

Phil's ashes are in my way and I drop them. The container hits the floor with a thud and the lid comes off. This is a story that's getting old by now, but I've got no time to worry about that.

Laser in one hand, gun in the other, I open fire. Bullets rip through the Medusa, rocking its borrowed shape, and for a moment hope rises that the thing has become human enough to die.

It's a short-lived hope. All the blood belongs to Eve.

So bullets won't work, but the laser is another story. Where I shine it, ragged holes appear in the creature's pseudo skin, black around the edges. The Medusa is one monstrous, bulging body now, part Vince, part Eve, but it still has two heads.

Under the assault of my weapons, the heads break apart. One mouth screams, human, terrified and in agony, the other lets out an inhuman wail.

I take a step closer, the laser blasting another hole into the Medusa's gelatinous flesh. Smoke curls up around the edges. The creature retreats, losing its human shape, dissolving into a shapeless mass. Jake approaches from the other side, ready to plug a round directly into its body.

And then Phil's flashlight dies.

I hit the On switch again. Nothing.

I shake it in desperation. Still nothing.

Maybe the battery has gone dead. Maybe something's wrong with the laser gizmo or a bulb has burnt out or the spirit interference is to blame. Whatever the reason, it only takes a few seconds for the Medusa to realize I've got nothing.

Over the sound of my own ragged breathing I watch the thing re-form. It loses human shape while it heals—a giant, oozing amoeba, with human bone and hair visible at the center. The bullet and laser holes fill in and knit together. Where my silver bullets struck, the jelly bulges and quivers, ejecting the silver out onto the floor, where they roll out of reach beneath one of the pews.

"What do I do?" Jake asks, holding his ground.

"All the bullets you've got. All at once." I reload, wishing for the first time that I carried something with a magazine. "Ready?"

I shift around to stand beside him, to make sure we don't die by friendly fire. But before either of us can pull the trigger, Sophronia sets herself between us and the thing.

"Sophronia!"

"You can't kill it," she says. "Not like that."

At her words, the Medusa reshapes itself around Eve's bones. It doesn't get the face quite right, but in the dim light it can pass for human.

"She's right," the Medusa says, in a close facsimile of Eve's voice. "I can't be killed."

"Sophie. Move out of the way." Jake sounds desperate. His weapon is steady, though. It's a comfort to have him solid and strong beside me.

Sophronia ignores him. "Why are you killing us?" she asks the Medusa.

"Souls," the thing wails. "Bodies. I called the Siren to the special place, but still her soul escaped me."

"But you took her memories," I say. "Her abilities."

"They aren't really yours," Sophie whispers. "Borrowed. Stolen."

"Mine. If I can use them, they are mine."

Which is when I finally see what is at risk, what I ought to have seen a long time ago. My blood runs cold. For the first time in my life, my hand holding the gun begins to tremble.

"Sophronia, please step away. It means you no good."

"Why borrow one soul when I can taste them all?" The lascivious smile on Eve's face is so incongruous it makes me twitch. I've been edging around to the side, trying to get to a point where I can get a clean shot without hitting anybody else.

Just when I'm there, my finger tightening on the trigger, Sophronia steps in front of me again. "No."

"Sophie, in case you've missed it, this is the Medusa."

"It's a monster," she says, agreeing with me. "So am I. Will you kill me, too, for doing what I was made to do?"

"What you were made to do is help spirits cross into the otherworld."

"And look how well I've succeeded."

I can see how the number of spirits filling the church just now wouldn't make her feel like a great success as a soul guide.

Sophronia turns from me back to the Medusa. "Do I have a soul?" she asks. "I was wondering. You asked me what I was praying for when you came in. I never said. Forgiveness. For the souls I have taken or misled."

The spirits raise a fuss at this. Wind swirls through the sanctuary. The lights flare and dim. Sophronia throws her hands up in the air in frustration. "If you want something, say it, for once. Or just get out of here and leave me alone."

"We're not going anywhere," a voice says from the stairs.

I damn near drop my gun. It's Phil's voice. Spinning around, I expect to see some revenant from the dead, but it's only Val, her body outlined in blue light. She descends the rest of the stairs and stands with her feet in Phil's ashes while his voice continues to come out of her mouth.

"We're not going anywhere until that thing is dead."

"How do we kill it?" I ask. "Have you figured that out?"

And then everything happens at once.

"Shut up!" The Medusa gathers itself together and lunges for Val. It hasn't quite got the hang of being Eve and trips over its own feet, stumbling. Jake takes advantage of the instant's reprieve to run in front of Val, shielding her with his body. He can't shoot, because bullets would go right through the Medusa to thud into me or Sophronia.

The Medusa staggers toward him, hands outstretched. Slow at first, but gaining in speed and coordination. If I shoot it, I might slow it down, but I'll hit Jake.

His eyes meet mine, and he dips his head in a nod of recognition. I'll shoot him dead rather than watch him be consumed. I hesitate. Not yet. Not while there's even the ghost of a chance.

"Phil!" I shout. "How do we kill it?"

The tips of the creature's fingers touch Jake's cheek. Jake stands his ground. "Maureen..."

I aim at his heart. My finger tightens on the trigger. "Val. Move."

She ducks and I take the opportunity.

The shot reverberates through the sanctuary.

The bullet tears a hole into the Medusa. Jake recoils as it slams into his chest. His face slackens, one hand comes up to touch the wetness welling out through the wound, and then he crumples. Blood vanishes as rapidly as it disappears, consumed by the Medusa who crouches down to lap at it with a human tongue.

This is more disturbing than watching blood vanish into

thin air, as it used to do when the creature was invisible, before it had a body and a voice.

Val, on the floor, grabs a handful of Phil's ashes and flings them at the Medusa's eyes.

It stops feeding and shrieks. Its eyes melt and mix with the ashes, forming a gray sludge that drips down over its cheeks.

Val flings another handful.

The creature throws both arms up over its face. One of the arms is slim and tattooed in green vines. The other is muscular with a badly done anchor on the bicep.

Blood gushing from Jake's chest makes a little stream through the heap of ash. Val mixes this into mud and flings handfuls at the Medusa.

The thing howls. Its features shift and morph. Alice's mouth. Aline's smooth forehead. Vince's sharp nose.

I lower myself to the floor beside Jake. His breathing is labored, accompanied by a wet, sucking sound from the hole in his chest. Blood stains his lips. He's going to die, and I'm the one who will have killed him.

There's nothing I can do for him in this moment, other than make his death worthwhile. Filling both hands with the mud I turn to the Medusa and smear it over that monstrous face. The effect is like hot water on jelly, melting its nose and lips into nothing. Another handful of muck. And another.

Headless now, still bearing a vaguely human shape with parts from all the people it has consumed, the Medusa attempts to retreat. Val and I both follow, our hands dripping with bloody ashes.

"Sophie," Jake's voice says behind me. I stop rubbing my handfuls of goo over the melting Medusa and spin around to see the girl on her knees beside him, her hands resting on his chest.

My blood runs cold. I'm in a nightmare. Everything in me rises up in horrified denial. I take a step toward them, powerless to stop what is about to happen.

Jake looks up into Sophronia's face. "I trust you. Take me across."

An unearthly wind swirls her hair; her eyes glow green. The flare of power nearly knocks me off my feet. She moves her hands to cover the bullet wound. "You're not going anywhere. Hang on. We'll get you to the hospital."

"Not. Going. To make. It."

The wind around them settles. Her eyes stop glowing. There are tears on her cheeks and she looks younger than her eighteen years, instead of ageless and supernatural. "Hold on, Jake. Please. Somebody call an ambulance!"

A cold wind whips down the aisle, stirring the ashes, raising goose bumps on my skin. Damned ghosts again, I'm thinking, but I look up to see that the church doors are open and Matt is standing there, the salt sprayer in one hand, a gun in the other. I'm torn between relief that he showed up and fear that he'll use his weapons against us.

Only an instant for me to doubt, before he's thundering up the aisle and spraying the twisted monstrosity at my feet with a mixture of salt and silver. It's the final death knell. The Medusa dissolves into a puddle of slime. It quivers and ripples and shudders as the salt mixture continues to pelt it, but finally goes inert.

"Ambulance is on the way," Matt says, turning his attention to Jake. "Hang on there, Sheriff."

"You found us." I lift my hand to push hair back from my

forehead, catch a glimpse of the mess coating it, and wipe both hands on my pants instead.

Jake's pulse is weak. He's too pale. His hand, when I take it in mine, is icy. His eyelids flicker, but don't open. I want to scream at him to stay here, not to leave me, but all my years of reserve don't let me do more than kneel here, covered in his blood and Phil's ashes, and think that I'm about to lose another strong man out of my life. I hear a siren and squeeze Jake's hand, willing him to hang on.

The ambulance crew comes up the aisle at a run, leaving a deputy to bring the gurney. They're the same two who responded when Jill fell and hit her head, and the look they give me is equal parts annoyance and suspicion. They are pros, though, and get down to work without asking questions.

The deputy is another story. Her eyes rove over the group of us, blood smeared and ashen. There's not much evidence left to back up our story. Not a trace of Vince or Eve. A bullet from my gun—a very specialized bullet—is lodged in Jake's chest. Unless he survives to tell the tale, no court in the world is going to believe that I shot him to save him from a monster I can't prove ever existed.

Matt smiles, ever so slightly.

"I shot the sheriff," he says, drawing my gun from its holster. "Borrowed Maureen's gun. It was an accident."

Val walks over and wraps her hands around the gun, tugging gently. It's loaded and the safety's off. I hold my breath waiting for her to shoot herself or Matt by accident as she takes the revolver into her own hands and sets her finger against the trigger. "But I did not shoot the deputy," she says.

"My God, give me that weapon. Is it loaded? You're going

to shoot somebody else if you're not careful." Deputy Grace approaches Val as if she were a cornered animal.

Out of my peripheral vision I watch the rescue team load Jake up onto the stretcher. They're not doing CPR and there's no sheet over his face, so he's still hanging in there. My eyes follow their progress to the door, intently enough that I don't realize what's happening until the first of the cuffs snaps onto my wrist.

"You have a right—"

"Yeah, yeah, yeah. Skip it."

Backup has arrived and a young male deputy is cuffing Matt. Our eyes meet and he shrugs. The most dangerous one of us all sits in a pew, alone. Tears slide down her cheeks and there's a bloody smear where she wiped one of them away.

"Are you all right?" Deputy Grace asks, her voice gentle. "Want me to call your dad?"

"What?" Sophie looks up, startled out of thought. "Oh, no. Thank you. No. I'll just—I'll take Val home."

"You can use my truck," Matt says. "Keys are in the ignition."

Sophie nods. "I'll take care of it. And this. I'll—clean up. Val will help me." Her eyes connect with mine and I read a promise there.

"Watch out for Jill."

"Got it," Sophie says. "Don't worry. It will all be fine."

Val crosses the room and takes one of Sophie's hands in hers. The girl flinches at her touch, but doesn't pull away.

"Val needs to come with us," Deputy Grace says, but her voice is hesitant.

Her partner glares at her. "Are you crazy? This old bird doesn't belong in jail. Obviously she didn't shoot Callahan. She was just copying the others with the gun. You're going to put her in a cell?"

Sophie's lips tighten, but Val pats her arm and she says nothing.

"You're right," Deputy Grace says. "Her prints will be on the gun, but we can explain that. Maybe call Adult Protective Services and have them look at getting her in a more appropriate placement. That Shadow Valley Manor is off the rails."

I'm too worried to raise a fuss about the comment. Who will take care of everything if I'm locked away? It occurs to me to resist, but I'm not in any condition to take out two deputies, not without shooting somebody else.

"Sophronia, you're in charge until we get back."

"Oh, I don't think that's a good idea, at all." She sounds frail and unsettled, not at all like her usual confident, sarcastic self.

"Val will help you. Jill may or may not be at the Manor, just so you know. Leave her for me to deal with."

Sophie blinks twice, but doesn't answer. Val smiles at me, though, and in her dark eyes I read a promise. I incline my head to her, closest I can come to a salute, and that's all I have time for.

The deputy frog marches me down the aisle and out into the car. Just before the door slams shut, I think I feel a light touch on my face, a caress and a whisper that sounds very much like goodbye.

TWENTY-EIGHT

Sophronia watches law enforcement lead Maureen and Matt out of the church. She's utterly exhausted and terrified of who she is and what she is capable of doing. Maureen actually trusts her to take care of things, which goes to show the older woman isn't quite as smart as she seems.

All Sophronia wants is to run back through the tunnels to her hideaway, crawl into her sleeping bag, and stay there. Only that wouldn't help at all, because it's impossible to run away from herself.

She knows who she is, now. She'd wanted to doubt the letters, but this encounter with the Medusa and with Eve have removed any hope that she might just be a normal human being. Or even just a Soul Guide.

She's the result of an experiment. A half human monster with the ability to suck the soul right out of a person and destroy it. The lure of power, of companionship from other beings more like her, the idea that she might escape the conscience that holds her and be free—all of that is still a huge temptation.

Jill is still out there, possibly back at the manor bossing everybody around. Sophronia shudders, remembering the way her hatred for Jill twisted into a hunger and a need, even as the spirit energy fed her strength and made her feel immortal. She was so close to taking Jill's soul for herself. What's to stop her the next time?

It was that fear that made her run away. She's known about the tunnels since she was a little girl. Her father's bomb shelter hideaway leads directly into the maze and this is not the first time she's used them as an escape. Maybe it would be better if she just stays underground, far away from people. Forever. Only she promised Maureen to take care of things.

"'The Walrus said.'" Val pats her arm and gestures at the multitude of ghosts, quiet now, waiting for something.

What on earth does Val mean? Sophronia sifts through songs and movies, finally locating the right line. "'*The time has come, the Walrus said.*' Is that it? They're ready to cross?"

Val nods.

Sophronia's heart feels too big for her chest. There are so many of them. Over half are children. The one that is Phil, Maureen's old friend, stands in front of them all and smiles at her.

All at once, she understands.

"You knew. You knew all along. What the Medusa was doing. That it would try to get to me so it could control all of you."

Phil's ghost inclines his head.

"So if I'd made you cross—if I'd eliminated you somehow..."

Val's brown eyes shine with sympathy. "Spilled milk," she says.

Sophronia chokes back a laugh. "Don't cry over spilled milk, you mean? We could all be dead. The spirits enslaved. That thing running free around the countryside gaining knowledge and power with every life it took."

She's begun shaking with reaction, so hard that her teeth rattle in her head.

Phil's ghost floats across the room and stops just in front of her. He has a waiting, questioning expression.

"You want to cross now?" she asks.

He nods. All the others drift toward him and form into a ragged line. Sophronia sucks in a deep breath. She's never taken more than one across at a time. But she owes them this, whatever rest there is for the dead. She has to try.

Reaching out she takes Phil's hand. To her it feels solid, warm even, although she knows to anybody else there would be only a sensation of cold. Pushing thoughts of Val and all the others out of her mind, she focuses on the veil that marks the crossing, holding it aside so that the dead can pass through.

Phil goes first, without a backward glance. The others follow, one by one. Toward the end of the line a girl about her own age pauses to look at her and she recognizes the face of Aline, the World Tree Girl.

"You do have a soul." Sophronia's eyes fill with hot tears that spill over her cheeks. If Aline has a soul, then maybe she does too.

Aline's spirit reaches out and traces a pattern on Sophronia's cheek with a fingertip. Then she turns and vanishes into the invisible beyond.

When the last of them is through, Sophronia sighs and

closes the door. Feeling as if she's waking from a dream, she turns to look for Val. The little woman is lugging a mop and bucket up the aisle, unearthed from a cleaning closet somewhere. Sophronia goes to take the bucket from her.

"This is empty," she says.

Val points at the baptistery. Sophronia hesitates. She's not Catholic, herself, but her father is. She came to this very church as a small child and watched the holy water administered in a sacred rite. It seems wrong to use it for something mundane like washing up a floor.

But then she takes another look at what's left of the Medusa and decides maybe holy water is best for what needs to be done.

"Sorry about all this," she says to the Virgin and anybody else who is listening. Val has thought of everything, including a smaller container for scooping up water. Between the two of them they drain the baptistery dry, pouring holy water over what's left of the Medusa and watching it melt away to nothing.

"Sure hope this thing stays dead," Sophronia says, when there is no trace of jelly left. They scoop up whatever they can of Phil's ashes and empty them out in the churchyard. It doesn't matter now. He's crossed. She's surprised to find she misses him.

Outside, the world has moved into velvety night. Sophronia pauses to breathe in the clear, cold air. It smells of snow, and also of hope.

"Hey," a voice demands. "How come nobody called me?"

A kid stands there on the steps, bundled into a jacket, a knitted hat pulled over her ears.

"Why would we?"

"Maureen promised. So I don't tell. About the spirits and all."

"Pretty sure that story is blown wide open," Sophronia says. "Who might you be?"

"You can call me G. Why is Val here? What happened? Is the sheriff okay? What are we doing next? What's that mark on your face?"

Sophronia's hand flies up to cover the place where the World Tree Girl traced a design. "It's nothing," she says. "And the sheriff will be okay." It's true. She can feel it, knew it before the ambulance took him away. His spirit isn't going anywhere, at least not today. And Maureen will find a way to get herself and Matt out of jail.

She looks from the girl to Val and something warm blossoms inside of her. It's an unfamiliar sensation, and she's not sure what to do with it at first, but then it comes to her. She smiles. "Anybody else in the mood for pizza?"

A NOTE FROM KERRY

On behalf of Maureen, Jake, Sophronia, Matt, and the other Shadow Valley characters, thank you so much for reading!

If you enjoyed the book, I'd love it if you'd pop onto Amazon and leave a review—this helps other readers discover the book! Even just a few words is so helpful and so much appreciated.

Happy reading,

Kerry

P.S. If you want to be sure you get in on new books in the series, sign up for my newsletter at www.kerryschafer.com/inboxmagic. You'll get a free down- load of the first novella in my Dream Wars series to say thank you!

ACKNOWLEDGMENTS

My first debt of gratitude goes to Maureen Keslyn herself, for showing up in my head and giving me the green light to write this tale.

I'd also like to thank my resident Viking—first, for putting up with the way my brain vanishes into an alternate dimension when I'm writing, and second, for providing the all-important Viking Read for issues of continuity and quality control.

Susan Spann, thank you for being my friend, my cheerleader, and my critique partner, and also for supplying me with penguins and chocolate. Chuck Harrelson, thank you for jumping on board and giving valuable feedback—remind me to buy you a drink (or two) next time we meet.

Much love to Patty Briggs and her truly awesome assistant, Ann Peters, for reading and offering encouragement.

Patti Hancock, thank you so much for explaining the ins and outs of the life of a rural coroner to me. This was invaluable information and I hope I've kept it straight.

I must not forget to mention all the active, creative people of my acquaintance who have taught me that life doesn't suddenly end when you reach a certain age. Specifically, to my mother who is continually exploring new areas of art. To my mother's friend Shirley, who is one of the most creative and fascinating women I have ever met. To my great-aunt, Harriet who was still teaching school at seventy. And to my irascible grandfather, who wanted to go deer farming in Bolivia when he was eighty, and who started taking piano lessons at that age so he could learn "before I get too old." All of you have been an inspiration to me and have found your way into this book, in one way or another.

Last, my thanks to you, the reader, for sharing your time with Maureen and company. Without readers, books would have no purpose.

ALSO BY KERRY SCHAFER

The Between Trilogy

Between

Wakeworld

The Nothing

Shadow Valley Manor Series

Dead Before Dying

World Tree Girl

The Dream Wars Series

The Dream Runner

The Dream Thief

The Dream Wars

Books by Alter Ego Kerry Anne King

Closer Home

I Wish You Happy

Whisper Me This

Everything You Are